GHOSTS AND ROBBERS

Daniel Corrick is an editor and literary historian with a specialist interest in nineteenth-century literature, especially the evolution of Gothicism and the Decadent movement. He has worked on a number of volumes including the collected fiction of Montague Summers, and unpublished works of Edgar Saltus and Edward Heron-Allen. In addition, he has edited several anthologies, including *Sorcery and Sanctity: A Homage to Arthur Machen* (Hieroglyphic Press, 2013), and *Drowning in Beauty: The Neo-Decadent Anthology* (Snuggly Books, 2018). He can be reached at: https://dccorick.com

I0584238

SNUGGLY BOOKS

GHOSTS AND ROBBERS

AN ANTHOLOGY OF
GERMAN GOTHIC FICTION

EDITED AND WITH AN INTRODUCTION BY
DANIEL CORRICK

THIS IS A SNUGGLY BOOK

ISBN: 978-1-64525-087-6

CONTENTS

INTRODUCTION

A T the turn of the nineteenth century British readers underwent a positive mania for those works of horror and
wonder Samuel Taylor Coleridge dubbed "speaking monsters
from the Danube". It was then that the German states were so
synonymous with Gothic literature that native writers of a less
than scrupulous bent were wont to preface their own works
with the label "from the German" as a way of testifying to their
bona fide terrifying nature.

In many ways Gothic fiction is a grotesque and splendid
mandrake growing off the spent corpse of the Enlightenment. It
can alternatively represent both the most strident expression of
that period's values in its anti-clericalism and rationalising ten-
dencies, and its dialectical overcoming in the medievalism and
mysticism of the Romantics. Its prominence in Germany was
the culmination of over half a century's worth of cultural and
artistic trends and the indicator of a philosophical revolution in
aesthetics. Although the Gothic novel had its birth outside of
that land, in Horace Walpole's *The Castle of Otranto* and in eighteenth century Orientalist fiction, many of the setting, themes
and plots we so associate with that genre have their origins in
German literature

During the period of its popularity between the 1780s and
1830s the Gothic underwent various evolutionary stages and
branches from the classical *Schauerroman* or "shudder-novel"

to the turbulent emotional exhalations of Romantic literature. This anthology presents a selection of its differing forms, many of which have not seen print since the Gothic's heyday. As a prelude, a brief lineage of these "speaking monsters" and the cultural upheavals they represent is called for.

For a genre long looked down on by critics as something vaguely disreputable, lurid and generally "horrid", the Gothic could scarcely have a more illustrious pedigree. The 1760s had seen the birth of the *Sturm und Drang* movement in German drama as a reaction against the French vogue for neo-classism. The writers of this movement stressed tumultuous emotional expression and the pursuit of desires over formal ideals, defending their use of the supernatural outside of a classical setting by citing Shakespeare as an exemplar for dramatic writing. It was given an intellectual justification by several philosophers and theologians, who argued that the metropolitan focus and universalised classicism of the Enlightenment had bred a dangerous contempt towards native folkloric subjects, often meaning that a peoples' spiritual heritage, its own mythology and legendary hero figures, were disregarded as subjects of art. The popularisation of the Middle Ages as a setting birthed a new species of novel, the *Ritterroman*, knightly novels often presented as medieval histories. Such works abounded in struggles between virtue and sin, magic, and the frequent appearances of the Devil, a presence which loomed larger over the genre since the publication of Goethe's *Faust*. It was this shift of emphasis towards the darker subject matter of diabolic bargains and fallen protagonists taken by writers such as Christian Heinrich Spiess, with his 1791 novel *The Dwarf of Westerbourg*, which gave the later *Ritterromane* their place as the first authentic *Schauerromane*. The "knightly gothic" remained a popular form, gradually giving way to the more romantic depictions of chivalrous adventure popular in continental art throughout the nineteenth century. Of the stories contained herein, Louise

Brachmann's "The Proscribed Knight" and the Prussian writer Ludwig von Baczko's "The Sorcerers" are examples of this school, with the latter being relatively unusual in its having a female protagonist. The extensive descriptions of a witch cult and its rites in Baczko's story typify the preoccupation with the occult many were to see in German art.

It was another of the canonical figures of German literature, Friedrich Schiller, who contributed more than any other to the genealogy of the Gothic. His early and wildly successful play, *The Robbers*, popularised the robber-chieftain as a literary trope, capable of alternatively encompassing rapacious amorality and Robin Hood-like defiance of corrupt authority. The dichotomous characters of Karl and Franz Moore, two brothers, one noble and the other base, were to provide a stock template for moral conflict throughout the genre. As with the *Ritterroman*, Schiller's play lead to another sub-genre of the novel, this time detailing the exploits of heroic or villainous bandits, the most famous example of which was England's own great high Gothic novel, Anne Radcliffe's *The Mysteries of Udolpho*. With this contribution alone the great poet had shaped the future of literature but he was to go further with another work, which heralded in the era of the *Schauerroman* and the horror novel as we know it today.

This was *The Ghost-Seer*, an episodic novel published in several instalments during the last years of the 1780s. The novel's plot involves a prince's encounters with a mysterious individual with seemingly occult powers, including the ability to raise spirits, who is later revealed to be the instrument of a Jesuitical plot to increase the power of the Catholic Church in the German countries. Its thrilling mixture of forensic mystery, secret societies, apparently supernatural phenomena, sinister monastic figures and perilous adventure was to start a craze for such novels, one which both dwarfed and absorbed the earlier knightly and robber genres. Here was the full emergence of the *Schauerroman* or

Gothic novel proper, with some of the earliest examples quickly translated and popularised in Britain such as Carl Grosse's *Der Genius* (*Horrid Mysteries*) and Karl Friedrich Kahlert's *Der Geisterbanner* (*The Necromancer*) consciously echoing Schiller. Unlike the earlier genres, which originally kept close to their exemplars, the *Schauerroman* encouraged thematic cross pollination between them; thus in "The Proscribed Knight" we have the knightly setting merging with the secret society plot in the appearance of the Secret Tribunal, a semi-mythical vigilante society controlled by the Holy Inquisition, and in Gottfried Peter Rauschnick's "The Warning", a skilful interweaving of the ghostly conspiracy and the bandit thriller complete with its morally dualistic siblings.

The novels patterned after *The Ghost Seer* with their rationalisation of supernatural phenomena were really the dying cries of the spirit of the age. It should be remembered that in some ways the eighteenth century was a very bigoted time, the views of the late Enlightenment being not so much a rejection of religious prejudices as a secularisation of the worst excesses of the Protestant reformers. The banishment of "superstition", meaning beliefs in ghosts, magic and miracles, and with them the implied authority of the Catholic Church, was seen as a socio-moral imperative to be expressed throughout all cultural mediums. Even Kant's Critical Philosophy was originally born of a desire to mock the mysticism of Swedenborg (that his polemic against that figure was entitled *Dreams of a Ghost-seer* says enough about the pedigree of Schiller's novel). For German and British writers, including the Gothic novelists, this desire was not materialistic, as it was with many of the French intellectuals; its connection to Protestantism leant it a kind of high moral seriousness. Although this attitude was still prevalent the popularity of the *Schauerroman* showed it was becoming uneasy. As critics of that genre pointed out why spend so much time reading of and writing about a subject if one is only to decry it?

Not only was there a fascination with stories of the supernatural, there was an appetite for the subject itself more than mere sensationalism.

The later development of *Schauerliteratur* is marked by changing views on supernaturalism and a wider range of settings prompted by ongoing world events. The period of the Gothic's popularity parallels some of the most cataclysmic social upheavals ever felt in Europe, civilizational trauma unsurpassed till the end of World War II. The cruelty and gore of the shudder novels were surpassed by current events: what Secret Tribunal could rule as brutally as the Committee for Public Safety and what feudal tyrant could boast a megalomania as grand as Napoleon's? Amongst these changes were the incorporation of the supernatural in more contemporary settings as well as a shift away from event-driven narratives to those focusing on character psychology. The Baroness Caroline de La Motte Fouqué's "Valerie" and Karl Theodor Körner's "The Harp" are examples of this more mature Gothic, as is Johann Heinrich Zschokke's "The Polish Inn". Of these, the first two use the manifestation of the ghostly in more "ordinary" settings than the traditional robbers' hideouts and secret caverns with a heavy emphasis on feelings of loss, whereas in the latter the rationalised supernatural is used to illustrate morbid psychological states in such a way as would later gain prominence through the works of Edgar Allen Poe and his disciples. As a result of the shift to a modern milieu the later Gothic also demonstrates an awareness of the Gothic as a genre—early shudder novels and romantic poetry will form part of the intellectual atmosphere in which the characters and provide a reference point in their own struggles to maintain faith in a hubristic Enlightenment *Weltanschauung*.

By the opening of the nineteenth century changing philosophical trends, particularly the rise of German Idealism, had led to a widespread culturally accepted interest in ghostly phenomena, what we would call the paranormal, both in the

German countries and in Britain. This had also lead to appreciation of the Gothic outside of the original shudder novel context, one example of which was in folktales or *Märchen*. The "Gothicising" potential of native legends had been recognised by earlier writers such as Johann Karl August Musäus, with his "The Elopement", a grotesque and darkly comically tale which was one of the main inspirations behind M.G. Lewis's *The Monk*; however, these were cast in a more formalised narrative style. The enthusiasm for "naïve" folk-culture, initiated by the *Sturm und Drang* movement and taken further by Romanticism, encouraged writers such as Körner, Friedrich Gottschalck and Alois Wilhelm Schreiber to compose anthologies of "traditions"; whilst many of such pieces did indeed derive from actual legend, the choice of subject matter and manner of presentation were heavily influenced by the knightly gothics, with Gottschalck's "The Castle Spectre of Scharzfeld" reading like the synopsis of a particular horrid *Schauerroman*. Schreiber took the appreciation of Gothic aesthetics further, often including such legends in the guidebooks he wrote about locations around the Rhine, as if each haunting was a matter of patriotic history.

With Romanticism's advent, the faint disdain in which the high priests of letters held Gothic fiction began to fall away, as the German-speaking countries came increasingly to be seen as an intellectual counter-weight to France. The relatively crude empiricist psychologies of the last century were replaced by new theories emphasising intuition, imagination and genius. The power of the human spirit, the supernatural, even the magical, all became major themes. Although it is not possible to draw a hard distinction between the Gothicism of the later *Schauerroman* writers and what some call Dark Romanticism ,Romantic writers did bring with them further elements of prose lyricism and spiritual angst. A highlight from this period is Ernst Raupach's justly famous "Wake Not the Dead," one of the first instances of Gothic vampire fiction and potentially a major influence on Poe's stories of grave defying heroines. Along with featuring a surprisingly modern depiction of vampirism as a beautiful evil, the character in question being presented as a kind of undead Über-woman, it is also where the cultural depiction of necromancy moves from divination via spirits to the art of raising the dead through dark magic now dominant in contemporary fantasy fiction and gaming.

For all the squeamishness of contemporary critics, the subsequent development of both mainstream literature and genre fiction is a testament to the enduring success and influence of Gothic fiction. Although German literature moved away from it as the decades wore on, it is still indelibly linked to those countries just as the Decadent movement is to France. Why did it grow so popular and why does it remain so? One reason is probably because, although often projected onto a mediaeval setting, the perils facing the heroes and heroines of the Gothic prefigured changes that were already occurring with various national psyche: the robber-chieftains and the corrupted knights representing the triumph of passion and the will over the abstracted intellect preached in then contemporary libertine writings. The overwrought sadism of the Gothic villains is a manifestation of that characteristic of man, which by the 1790s, many intellectuals saw as having torn down the dreams of the Enlightenment: the *libido dominandi*, the lust for power. More universally the extremes of good and evil seem to have a tendency to overstep the bounds of the natural, inviting the angels, resplendent and fallen, into art, a more individualist take on morality than the merely "civic" concept of virtue the Romantics were to rebel so strongly against.

Neither should the increased aesthetic scope these writers opened up by locating their speaking monsters in the Middle Ages be overlooked. Whilst we are used to settings at least inspired by that period from fantasy and historical fiction back in the Gothic's heyday the vogue for classical backdrops was still so strong that the sudden intrusion of the age of the Crusades, even in a caricatured sense, was an invigorating draft for the literary imagination. And where better for this to start than the German countries, the centre of Christendom at that period? It is tempting to draw analogies between the quintessential Gothic edifice and the state of the Holy Roman Empire, itself a ruin, grotesquely archaic, upheld by semi-legendary divinely sanctioned customs, and awaiting final prophetic collapse. Beyond simply the scope of folk history the writers of the German Gothic are responsible for taking the powerful subjects and figures of European folklore and setting them into the full length literary form, thereby both raising supernatural horror into a genre and helping society rediscover alternative mythologies.

—Daniel Corrick

GHOSTS AND ROBBERS

THE GREY CHAMBER

by Heinrich Clauren

YOUNG Blendau was travelling to Italy in the suite of a German princess to whom he acted as secretary. Arrived in the town in the north of Germany where the princess had decided to remain several days, he obtained permission to visit a certain M. Rebmann, who then held the office of chancellor to an adjacent royal estate. This gentleman lived several miles from the town where the princess and her train had halted.

Blendau had been educated with him and had not seen him since he was fourteen years old, that is to say, for about seven years. He thought, therefore, that he would make this visit a surprise to this friend and his family, and as he knew the country perfectly well he hired a horse and set out alone across the forests although it was the middle of winter.

The weather was very fine in the morning, but in the afternoon he perceived that the sky became covered over, and towards evening a heavy snow began to fall. This caused a considerable delay to Blendau: the path became heavy, large snowflakes blew into his eyes and blinded him so that he could not guide his horse properly; he mistook his way several times, and though he calculated on reaching M. Rebmann's early in the afternoon, it was not till nine o'clock at night that he at last arrived, cold and exhausted, at this friend's, having made a detour of twenty miles.

M. Rebmann hardly recognised him, so much had he changed since he had last seen him. When, however, he discovered who was his late guest he received him with great pleasure and only regretted that his wife and children had gone to the neighbouring town on the occasion of the marriage of a relative and would not return for several days.

He ordered a good meal for his friend and some of the best wine in his cellar, and after Blendau had drunk three bottles of Meersteiner and gossiped over all that had happened to him during the last seven years he felt the fatigue and vexation of his long cold ride pass. Nevertheless, an extreme lassitude overcame his spirits and he was forced at last to break off the hilarious conversation and demand permission to retire to bed.

M. Rebmann admitted with a laugh that this put him in a difficulty. His lady was away and all the chambers save those occupied by the family were dismantled, while the prudent housewife had taken with her the key to the coffers which held the sheets, the coverlets, and the mattresses. On calling the old servant, Bridget, and putting to her his difficulty, she replied: "There is a bed already made in the Grey Chamber—you know, sir, the guest chamber. M. Blendau can sleep there if he pleases."

"No," replied Rebmann. "My friend Blendau would not wish to pass the night in the Grey Chamber, of that I am sure."

"And why not, sir?" asked the old woman.

"What, in the Grey Chamber! Have you already forgotten the Lady Gertrude?" Mr. Rebmann turned slyly to his guest.

"Bah! That's such a long time ago that I thought no more of it," cried Blendau. "What, do you think I am still troubled by such childish follies? Go along with you! Let me pass the night in this famous chamber. I am no longer afraid of ghosts or evil spirits, and if the beautiful Gertrude should come to keep me company I am so tired that I don't think she'll prevent me from sleeping."

M. Rebmann gave the young man a doubtful glance.

"Well, my friend, you've certainly singularly changed. Seven years ago nothing in the world would have made you consent to sleep in the Grey Chamber, even if you'd had two people to keep you company. Where did you find so much courage?"

"Seven years ago is seven years ago," laughed Blendau. "I have grown up since then. For five years I have lived in the capital, remember. Believe me, I now know too much to give any credit to old legends."

"Very well, my friend, I've no more objection to make. May Heaven watch upon your rest. Bridget, take the light and conduct M. Blendau into the Grey Chamber."

Blendau said good night to his old friend, then he followed Bridget to the famous Grey Chamber, situated at the second stage of the extremity of one of the wings of the castle.

Bridget put her two candles on a dressing-table on either side of a mirror of oval form surrounded by an interlaced antique border. The old woman seemed ill at ease in this vast chamber; she made a slight curtsey to Blendau and hurried away.

The young traveller stood for a moment considering the apartment which had once been familiar enough to him and had always, in the days of his youth, filled him with terror. It was still in the same state as it had been when he had seen it last. The enormous iron stove bore the date of 1616; a little beyond this, in the corner, was a narrow door the upper part of which was composed of squares of ancient glass, heavily leaded. This led to a long, sombre passage which wound round the tower to the subterranean dungeons.

The furniture consisted of six ormolu chairs, two tables in heavy brasswork supported by finely carved stag's feet, and a great bed with a baldaquin which was hung with curtains of heavy grey silk embroidered in tarnished gold. Nothing in the room had been changed for perhaps more than a hundred years, for the chancellorship of this royal domain had been confided from time immemorial to the family Rebmann.

The châtelaine Gertrude was of an even greater antiquity. How often had not Blendau heard her horrible story! According to this old legend, which he had heard whispered fearfully by his nurse in his boyhood, Gertrude had from an early age vowed to God her youth and beauty, and had been about to enclose herself forever in a convent when the splendours of her youthful loveliness had aroused the base desires of a certain Graf Hugues, who one night broke into her room, this very Grey Chamber, and despoiled her by force of her honour.

Gertrude swore on the crucifix that she had called for help, but in this lonely part of the castle, so far from the other apartments, who could hear the cries of agony and innocence? The wickedness of Hugues did not entail any consequences that could reveal it, but the unhappy Gertrude avowed the crime to her confessor, who refused her permission to enter the convent and closed to her the door of the sanctuary of the virgins of the Lord. And as she had intended to tempt God by concealing her fault and taking the veil, he told her that in expiation she must suffer the torments of purgatory during three hundred years.

The wretched girl, a prey to despair, poisoned herself and expired in the Grey Chamber at the age of nineteen years. Her rigorous penitence was still lasting and would not be terminated for another forty years, that is to say in 1850, and until the expiration of the fatal term, Gertrude would continue to appear every night in the Grey Chamber.

Blendau had frequently heard this tale and he had even met several people who were ready to swear that they had seen Gertrude in the Grey Chamber. All these tales agreed that the phantom had a dagger in one hand, probably to pierce the heart of the perfidious lover, and a crucifix in the other, destined without doubt to reconcile the criminal with Heaven in offering him the image of the Saviour who died to expiate the sins of mankind.

The ghostly apparition only showed itself in the Grey Chamber, and for this reason this apartment had long remained uninhabited. But when M. Rebmann inherited the castle and the post of chancellor, he had turned the haunted room into a guest-chamber as a proof of his complete disbelief in phantom or legend.

Blendau looked steadily round the room. Although he had boasted of not believing any longer in ghosts, he was not too much at ease. He locked the door by which he had entered and the glass door which gave on to the long, obscure passage. He put out one of the candles, placed the other near the bed, undressed, and slipped beneath the sheets and under the warm coverlet, recommending his soul to God, then extinguished the other candle, sunk his head upon the pillow, and at once fell into a profound sleep.

But about two hours afterwards he woke and heard a clock in the neighbouring tower strike midnight. He opened his eyes and saw that there was a faint light in the chamber. He raised himself on his elbow—extreme terror caused him to become immediately wide awake. The curtains at the end of the bed were half-pulled and his glance fell on the mirror on the dressing-table directly in front of him. In this he could see the reflection of the spectre of Gertrude wrapped in a shroud, a crucifix in the left hand and a dagger in the right.

Blendau's blood froze in his veins: this that he saw before him was not a dream, a vision, but a frightful reality, it was not a skeleton or a shade, it was Gertrude herself, the face discoloured with the livid tint of death. A garland of ivy and rosemary was interlaced among her dry, colourless locks, and as she moved Blendau heard the rustle of the leaves of this dead chaplet and the sound of the hem of the shroud dragging on the floor. He saw in the mirror by the light of the two candles, both of which were now brightly burning, the fixed brilliancy of the eyes of Gertrude, the pallor of her lips.

He tried to leap from his bed and to run to the door by which he had entered, but the fright had paralysed him—he found that he could not move.

Gertrude kissed the crucifix. She seemed to be praying under her breath; Blendau distinguished the movement of her lips which still carried the marks of the burning poison. He saw the eyes of the unfortunate wretch turned towards heaven; she raised her dagger and advanced towards the bed with a terrible glance.

Blendau was about to lose consciousness as she opened the curtains of the bed. Horror was painted in her fixed and inanimate eyes as she perceived a man crouching on the pillows, and she pressed her little dagger on the bosom of him whom she took for her false lover. As she did so a cold drop of poison fell from her garland on to Blendau's pallid face. At this he gave a piercing cry, flung himself from the bed, and rushed to the window to cry for help.

But Gertrude prevented him. When he reached the window she was there with one hand on the catch so that he could not open it. With the other she caught him round the waist and he gave a piercing cry, for he felt through his nightshirt the glacial impression of the cold sweat of death coming from her clasp.

He observed that she had now neither crucifix nor dagger, and that she seemed no longer to wish for the life of the unhappy Blendau, but, what was more horrible, that she appeared to offer and to expect the embraces of love.

As the icy spectre folded him in her arms Blendau dragged himself away with long shudders of terror and hurled himself towards the little glass door.

As he opened this (it was not locked, though he had turned the key himself the night before) he found himself face to face with a skeleton that blocked the long passage—that of Graf Hugues, without doubt. His ghastly face, on which still clung a remnant of skin and muscle, was distorted in a frightful grimace. He entered the chamber, letting the door fall behind him with a sound that echoed like thunder throughout the tower.

Blendau, between the two phantoms, that of Gertrude and that of the skeleton, sank to the ground unconscious into darkness.

When he recovered, the cold wintry dawn was showing through the unshuttered windows. Blendau, stiff and chilled, his shirt still bathed with sweat, rose from the floor and with trembling hands searched for his clothes. Though unutterably weary and shaken by nausea, nothing would have persuaded him to endeavour to obtain any repose in that apartment.

At first he endeavoured to persuade himself he had been the victim of some frightful dream, but such an idea was no longer plausible when he perceived, on the dressing-table in front of the mirror, the second candle that he had placed near his bed and put out after he had got between the sheets. He remarked that these candles were half burnt down, although they had only just been lit for a second the night before. He also discovered that the two doors which he had locked the night before were again fastened as he had left them.

Blendau had not the courage to relate his adventure to anyone. He did not wish to be laughed at for a susceptible fool and made the subject of the pleasantries of the family of Rebmann. On the other hand, if he was able to persuade his host of the reality of his vision, who would dare to continue to inhabit the castle where Gertrude and the hideous skeleton of her lover had a rendezvous every evening?

Then, again, if he was silent, he would be asked to spend another night in the Grey Chamber and that he felt he had not the strength to do.

He therefore dressed himself in haste, crept through the castle while everyone was still asleep, went to the stable, mounted his horse, and without taking leave of anyone rode away through the snowy forest towards the city.

THE BOTTLE IMP

by Baron Friedrich de La Motte Fouqué

IT was a lovely Italian evening, when a young German merchant, named Richard, entered Venice, the widely celebrated
seat of traffic and commerce. In consequence of it being then
the period of the Thirty Years War, all Germany was, at that
time, a scene of dissension; no wonder, therefore, if the young
merchant, who was a gallant more inclined to banqueting and
luxurious indulgence, than feats of chivalry, was not greatly
displeased at his affairs calling him for some time towards Italy,
where things wore a less hostile appearance, and where too, he
had heard, there was no lack either of the richest mines, or the
most delicate fruits—to say nothing of fascinating beauties,
in which latter article our gallant piqued himself on being no
ordinary connoisseur.

Seated in his gondola, he traversed the various canals of
the city, struck with admiration at the beautiful buildings, and
still more so at the lovely tenants, whom he frequently beheld,
peeping from their lattices. At length he arrived at a magnificent
mansion, at whose windows he saw some ten or twelve charming girls.

"Now, would to heaven," exclaimed the captivated German,
"that I had but the opportunity of saying a few words to one of
those rare creatures!"

"Well!" returned his gondolier, "and that be all, you have only to step out, and go boldly into the house at once—your time, I warrant me, will pass pleasantly enough."

"It may be pleasant enough, friend, to thee, to put thy jeers upon strangers; but dost thou suppose that I am such an errant loon as to follow thy knavish counsel, and to venture where l should not only be hooted out, but receive too a sound drubbing into the bargain?"

"My good master," replied the other, "do not think to teach me the customs of our city; only follow my advice, and, if you are not welcomed with open arms, why then I am well content to lose my labour and my fare."

The youth now began to think the experiment worth trying; and soon found that the gondolier had not imposed upon him. These beauties, he quickly discovered, were far from being prudish or tyrannical; on the contrary, they were of that courteous sort who are never backward in shewing hospitality to the stranger, but ready to extend their consideration to the utmost, for the trifling consideration of some fifty ducats. "This same Italy," thought the unwary youth, intoxicated by their voluptuous caresses, "is assuredly the most delightful place beneath heaven;" for he did not fail to impute the flattering reception he had experienced, in no small degree to the comely person with which nature had favoured him. The demand, however, that was made upon his purse, soon dissipated some of these pleasing reflections, as he discovered that, instead of having made a conquest of some princess, he had only been entertained by a courtesan, who now made demand that nearly drained his purse. Yet did he not lose all his patience, since he was a gallant that did not consider the cost bestowed upon his pleasures flung away: he therefore retired with as good a grace as he could muster on such an occasion, and repaired to a tavern for the sake of diverting his spleen.

Having commenced his affairs in so notable a manner, the wild youth continued daily to indulge in revels, and in the society of mirthful faces. In all the company of brave gallants, with whom Richard now constantly associated, there was but one countenance overcast with gloom. It was that of a Spanish captain, who, though he never failed to be present at these scenes of riot, rarely bestowed a word upon the company, while his dark features were rendered still more gloomy by the visible uneasiness that sat upon them. Still his presence was endured, as he was a man of rank or wealth, and one too who regarded lightly the expense of treating his friends evening after evening.

Richard, in the meanwhile, although less liberal of his purse than on the first evening of his arrival at Venice, found his finances rapidly decreasing, and reflected with no small sorrow that this gay and joyous life must quickly terminate. His associates were not slow in observing his melancholy, or in divining the cause of it, this being, by no means, the first instance of the kind that had occurred within their society—neither did they spare their taunts upon the occasion, so that our hero was fain to venture among them the last precious relics of his purse. At this prosperous period of his history, the Spaniard called him, one evening aside, and, with unexpected courtesy, requesting that he would accompany him abroad, conducted him to a lone and retired spot. The poor youth was at first rather alarmed; but at length he somewhat quieted his apprehensions by reflecting, that his companion well knew that he had little about him of value, save his skin, and in that he was determined a hole should not be picked without returning the compliment.

The Spaniard, however, having first seated himself on the ruins of an old building, and compelled his companion to do the same, addressed him as follows:—

"I cannot help imagining, my dear young friend, that you stand greatly in need of that which has long become a burden to myself—namely, the power of procuring whatever sum of money you choose, and whenever you please. This power, such as it is, I am willing to dispose of to you for a trifling consideration, besides some other advantages into the bargain."

"What occasion," inquired Richard, "can you possibly have for money, if you wish to part with the power of obtaining it yourself?"

"The case stands thus," returned the captain. "I know not whether you are acquainted with certain little spirits that are called 'Bottle Imps;' they are small black devils, enclosed in a little phial. Whoever possesses one of these can command from it whatever worldly possession he desires most, especially abundance of gold. In return for those services, the soul of the person who possesses the imp becomes forfeit to Lucifer, in case he dies without having previously disposed of it. But this can be done only by receiving a less sum than that which he first paid for the spirit. Mine cost me ten ducats—for nine it is yours."

While the youth was reflecting on this extraordinary offer, the Spaniard continued, "I could, if I pleased, easily get rid of the thing, by palming it upon someone as a mere curiosity, in which manner a knavish fellow inveigled me to purchase it. But I wish not to have the weight of such an ill deed upon my conscience, and therefore, very honestly and fairly, acquaint you with the bargain. You are still young and high-spirited, and will not fail to meet with opportunities enough of disposing of your purchase, whenever you may become as weary of it as I am even now."

"My noble sir," replied Richard, "if you would not take it ill at my hands, I could inform you how often I have been imposed upon already in this good city of Venice."

"Why, thou foolish varlet," exclaimed the enraged Spaniard, "thou need'st but call to mind the brave entertainment I gave last evening, to judge whether I would cheat thee for the sake of a paltry nine ducats."

"Who spends much, wants much," gently observed the young merchant, "and the longest purse we know has a bottom, although not a golden one. If, therefore, you yesterday spent your last ducat, today you may be hankering after mine."

"Excuse me if I do not chastise thee with a cold steel for this insolence—that I do not do it, is because I still hope that you will help to rid me of my bottle devil. Besides it is my intention to perform penance which would only be rendered still heavier thereby."

"Might we not, at least, be, favoured with some specimens of the thing's abilities?" inquire the wary merchant.

"How may that be?" answered the other. "It will not remain with anyone nor aid anyone save him who has fairly purchased and paid for it."

The youth could not help feeling some alarm, for the place where they were sitting seemed a particularly lone and gloomy spot—although the Spaniard assured him that he would not employ compulsive means. Yet, in spite of his fears, his imagination dwelt upon the enjoyments that would be in his power, should he once become possessor of the little spirit: he determined, therefore, to try whether he could obtain the bargain at a cheaper rate.

"Witless fellow that thou art," with a laugh, "it is for thy sake, and for the sake of those who shall come after thee, that I demand the highest sum I can, that I may delay, as long as possible, the time when it shall be purchased for the smallest coin possible, and the purchaser thereby become inevitably forfeited to the devil, even because he cannot sell it again at a lower price.'

"Well," said Richard, with a tone of delight, "let me but have it. I warrant me I shall not be very eager to get quit of my purchase in a hurry. If therefore I could have it for five ducats——"

"It is all one to me," returned the Spaniard, "but remember you are hastening on the minute when the evil spirit shall claim the last unhappy possessor as his own."

With these words he delivered up to his companion, in return for his gold, a small glass phial, wherein Richard could just discern by the light of the stars something dark that kept leaping, up and down.

By way of making an experiment he demanded, although but mentally, to have double the amount of the sum he had just expended in his right hand, when he instantly felt ten ducats there. He now returned in glee to the tavern, and the rest of the company, who were still carousing there, were not a little astonished at perceiving what cheerful countenances were now worn by those who were lately in so melancholy a mood. But the Spaniard quickly retired without awaiting the costly banquet which, late as it was, Richard had ordered to be prepared, having first satisfied the demands of the wary host beforehand, for his pockets were well lined with brave new ducats, which flocked thither merely at his wishing.

Those who are most anxious for a similar bargain will best imagine what kind of a life our wild gallant now led; unless, indeed, they should be devoted to mere sordid avarice. Even the most charitable may well suppose that he spent not his days or nights in abstinence and fasting; the first thing he did was to choose, as the minion of his pleasures, the courtesan whose acquaintance cost him so dear at his first arrival at Venice. On this worthless creature did he lavish unheard of sums, purchasing for her a mansion in the city, and two villas, all of which he furnished with the utmost sumptuousness.

It chanced one day, as he was sitting with Lucretia, such was the name of his mistress, in the beautiful garden of one of his villas, upon the bank of a little stream, that she suddenly snatched the phial which Richard constantly wore in his bosom, attached to his neck by a chain of gold. She had seized it before he was aware, and now held the little bottle up against the light. At first she was highly amused at beholding the antics of the little black figure; but at length she shrieked out in a voice of terror,—"Ah! the nasty creature is a toad!" and immediately flung chain, phial, and bottle devil, altogether into the water, where the current as quickly carried them away.

The youth endeavoured as well as he could to conceal his distress, lest his mistress should inquire farther into the matter, and perhaps accuse him publicly of witchcraft. He pretended, therefore, that it was merely a curious toy, then as soon as he could he quitted Lucretia, in order to consider what was best for him now to do. He was still in possession of his palace and villas, and had, moreover, in his pockets, no inconsiderable sum in the shape of bright ducats. But how great was his joy when, on putting his hand into his pocket to examine the latter, he discovered there his lost phial. The chain probably remained at the bottom of the stream, but the phial and its little black tenant had faithfully returned back to their owner.—"Now then," exclaimed he, in a burst of transport, "now then I find that I possess here a treasure, of which no accident, no earthly power, can possibly deprive me!" Nay, he had even kissed the very phial, had not the little jumping black figure excited his aversion, so loathsome did it appear.

If his doings were wild and mad enough before, they were now ten times worse. The infatuated youth regarded even the potentates and princes of the world with a disdainful compassion, convinced that not one of them was able to indulge in such a luxurious life as himself. Even Venice, the most opulent mart in the world, could hardly find dainties enough for his extravagant banquets. Did a well-meaning friend hint at the folly of this continual rioting, he would indignantly reply, "Richard is my name, and my riches are boundless." Often would he, in a fit of intemperate mirth, rudely jest at the folly of the Spaniard, who had cast such a prize from him, and as he had heard it reported, had retired into a monastery.

On this earth, however, there is nothing that lasts forever. This too our gallant soon experienced to be true, much sooner, indeed, than he would otherwise have done, in consequence of the intemperance with which he plunged into all sensual delights. A languor like that of death seized his exhausted frame, in spite of all the virtue of his phial, which he vainly kept invoking for health, at the first attack of his disease. Recovery visited him not, but on the contrary frightful dreams.

It seemed to him that one of the phials, which were standing by his bedside, began to set up a wild dance, jostling against the rest in a furious manner. After gazing at it for some minutes, Richard recognised it to be that in which the little Spirit was enclosed, and exclaimed, "Bottle devil, bottle devil, thou assistest me no more, but rather destroyest that which should work my cure," whereupon the little black thing sang in a hoarse voice;

"Richard! Richard! thou prayest in vain;
Prepare thee now for eternal pain;
Therein must thou abide and endure,
Since spirit's power can work no cure,
No herb that groweth, death can heal;
I joy, for that thou art mine I feel."

After which it immediately stretched itself out, quite long and thin, and, notwithstanding that Richard held the phial stopped as closely as possible, it crept out between his thumb and the cork; it then suddenly became a large black man, who began to dance in the most hideous manner, clapping to and fro, at the same time, his huge dusky wings; and at length placed his hairy, leathern breast upon Richard's bosom, and his grinning face upon Richard's face, so that the latter felt as if he were himself assuming the hideous figure, and in a tone of wild agony screamed out for a mirror.

A cold sweat stood upon his brow as he awoke out of the ghastly dream, and he thought that he perceived a monstrous black toad creep down beside him into his bed; but, upon putting down his hand, he felt only the phial, in which the little black figure lay panting and apparently exhausted.

How awfully long did the remainder of this horrible night seem to the sick and frenzied wretch. He dared not again resign himself to sleep, lest the terrific vision should reappear; hardly, too, did he venture to open his wearied eyes even in the dark, lest he should perceive the monstrous fiend squatted in some quarter of the apartment. Yet did he shut his eyes but for a moment, he thought that it was again upon him, and started up with horror. He rang aloud for his attendants but no one came, all was still as the grave; as for Lucretia, he had not beheld her since he was first attacked by his disorder.

Thus did he lay in a state of torturing horror throughout the whole of that long, dreary night, the terror of which was increased, when he reflected that, if this single night appeared almost an eternity of terrors, what must seem the eternal night of hell on which no day would ever dawn that—night to whose dreadful visions there would be no end? He determined, at all events, upon getting rid of the fatal phial the very next morning.

When, however, the morning came, he felt his spirits so much revived that he began to ask himself whether he had yet turned the "Bottle Imp" sufficiently to account. Palace and villas, and all the luxuries wherewith they were furnished, seemed hardly enough; he, therefore, instantly demanded a great heap of ducats to be placed beneath his pillow, and, on finding them there instantaneously, he then began to reflect how best to dispose of the talisman. He knew that his physician was a great naturalist, and one who sought much after all monsters, and all such wonderful productions as are generally kept in spirits; he hoped, therefore, that he should be able to pass off the "Bottle Imp" to the learned man as a curiosity of this description; for else the doctor was too good a Christian to have anything to do with the evil creature. The deceit, indeed, could hardly be termed an innocent one, but need knows no niceties.

Accordingly, he offered the doctor the little spirit, which was now become again exceeding lively, jumping to and fro in the bottle with great vivacity; insomuch that, anxious to examine what he considered a wonderful *lusus naturæ*, the learned man agreed to purchase it, if the price demanded for it were not too high. In order to satisfy his conscience as well as he could, Richard asked a sum as nearly approaching to five ducats as was possible: the doctor, however, would give only three, which, fearing to lose his customer altogether, the other at last accepted, taking care, however, to bestow it all in alms upon the poor. But the money which he had found under his pillow, he carefully laid by, as the only fund upon which his future wealth and prosperity depended.

In the meanwhile his disorder continued to increase; he lay in a constant delirium, and had he still been tormented by the possession of the bottle devil, there is no doubt but that he would have actually died with terror and anxiety. At length, however, he gradually grew better: and now the only thing that seemed to retard his recovery, was his solicitude about the ducats, which he could no longer find beneath his pillow. At first he was very loath to make any inquiry after them; when, however, he did so, no one could give any account of them. Being able to obtain no information respecting the gold, it now remained for him to consider how he might best convert his mansion and villas into money. But here, too, he was reckoning without his host, for a throng of creditors appeared with various claims upon his estates, all duly signed by himself, and sealed with his own signet, he having, at the time of his boundless prosperity, given these papers to Lucretia to fill up as she judged proper: all that he could do, therefore, was to depart as quickly as possible with the little he could save from the fangs of these harpies; so that he quitted all his splendour very nearly a beggar.

At this juncture his physician made his appearance, with a countenance betokening serious displeasure. "Doctor," exclaimed the unfortunate young merchant, "if it so be, that you are come hither like the rest of your fraternity with a large bill, I prithee, add another item to the account, and see, good doctor, that it be for opium, or some equally potent drug; for my last bread is now baked, as I know but too well I have no money to buy more."

"Nay, nay," replied the physician, "things are not yet so bad as that. I am not only ready to renounce every demand upon you, but have also prepared a certain, most efficacious medicine, that will quickly revive you from this despondency; all that I ask for it is two ducats."

"And most readily will I pay them," replied the youth, which having done, the doctor forthwith departed. On opening the box wherein he expected to find this cordial restorative, he discovered a phial, but how great was his dismay on perceiving that it was that which contained the little bottle devil; and that, affixed to it, it had a label containing the following lines:

> Thy body I strove to cure from ill,
> But thou my soul hast sought to kill;
> Yet, an my art, 'buve craft of thine,
> Perceived full soon thy base design,
> Let me then now retaliate,
> To thee again revert thy fate;
> Be thine once more the dreadful sprite;
> And may'st thou feel his fellest might.

Great, indeed, was Richard's alarm, at finding that he had re-purchased his phial at so much lower a price. The only consolation that now remained, was to employ it as an instrument of revenging himself upon his treacherous paramour, which he effected in the following manner.

Having first of all summoned, by a wish, a sum of money double to that which he had lost, he carried and deposited it all with the nearest scrivener, excepting one hundred and twenty pieces, with which he betook himself to the abode of the faithless Lucretia. His reception was exactly such as he supposed his gold would procure him: his mistress was as lavish of her caresses towards him as she had ever been on any former occasion. After some time he displayed the curious toy he had brought, making the little black puppet, enclosed in the phial, perform abundant antics and tricks. This, he informed Lucretia, was exactly like the one which she had once flung into the water. She, like the rest of her sex, was desirous of obtaining such a droll play-thing: and, on the youth's sportively demanding a ducat for it, she paid it without hesitation. This bargain being completed, Richard hastened away as quickly as he could, and repaired to the scrivener, with whom he had deposited his money. He now found, however, that gold sticks so fast to certain people's fingers, that they cannot shake it off. The honest man stared with the utmost astonishment, protesting most vehemently that he had never clapped his eyes upon the young man before. This worthy specimen of probity had written his receipt for the sum deposited with him with a kind of ink that totally disappeared in the course of a few hours: therefore, when Richard produced his voucher, be found that he had merely a piece of plain paper. He thus found himself suddenly reduced to poverty, and would, indeed, have been completely a beggar, had he not still thirty ducats remaining from what he had been squandering at Lucretia's.

He who lies in too short a bed, must even pull up his legs: he who has no bed, must couch on the bare floor; who cannot afford to ride, must walk: so was it with our merchant, who was now fain to become a pedlar.

For this purpose he provided himself with a suitable box; but with what a heavy heart did he first buckle it on, to take his stand with some ware in those very streets where, but a few weeks before, he used to pass with a splendid retinue. In a little while, however, he became somewhat reconciled to his new occupation, having no lack of customers. "If I proceed at this rate," thought he, "I may yet again become a prosperous man, and that too at no very distant time. I will then return to my native Germany, where I shall find myself more comfortable than ever, after having been in the power of the accursed bottle devil, and having got out of his clutches by my own skill and dexterity."

With such thoughts did our newly-made pedlar cheer and console himself, on retiring for the night to an obscure inn. On his taking off his box, several of the guests, attracted by curiosity, began to examine the various wares it contained.

"My good friend," inquired one of these inquisitive gentry, "prithee, what queer kind of animal is this which you have got here in this phial, and which keeps jumping about at so strange a rate?"

To his great terror Richard now, for the first time, perceived that along with the other articles in his box, he had purchased the fatal bottle devil.

Instantly did he offer it to the bystanders for a mere trifling sum, but not one of them could endure the hideous creature, neither could Richard inform them of any particular use it was of; he, nevertheless, continued to harass them at such a rate with his entreaties to purchase it, that at length they thrust the impertinent chapman and his wares into the street.

In the anguish of his distress he now returned to the person who had sold him the box, and pressed him to take back the little imp at a lower price. The fellow, however, quite out of temper at being disturbed at such an unseasonable hour, and little disposed to become a dealer in such strange commodities, bade him be gone, and take his trumpery to Lucretia, for she was the person that had lately sold him the stock of trinkets, among which was that queer-looking phial.

Without waiting to hear another syllable, Richard ran off to Lucretia, as quickly as if he had a devil driving him instead of himself carrying a devil. He found the lady along with a couple of young noblemen. At first they railed at the uncourteous pedlar for daring to intrude upon them; but afterwards they purchased nearly his whole stock, for Lucretia had now recognized some of her old valuables, and also their present vendor: nor did the sight of him, in such a condition, seem by any means to damp her mirth. As to the "Bottle Imp," no one would purchase it; for Lucretia protested that she could not endure to look at the ugly thing.

"Say not so," replied Richard, "my fair inconsiderate: permit me but to whisper in your ear some of its virtues, and I am sure you will hesitate no longer."

She now retired a little aside, and the pedlar disclosed to her all the powerful, occult qualities of his little "Bottle Imp."

"How now! thou cheating varlet," cried the incredulous dame, "dost thou think to impose upon people by such fine tales as these? Were it true, I warrant me, thou hadst taken care first to provide thyself with something better than those filthy rags. Out with thee, for a knave! Begone, or I'll denounce thee for a sorcerer and dealer in the black art, and then both thyself and thy devil may be burnt together."

Both the gallants now took part in the fray, and kicked the unfortunate pedlar and his wares down stairs: where upon the poor wright, unable to resent the indignity, and terrified at the idea of being roasted for a wizard, hastened to leave Venice with all possible expedition; insomuch that, on the following day, he had quitted a territory which he now regarded as the land of all his misfortunes.

In the meanwhile he did not forget a nearer cause of his unhappiness, but, drawing the little dusky imp from his pocket, he cried,—"Thou miscreant devil! If I again call on thee for thy services, it is that I may rid myself of thee forever."

Having thus vented the bitterness of his feelings, he forthwith desired to have a sum much more considerable than the last, and then, almost sinking under its weight, he proceeded to the next town. Here he purchased a splendid equipage, hired a numerous retinue, and set out for home, convinced that there he should soon be able to find someone who would not scruple to take his unwelcome little companion off his hands. As often as he expended a ducat, did he require the imp to replace it by another, in order that, after selling his phial, he might still have the entire sum. This seemed to him no more than a fair compensation for the horrors he constantly endured; for in addition to the nightly visits of the black apparition, that never failed to come, and lay upon his breast, he saw also the bottle devil constantly frisking about the phial, with the most horrible glee, as if now quite certain of his prey at the expiration of the due period of his service.

Hardly had his wealth and the figure which he made procured him admission into the first circles of Roman society, than his constant dread would not allow him to wait until a proper opportunity should offer of freeing himself from his tormentor. He was continually offering his phial to every person, demanding for it three groschen in German money; insomuch that he, in a short time, became to be considered as a lunatic, and was a subject of ridicule to everyone. Money makes a good mood, and many a fair friend withal: so was it with our Richard; yet no sooner did he produce his phial, and begin to talk of three groschens, than all present were glad to escape his importunity.

So great, at length, was his despair, that he could no longer endure to remain at Rome, but determined to try his fate in war, hoping that by some chance he might there, at least, get rid of the cause of his misery. He had heard that two small Indian states were engaged in hostilities towards each other, and prepared to espouse the cause of one party. Adorned with a rich golden cuirass, and a superb crest of plumes, and armed with two light hunting pieces, an admirably tempered sword, and two beautiful daggers, did he set out, mounted on a noble Spanish steed, and attended by three followers, all of whom were bravely equipped.

A volunteer of so gallant a bearing needed not to offer his services in vain. Richard soon saw himself, therefore, attached to a troop of brave comrades, and led such a jovial life in camp, with drinking and singing, that his mortal apprehensions, and nocturnal visions, gradually left him. Having received a good lesson from what he had experienced at Rome, he was now cautious in offering his strange ware to sale; observing not to urge it with such suspicious earnestness. Indeed, he had hardly spoken of it to any one, hoping thereby to have an opportunity of meeting with someone who would not refuse it, if offered quite unawares, and with seeming indifference.

One morning as Richard was playing at dice with some companions, they were suddenly summoned to battle, by an alarm sounded on the trumpet. The cry was instantly "to horse!" With joyous spirits did our warrior leap upon his steed as it neighed and pawed the ground: the leaders encouraged on their troops, the signal sounded for the combat. A troop of the enemy's cavalry advanced, apparently for the purpose of hindering their attack: yet they soon retired before the powerful charge of their adversaries, nor were Richard and his followers last among the pursuers. The balls now began to whiz in the air, and many a rider fell from his horse, rolling to the earth in his blood. In spite of his personal courage, Richard could not think without shuddering of the immediate peril in which he was placed, fearing that some fatal ball might, in a single moment, deliver him into the power not only of the bottle devil, but of Lucifer himself. Scarcely, however, had he expressed a wish to escape the scene of danger, ere his steed bore him away to a wood, which was situated at no great distance.

So hard did he spur the animal, and urge him to flight, that it at length stopped quite exhausted. He then alighted, being himself greatly fatigued; unbuckled his own cuirass and sword, and laying himself down on the grass, said,—"This fighting is dangerous work at the best, but much more so with an imp in one's pocket!" He now wished to devise what course it would behove him next to pursue, but fell into a profound sleep.

After he had indulged in a repose of several hours he was awakened by the sound of voices and approaching foot-steps. He stirred not, in hopes that he might be passed by unnoticed, but soon found that the attempt would not succeed, for a voice, of no very friendly or musical tone, thundered out—"Ho! Fellow, art thou already dead, or are we to have the honour of killing you?" Looking up perforce at this uncourteous address, the unfortunate Richard perceived a musket levelled at his breast. The fellow who held it was a ruffianly looking foot-soldier, and the others had already seized upon his steed and equipments as their booty. Struck with terror, he supplicated most earnestly for mercy, but if they were determined upon shooting him, requested that one of them would first purchase a little phial which he had in his pocket.

"Senseless poltreon that thou art!" cried one of the fellows, with a grin, "to suppose that we here barter for anything; although that we will take the bargain off thy hands thou needest not fear:" and so saying he seized hold of the phial and thrust it into his bosom.

"In God's name thou art welcome to it," cried Richard, "if thou canst keep it. Yet that thou canst not do unless thou first purchase it."

The soldiers laughed at hearing him speak thus, and thinking him somewhat crack-brained, rode off without paying further attention to him. On feeling in his pocket, however, Richard found that the phial was there again. Whereupon holding it up that they might see it, he called after them. The fellow who had taken it was struck with amazement; and as, on thrusting his hand into his bosom, he did not feel it, he ran back in order to recover his booty.

"Did I not tell thee," said Richard mournfully, "that it would not continue with thee? Pay me but the trifle I demand, and it is thy own."

"Juggler!" returned the soldier, "dost thou think to defraud me of my well-earned spoils by these conjuring tricks of thine?"

And holding the phial carefully in his hand away he ran to overtake his companions; suddenly, however, he stopped short, exclaiming, with an oath, that it was gone again. Whilst he was searching for it on the ground, Richard called out to him once more, "Return hither, my good friend, for it is again in my pocket."

On finding this really to be the case, the soldier became more desirous of possessing so curious and wonderful a thing. On these occasions indeed it always manifested more than usual liveliness and agility, knowing that such bargains accelerated the final term of its servitude. Three groschen, however, still seemed too much to the soldier. "Well then, since thou art so unwilling to part with thy coin, let it be a single groschen, and take away thy purchase in good hour." Thereupon was the bargain concluded, the money paid, and the little bottle imp delivered up to its new master. While the soldier and his companions were examining the singular creature, and amusing themselves with its grim antics, Richard was reflecting upon his future destiny. His heart now felt quite light; but unfortunately, his purse was quite as light as his heart; nor did he know to what to betake himself, since he would not venture to his troop, although he left there not only his followers and his equipments, but all his money. He was partly ashamed of his disgraceful flight, and partly afraid lest, if he returned, he should be put to death as a deserter. It then occurred to him that it would not be amiss were he to accompany these troopers, having gathered from their discourse that they belonged to the other party, among whom he was certain of remaining unknown; and now that he had lost all his cash, and gotten rid of his little imp to boot, he felt that he had had returned some of his courage in exchange, and was by no means disinclined to venture his life once again, in the hope of obtaining some valuable spoil. He accordingly gave utterance to his wishes; and his proposal being accepted, he forthwith set off with his new comrades.

The captain was not very scrupulous in taking into his service such a tall and well-built young fellow as Richard, who was therefore considered as fairly enlisted among them. He was still, however, displeased with his lot: for, since the last battle, the two armies remained quite inactive, without either attacking the other, a treaty of peace being in agitation. Under these circumstances there was little danger of wounds, but, at the same time, very little opportunity of fattening on booty and plunder. Instead of the latter, the troops must perforce content themselves with their camp fare and their scanty pay. In addition to this, while most of his comrades had already enriched themselves in the preceding engagements, Richard, the once wealthy merchant, was almost the only one who was a beggar among opulent neighbours. Very naturally, therefore, he grew weary of such a life, so that once having received his monthly pay—too inconsiderable for his wants, and yet too much for him not to attempt something with it—he determined to go to a 'suttling booth, and seek whether the dice would not befriend him more than either traffic or war had hitherto done.

His success at play was as chequered as usual, now winning, now losing; and so did it continue until late at night, when all the dice turned up against Richard, whose cash was quite gone, nor would any one give him credit for a doit. He now offered to stake his cartridges, having nothing else to offer; the proposal was accepted, and, as the throw was about to be made, Richard perceived that the soldier who had accepted the stake, was the very same one who had purchased the bottle imp, by the assistance of which he would, doubtless, be certain of winning. He would fain have cried "Hold!" but the dice had already decided in favour of his opponent. Uttering curses at his ill fate, he quitted the company, and retired in the dark to his tent. A comrade who had been equally unfortunate, but whose brain was less heated by wine, now took him by the arm, and, as they were proceeding together, inquired whether he had any more cartridges in his tent?—"No," returned Richard, furiously: "did I possess any, they should serve me for the same purpose."

"Then," said his companion, "you would do well to provide yourself with fresh ones, for should the commissary come to examine you, and find you without them, he will order you to be shot."

"Zounds! that were plaguy work indeed! but I have neither cartridges nor the wherewithal to procure them."

"Thine is a sorry case indeed, then," replied the other, "for the commissary comes hither on the morrow."

This intelligence, although it did not tend greatly to tranquillize Richard, served in some degree to sober him; he went, therefore, to inquire of his comrades, if any one would lend him some cartridges. All, however, flouted him as a wild idle fellow, and bade him not interrupt them with unseasonable nonsense. In the utmost apprehension lest he should be ordered to be shot the very next day, he rumaged everywhere in the hope of finding some loose coin, but could meet with no more than five hellers. Late as it now was, he hurried from tent to tent, in order to find someone who would supply him with the cartridges. Some laughed at him, others abused him, but not one made any reply to his demand. At length he came to a tent, the occupant of which he discovered to be the very soldier who had so lately stripped him of his cartridges at play.

"Comrade," cried Richard, with great agitation, "if any one, it is yourself who must assist me in this extremity. But just now you have plundered me of all my cartridges, nor is it the first time in my life that you have proved the cause of my misfortunes. On the morrow the commissary comes, and he, unless I can produce my cartridges, will certainly give orders for me to be shot; you must, therefore, either give or lend—at least sell me some."

"As to either giving or lending, that I have long ago for-sworn; yet, to ease your distress, I will agree to sell you some. What money, therefore, have you?"

"But five hellers," replied Richard, in a melancholy tone.

"Well," said the soldier, "to show thee that I am willing to do thee a comrade's turn, there are five cartridges for thy five hellers. Now then betake thyself to thy rest, and disturb neither me nor my neighbours any longer." Which request, as soon as he had received what he sought, Richard instantly hastened to comply with.

On the following day the troops were examined, and Richard passed muster with his five cartridges, at which he, for a while, considered himself supremely happy, in spite of all the misfortunes he had undergone. His felicity was, however, but of very short duration; the joy he had first felt at finding himself out of actual danger soon subsided, when, on retiring to his tent, he found himself obliged to dine off coarse bread, without any better sauce to it than his own reflections. "What would I now give," sighed he, "had I but one of all the ducats which in the days of my folly I so wantonly squandered away?"—Hardly had he formed the wish, when, lo! a beautiful bright golden ducat was in his hand. But, alas! he thought of the bottle imp, which instantly flashed across his mind, damped all the satisfaction he had otherwise felt at finding himself the possessor of so acceptable a piece of gold.

At this instant, the comrade of whom he had purchased the cartridges entered the tent with a look of anxiety, and said,—"Friend, I have missed the phial with the little black creature; you must remember it well; it is the same that I formerly purchased of yourself. Has it happened that I sold it to you by mistake for a cartridge, for I wrapped it up in a piece of paper, and it was lying close beside them?" With a trembling hand did Richard now search in his cartridge-box, and found, the first thing he took hold of, to be the fatal phial wrapped up in the form of a cartridge.

"Ha!" cried the soldier, "this is all right. To say the truth, ugly as the creature is, I should be exceedingly loath to lose it, since I somehow cannot help fancying that it helps me to good luck. So, comrade, take one of thy hellers back, and return me my bottle." Most readily did Richard accede to this demand, and the soldier departed equally pleased.

Yet was poor Richard ill at ease, after having met with his bottle imp once more, and having had it again in his own possession; he could not help imagining that he saw it grinning at him between the folds of his tent, and that it would strangle him in his sleep. Much as he stood in need of refreshment, he now flung the piece of money from him; and at length his terror lest the accursed being should once more return while he continued there arose to such a pitch, that he led from the camp, and entered a thick wood, where, exhausted by alarm and fatigue, he sunk down in a wild, lonesome spot.

"Ah me!" he exclaimed as he lay there panting, "that I had but a camp-bottle with water to keep me from dying with faintness!" And the bottle with the water stood beside him. It was not till after he had drunk at hearty draught out of it, that he thought of asking himself by what means it came there. The bottle imp now occurred to him; when, putting his hands into his pockets, and finding the phial there, overcome with sudden horror, he fell down in a deep swoon.

While he continued in this state, his former horrible dream returned, wherein he beheld the little bottle imp stretch himself out longer, and at last fix himself, grinning most hideously, upon his breast; he expostulated with the monster, asserting that it no longer belonged to him; but the creature replied, with a hollow satanic laugh, "Thou boughtest me for a heller, and thou must therefore sell me for less, or the bargain will not hold good."

Richard leaped up in horror, and thought he still beheld the terrific figure, as it re-entered the phial in his pocket. In a state of agonized frenzy he dashed the phial from him down in a steep hollow, but instantly afterwards felt it again in his pocket. "Alas! alas!" screamed the unhappy wretch, "how fortunate did I at one time consider myself at finding, that let me cast away the phial ever so far, it always returned to me—but that it does so, is now my misery—yes, my everlasting misery." And he thereupon began to run furiously among the wild bush-wood, dashing in the dark against trunks of trees and pieces of rock, and hearing, at every step he took, the phial clinking in his pocket.

At day-break he arrived at an open plain, which had the appearance of being well cultivated, and had a cheerful appearance; somewhat revived by this prospect, he began to hope that what he had experienced was merely a wild dream, and that the phial would prove to be no more than a common bottle. He took it out, therefore, and held it up against the sun; but, alas! he still perceived the little black monster dancing up and down, and stretching out towards him, as usual, its little ugly misshapen arms, as if it would seize hold of him. Uttering a loud cry of agony, he let the phial fall on the ground, but only to feel it in his pocket immediately afterwards. The thing of the utmost consequence for him now to do was to inquire everywhere for some coin of less value than a heller. Nowhere, however, could he meet with any such piece of money; so that, at length, despairing of being ever able to get rid of the monster that now threatened inevitably to become his master, he no longer thought of calling upon it for its services; his increasing horror, on the contrary, would permit him to think of nothing but his miserable situation. Thus did he wander up and down, subsisting upon charity and alms: and as he had a wild, crazed appearance, and was continually beseeching everyone for some piece of money less than a heller, he was considered as a madman, and was called "Crazy Half-heller," by which appellation he was soon known far and wide.

It is said that the vulture sometimes fixes itself with its talons into the back of a young deer, and thus hunts to death the poor animal, which, as it flees in agony, still carries along with it its savage, relentless enemy. Thus was it with poor Richard, and the Satanic imp in his phial—but instead of accompanying him through his continual and unvaried misery, let us pass over a considerable interval and arrive at an important event.

He had one day lost himself in a wild rocky country, and had set down to rest beside a little stream, whose murmuring seemed to sympathize with his affliction. A loud sound of a horse's hooves rung on the rocky surface of the ground, when there came, riding upon a large black wild looking steed, a man of gigantic figure, and exceedingly terrific countenance; he was attired in a deep blood-red garment, and approached the spot where Richard was sitting.

"Wherefore so melancholy, young stranger?" said he, addressing himself to the youth, who involuntarily shuddered at his voice, as if with a vague presentiment of something evil—"I should take thee to be a merchant: hast thou then been making a bad bargain?—Hast purchased anything at too high a price?"

"Alas! no—rather at too low a one," returned Richard in a tremulous tone.

"Ay, so I should think indeed," rejoined the grim horseman with a horrible laugh. "And hast thou then got for sale a thing that they call a bottle imp?—or am I mistaken in conjecturing you to be a crazy Half-heller?'"

The poor youth was hardly able to say "yes," so great was his horror, expecting every instant to behold the apparition's mantle expand itself into a pair of bloody wings, and his steed to assume a more terrific, spectral appearance, breathing forth infernal flames from its nostrils; and, lastly, that the monster would carry off his wretched soul to the regions of eternal misery.

But the ghastly horseman said, in a somewhat milder voice, and with less appalling mien—"I perceive for whom you take me: yet be comforted, for I am not he, I rather present myself to rescue you, if so may be, from his power; having for some days past been searching for you, in order to become the purchaser of your phial. To confess the truth, my friend, thou hast paid indeed a most terrible small sum for it, nor can even I myself inform you where it is possible to meet a coin of less value. But, listen and obey me. On the other side of this mountain there resides a prince who is a sad dissolute young fellow. When he comes to the chase on the morrow I will first withdraw him from his attendants, and then cause a frightful monster to fall upon him. Wait thou here till midnight, and then proceed just as the moon rises above that jagged rock, towards that gloomy defile to the left, but neither hurry nor loiter in thy pace, so wilt thou arrive at the spot precisely as the monster has seized the prince in his frightful paws. Attack it, but courageously—it must yield to thee; and drive it down the steep cliff into the sea. Then, as a recompense for having delivered him, demand of the prince that he cause two half hellers to be coined for thee; let me have them, in order that, with one, I may become the purchaser of thy bottle imp."

So spoke the grisly horseman, and then, without waiting for any reply, rode off slowly into the wood.

"But where am I to find thee when I have obtained the half hellers?" cried out Richard.—"At the Black Fountain, of which each old crone hereabouts will be able to inform thee;" and then with solemn, but wide outstretching pace, did the horrible steed bear away its no less terrific rider.

He who has already lost nearly everything, ventures not much by any further risk: Richard, therefore, determined, as his situation was so desperate, to follow the councils of the grisly spectre.

Night closed in, and the rising moon shortly after appeared above the craggy tops of the rocks which had been marked out to him. The pale wanderer then raised himself tremblingly, and entered the dark defile. All seemed there cheerless and gloomy;

seldom was a pale moon-beam able to penetrate above the lofty precipices; a dark oppressive vapour too, as if exhaled from graves, seemed to fill the narrow pass; in other respects there was nothing particularly terrible in its appearance. Richard felt himself by no means disposed to linger in the gloomy valley; yet, adhering to the strict injunction laid upon him by the mysterious horseman, he did not venture to quicken his pace, resolutely determined not to snap short at once the only slender thread that still attached him to light and hope.

After the lapse of several hours some red streaks of dawn cast a glimmering light across his path; a reviving breeze played upon his forehead. But, just as he was about to emerge from the deep valley, and enjoy the forest scenery, and the azure waters of the sea that lay expanded at no great distance before him, he was disturbed by a piercing cry of distress. On looking round he perceived a horrible animal attacking a youth in a magnificent hunting dress, who had fallen on the ground. Richard's first impulse was to rush instantly to the stranger's rescue, yet his courage failed him as soon as he clearly discerned the monster, and saw that it resembled a huge grisly baboon, with a stag's antlers on its forehead; and, notwithstanding the cries of the wretched man for succour, he was about to turn back. But suddenly calling to mind all the horseman had said, and inspired by the dread of his eternal doom, he ran and attacked the monster of an ape with a knotty club, just as it had seized the unfortunate hunter in its paws to fling him up into the air, and then catch him upon his branching horns as he descended to the ground. At the approach of Richard, however, it let fall its prey, and began to flee with a hideous, terrifying cry; he pursuing it all the while, till, leaping from a precipice into the sea, it turned its frightful visage upon him, and then disappeared beneath the waves.

Flushed with success, the youth now returned triumphantly to the hunter whom he had just rescued, and who, as he expected it would be, announced himself the prince of that territory.

After extolling the bravery of his deliverer, he requested that he would boldly demand whatever boon he should think fit.

"What!" exclaimed Richard, in a transport of joyous hope, "and are you serious? and will you pledge me your princely word that you will grant what I shall demand of you?"

Again the prince confirmed his promise, assuring him, in the most solemn manner, that he would gladly comply with whatever he should request.

"Then I supplicate you, for the love of God, to order that some half-hellers be immediately struck for me, even though it be only two." Whilst the prince was regarding his strange petitioner with fixed astonishment, some of his train came up, and, on hearing the adventure, and the singular boon that had been craved, one of them recognised, in the person of the suitor, the poor crazed Half-heller.

The prince began thereupon to laugh, whilst Richard, clasping his knees, conjured him in the most moving manner, protesting that unless he obtained the half-hellers his soul was doomed to everlasting perdition.

To this the prince replied, while he still continued to laugh, "Rise up, my friend, I have pledged my princely word, and if you persist in demanding them, I will engage to supply thee with half-hellers to thy very heart's content. But, if a still lesser coin will suit your purpose, I can accommodate thee without the aid of my mint-master, for the neighbouring provinces all maintain that my hellers are so light that three of them are requisite to pass for a single ordinary one."

"Were that, indeed, the case——" said Richard.

"Thou art, indeed, the first," returned the prince, "that has ever doubted it. Should they, however, upon trial, prove not suitable for your purpose, I here promise to order some less valuable to be coined for your especial use—provided, however, that it be possible so to do."

Having said this, he gave orders that Richard should forthwith receive a whole bag full of hellers. The latter instantly set off at a furious rate towards the adjoining province, where he became more delighted than he had been with any occurrence for a long time past, at finding, at the very first inn, that the people were exceedingly unwilling to exchange one heller in return for three which he offered them, by way of experiment.

He now inquired his way towards the Black Fountain, when some children who were present ran away, shrieking with affright; and the host informed him, not without shuddering himself, that it was a place frequented by demons and evil spirits, but hardly ever visited by mortal being. He knew perfectly well, however, that the entrance to it was at no very great distance, through a cavern, at the mouth of which stood two decayed cypress trees, so that Richard could not mistake finding it: "yet, God forbid that he, or any other Christian person, should ever seek it!"

At hearing this account, Richard was again greatly disturbed, but let the event be what it would, he must make the attempt, and therefore set out to discover it. Even at a distance the cavern had a most dismal and terrifying appearance: it seemed as if the two cypresses had died with horror at the ghastly hollow, which, as he approached it, displayed just above its mouth a singular stone. It seemed to be entirely covered with grim countenances, some of which bore a resemblance to the hideous baboon-monster on the sea-shore. Yet, on looking fearlessly and attentively, one might perceive that it was merely the rugged stone. Not without trembling did Richard pass beneath these horrible visages. The Bottle Imp now became so heavy in his pocket, that it seemed as if it wished to prevent his advancing further. This circumstance inspired him with courage to proceed: "for," thought he, "it behoves me to do that which this creature wishes I should not do." On penetrating farther into the cavern the darkness became so great that he could no longer discern any terrifying shapes. He now proceeded with the utmost caution, groping his way with a stick lest he should fall into some abyss, yet found nothing but is soft mossy turf; and had he not heard at times a strange groaning noise, his fears would have ceased altogether. At length he reached the outlet of the cavern. He now found himself in a dreary hollow, quite enclosed by steep hills. To one side he perceived the large sable steed of the mysterious customer for his phial, which was standing motionless as a brazen statue. Opposite to him was a spring, gushing from the rock; and in this the grim horseman was washing both his face and hands, but the horrid stream was of an inky hue, with which it stained whatever it touched; for when the gigantic figure turned round towards Richard, the latter perceived that his visage was become like that of a Moor, and thereby formed a terrific contrast to his blood-red garments.

"Shudder not," cried the hideous being; "this is only one of the ceremonies which I am obliged to perform in honour of the devil. Each Friday I am bound to wash myself thus, on account of the sins of earlier days. I am also compelled to stain my garment afresh with my own blood—it is this which gives it a hue of so much deadly lustre; besides a number of still more horrible ceremonies which I am obliged to undergo, I have, moreover, formed so strong a compact with the powers of darkness—both for body and soul, that it is now utterly impossible for me to obtain redemption on any terms. And what do you imagine are the terms on which I have sold myself?—for a hundred thousand pieces yearly. Thus seeing how desperate is my own condition, still I am willing to serve thee, by purchasing the imp thou carriest in thy phial, to thus to frustrate the end of all his long servitude; besides the rescuing thee from the powers of darkness, will so enrage them, that, reckless of ought else, I'll do it. Then how will their impotent curses peal through their deepest vaults; ha! ha! ha!" So saying, he began to laugh in the most frightful manner, that the very rocks re-echoed, and the sable steed, which had hitherto stood motionless, seemed to shrink with terror at the awful sound.

"Now then, friend," added he, after a while, "hast thou brought me any half-hellers?"

Upon Richard showing him his purse he took three of the pieces and gave him a heller in exchange; one of which he directly paid back again, as the purchase money for the Bottle Imp, that now lay crouched up melancholy at the bottom of the phial, so that he felt quite heavy. At perceiving this the unknown purchaser laughed again most violently, and exclaimed, "Nothing can avail thee, fiend; all resistance is in vain. In token, therefore, of thy obedience, let me have, instantly, as much gold as my strong steed can bear." And no sooner had he uttered the command, then the enormous beast stood panting beneath the golden load. Then the blood-red horseman having mounted on its back, it began to crawl up the perpendicular sides of the rock, just as a fly does up a wall, and disappeared forever.

THE ELOPEMENT

by Johann Karl August Musäus

O N the banks of a small river, called Lokwitz, in Vogtland, is situated the castle of Lauenstein, which was formerly a nunnery that was destroyed in the Hussite Wars. The holy domain passed again as an abandoned property into the hands of the laity, and was let by the count of Orzonumda, the former lord of the manor, to one of his vassals, who built a castle on the ruins of the cloister, to which he probably gave his own name— he was called lord of Lauenstein. The event soon fatally proved to him that church property is never prosperous in the hands of laymen, and that sacrilege, however clandestinely committed, will always meet with punishment in the end.

The bones of the deceased nuns were roused from their peaceful abode. Rattling noises perpetually disturbed the tranquillity of the family. Processions of nuns with flaming images were seen passing to and fro, opening and shutting the doors. They would often follow the servants wherever they went, in the stables, and different apartments of the castle, pinching them, nodding at them, and tormenting them with frightful noises. The terror and dismay which these disturbances produced, spread among all the domestics, who were afraid of moving from the spot where they were fixed, for fear of meeting something more horrible. Nor was the lord himself proof against this host of spirits. The resentment of the nuns did not confine itself to these outrages. They would likewise attack the cattle, dry up the milk of the cows, and flit about the horses, so that both men and beasts were kept in a continual state of affright, from the annoyances of the spirits.

The lord of the manor spared no expense to obtain, by means of exorcisms, a cessation of the tumults. But the most powerful enchantment, before which the whole empire used to tremble, and the sprinkling brush dipped in holy water which drives away spirits as the flap drives away flies, had no effect on these Amazonian spectres, who defended their claim to the property of the castle so firmly, that the exorcists with their holy vessels and relics were sometimes obliged to quit the field.

There was a certain famous man by the name of Gessner, who travelled about the country to lay spirits, and relieve the injuries which their nocturnal revels had produced.

To him was reserved the task of reducing these troublesome visitors to obedience, and confining them again in the gloomy regions of death, where they might roll their skulls and rattle their bones without molestation.

Tranquillity was now restored in the castle. The nuns now slept again the still sleep of death, but after the period of seven years, a restless spirit of the sisterhood made her appearance in the night, renewed the former disturbances for a long time, till she was weary, then having rested another seven years, re-peated her visits. So that the family in course of time began to be habituated to her appearance at stated periods, and left the apartments whenever that happened.

Upon the decease of the first possessor, the inheritance fell by a regular succession into the hands of the male heir, which did not fail till the Thirty Years War, when the last branch of the Lauenstein family flourished, in whose formation nature seemed to have exhausted all her powers; she had so prodigally lavished her materials upon him, that at the time he was arrived at years of maturity, his corpulence and weight almost equalled that of the famous Irishman, who some years ago exhibited the enormous bulk of his body in the principal towns of Germany; at the same time the young lord, Siegmund, to rusticated manners united an uncommon share of pride: he was determined to enjoy life, while he carefully avoided any extravagance which would diminish the paternal estate, that had been hoarded up by parsimony.

After the example of his ancestors, he fixed upon a wife, as soon as his parents were deceased; and began to look forward with pleasure to the prospect of an heir to his estate.

In this, however, he was disappointed; for the wished for child proved a lovely girl. He afterwards sought no other enjoyments but that of eating, so that all the hopes of a male successor were buried in his corpulence. His wife, who from the beginning had the management of the family, fixed all her affections on her daughter, and left her husband to revel in his sensual indulgencies, till at last he regarded nothing, but the luxuries of the table. The education of Emily was, therefore, entrusted to the care of her mother, who spared no pains in adorning her person, and cultivating her understanding, of which she had no small share.

In proportion as the charms of her fair Emily began to expand, her views were extended, and her hopes flattered with seeing her daughter the ornament of her family. She indulged latent pride, which consisted in an extravagant attachment to her pedigree.

No family in all Vogtland, except the *** were in her opinion of sufficient antiquity, and noble birth to be allied to the last branch of the Lauenstein family; when, therefore, the youths of the neighbourhood were eager to pay their respects to this young lady, whose affections they wished to gain, the weary mother gave them such reception as effectually put a stop to any further intercourse. She likewise carefully guarded the heart of Emily against what she called smuggled goods, and railed greatly against the speculations of cousins and aunts, who busied themselves in forming matrimonial connections. This had the desired effect upon the daughter, who united with her mother in rejecting every offer.

So long as the heart of a maid yields to instruction, it may be compared to a small boat in the ocean, which suffers itself to be steered wherever the rudder guides it, but when the wind rises and the waves toss the light bark to and fro, it regards no longer the rudder, but yields to the violence of the winds and dashing of the waters. Thus the docile Emily submitted to the guidance of maternal instruction and walked with cheerfulness in the path of pride. The heart was yet untainted with guile. She expected some prince or count to do homage to her charms, and therefore treated every inferior person with a contempt truly gratifying to her mother.

Before a suitable successor could be found for the Lauenstein estate, a circumstance happened to frustrate the views of the mother, and proved that all the princes and counts in the Roman empire would have come too late to gain the heart of Emily.

During the disturbances of the Thirty Years War, the army of the brave Wallenstein took its winter quarters in Vogtland; and Siegmund received many uninvited guests, who committed more outrages in the castle than the former nocturnal visitors. If they did not lay claim to it, as their just property, in the same manner as the latter, neither did they suffer themselves to be expelled by exorcists; and Siegmund saw himself compelled to make his guests comfortable, that they might preserve discipline.

Entertainments and balls succeeded each other, without intermission; the former were superintended by madame Siegmund and the latter by Emily. The officers were pleased with the hospitality with which they were treated, and their host with the good temper and respect with which they returned it.

Among them were many who might have attracted Venus herself; one, however, who was called the beautiful Frederic, eclipsed the rest. To a fine form he united insinuating manners. He was gentle, modest, agreeable, lively, and a charming dancer. No man had yet made an impression up on the heart of Emily, but she could not resist these fascinations when united to a red coat.

Her heart became susceptible of feelings, of which she was not at first conscious, and they filled her soul with an inexpressible pleasure. The only thing that surprised her was, that such attractions should be found in a person who was neither a prince nor a count.

Upon a nearer acquaintance she frequently questioned his companions respecting his family and prospects: but no one could give her any satisfaction on a subject which occupied all her thoughts. Everyone praised him as a brave and amiable man, but his truth seemed to be buried in perfect oblivion.

The secret enquiries of the anxious Emily did not remain long concealed from him. His friends thought to flatter him with this information, and accompanied it with many favourable conjectures. His modesty would not permit him to consider this anything but a joke. At the same time he felt a secret pleasure in supposing himself the subject of a young lady's thoughts, who was by no means indifferent to him. The first view of her had excited in him an enthusiasm which is the precursor of love.

No words are so forcible or intelligent as the looks which excite the sympathy of a tender attachment. A verbal explanation did not take place for some time, but both parties could divine each other's thoughts; their countenances declared what the bashfulness of love forbade them to utter.

The unsuspecting mother was now so immersed in the care of providing for her guests, that she had not leisure to guard with her usual diligence every avenue to the heart of Emily: Friz perceiving this, did not fail to turn it to his own advantage, by insinuating himself in her favour. As soon as he had gained her confidence, he gave her very different instructions from those she had received from her mother. As he was the avowed enemy of distinctions, his care was to free the mind of Emily from the prejudices she had received upon this subject; teaching her that birth and rank must not be put in competition with the softest and most pleasing passion.

The enamoured Emily suffered her pride, therefore, to fall before her attachment, and excused in her lover the want of nobility and titles; she even carried her political heresy so far as to conceive that the prerogatives of birth, with regard to love, were a yoke which human freedom should be permitted to shake off.

The affections of Frederic were now fixed on her and from every circumstance he was satisfied that his lover would meet an ample return. He sought, therefore, an opportunity to open to her the state of his heart! She received his professions with blushes, but with real pleasure; and their confiding souls were united by mutual vows of inviolable fidelity.

They were now happy for the present instant, but shuddered at their future prospects! The return of the spring recalled the army to the field, and the melancholy period in which the lovers were to part quickly approached.

Consultations were now begun, how an intercourse might be kept up between the two lovers, who resolved that nothing but death should separate them forever. Emily informed him of her mother's sentiments on the choice of a husband for her, and the improbability that her pride would yield in a single point to affection.

A hundred schemes were alternately fixed upon and rejected, as the difficulties of each preponderated in their minds. When the young warrior perceived the willingness of his mistress to embrace any plan that would contribute to the completion of his wishes, he proposed an elopement as the securest method which love ever suggested, and by means of which it had often succeeded in frustrating the views of parsimonious pride. Emily after a little reflection consented. The only subject of consideration was the method of escaping from the strongly guarded castle, and the scrutinizing vigilance of her mother, which would be redoubled upon the departure of Wallenstein's army.

But the inventions of love surmount every obstacle, Emily was well acquainted with the periodical visits of the spirits, and that on All Saints day, in the ensuing autumn, when seven years would be elapsed since their last appearance, they were expected to be renewed. The terror of all the inhabitants she knew likewise to be very great on these occasions, which gave her an idea of the possibility of passing for one of the ghosts. For this purpose, she proposed to keep a nun's dress in readiness for herself, and, under this disguise to make her escape. Frederic was enchanted at the happy thought and joyfully clasped her in his arms. Although at the time of the Thirty Years War heterodoxy was but in its infancy, yet the young hero was philosopher enough to disbelieve the existence of ghosts or at least to deny their interference with human affairs.

When everything was prepared for her departure Frederic mounted his horse, committed himself to the protection of fortune, and put himself at the head of his squadron. The campaign terminated fortunately for him: love seemed to have listened to his prayers and taken him under her protection.

In the meantime, Emily, who was alternately agitated with hope and fear, trembled for the life of her faithful Amadis, and took particular care to make herself acquainted with the safety of their winter guests. Every report of a skirmish terrified her, which her mother attributed to the humanity of her disposition, not suspecting the real cause of solicitude.

Frederic did not omit to convey information to his mistress of his situation from time to time, by private letters, which reached her through the means of a faithful chambermaid, by whom she returned intelligence of herself.

As soon as the campaign was at an end, he began to make every preparation for his expedition, and waited with the most restless impatience for the joyful day when he was to repair to a little wood near the castle.

On the day of All-Souls, Emily prepared herself for putting her scheme into execution, with the assistance of her chambermaid. She affected a slight indisposition, retired to her chamber at an early hour, and converted herself into one of the handsomest nuns whose spirit had ever appeared.

The tedious hours moved on leaden wheels. Every moment increased her eagerness to commence the adventure.

In the meantime, the moon, a friend to lovers, threw her pale light over the castle, where the bustle of the busy day had given way to awful stillness.

No one was awake but the housekeeper, who was summing up the domestic expenses, by the dim light of a candle; the porter, who also served as watchman, and the dog Hector, who, barking, saluted the rising moon.

When the midnight hour arrived, the undaunted Emily sallied forth. Provided with a large key that unlocked the doors, she slid gently down the stairs into the hall. Descrying here unexpectedly a light in the kitchen, she began to rattle a bundle of keys with all her might, threw down the chimney board with violence, opened the house door, and entered the small porch.

As soon as the three watches heard this rattling they thought of the ghosts, and took refuge in different places. The housekeeper ran into bed, the dog into his kennel, and the porter to his wife, on the straw; by which means Emily obtained her liberty, and hastened to the wood where she fancied she already saw at a distance the carriages and horses. But what was her amazement when upon a nearer approach it proved to be the shade of a tree. She thought of course that she had mistaken the place of rendezvous, and traversed, therefore, every part of the wood from one end to the other. But all her searching terminated in the most grievous disappointment: her knight and his equipage was nowhere to be found.

Amazed at this event she was incapable of thinking or acting. Not to attend to engagements of this kind is a crime amongst all lovers, but in the present case it was unpardonable. The affair was to her inexplicable. After waiting an hour in the most cruel anxiety, in which her heart was torn with conflicting passions of grief, shame, and vexation, she began to weep and utter the bitterest complaints, when at length the reflections suddenly led her to recall her long lost family pride; she was ashamed of her condescension in making choice of a man of unknown family. The ecstasy of passion had now forsaken her. Her reason had gained the ascendency, and she resolved to retract the false step she had taken, by returning immediately to the castle and forgetting her lover. Upon her arrival there she was met by her maid who received her with a mixture of joy and surprise. Everything however was buried in the profoundest silence.

Her lover was not however so culpable as the incensed Emily imagined. He had not failed to attend at the appointed place, even earlier than necessary, in order to be in perfect readiness to receive his beloved mistress. While waiting with anxious impatience, the form of a nun presented itself before him. He sprang from his place of ambush, clasped it in his arms, and cried out—"I have you; I hold you; I will never let you go, dear Emily, now thou art mine and I am thine, with heart and soul." Upon these words he joyfully carried the lovely burden, and placed it in the carriage, which drove off with the utmost speed.

The horses snorted, kicked, and shook their manes, one of the wheels broke, and by a violent jerk the horses, carriage, and man, were thrown down a precipice into a deep ditch; our hero became insensible from the violence of the fall, and, upon his recovery, found himself in a village, whither he had been carried by some country people, who discovered him in the morning in a deplorable condition. He had lost all his equipage, together with his fair companion. This circumstance afflicted him more than all the rest. He sent people to different parts in pursuit of Emily, but could obtain no information. Midnight set him free from the anxiety of suspense: when the clock struck twelve his door was opened, and his fellow traveller made her appearance, not in the form of the enchanting Emily, but of the ghostly nun, as a horrible skeleton. The beautiful Frederic became sensible of his mistake, blessed and crossed himself, and uttered many ejaculations.

The ghost turned itself towards him, walked to his bed, stroked his cheeks with her ice-cold hands, crying "Freddy! Freddy! I am thine, thou art mine with heart and soul." Having persecuted him for a whole tedious hour with her presence, she at length disappeared. In this manner she continued her persecution every night, and followed him to Eichsfeld, where he was quartered. He had there no respite from the irksome caresses of the ghost, which afflicted him to the destruction of his spirits. His melancholy became the subject of conversation among his companions, who felt compassion for him, without being able to conjecture the cause of his anxiety, for he had not ventured to divulge his unfortunate secret. He had, however, one confidential friend among his comrades, an old lieutenant, who was reputed to be expert in laying spirits; to him the beautiful Frederic explained the grounds of his uneasiness. "Is that all?" said the exorcist with a smile. "I wilt relieve you from this impertinent visitor; follow me to my quarters." Upon entering, he observed many magical preparations and characters marked upon the floor, and as soon the lieutenant called, the midnight spirit appeared in a dark room, lighted by the dull glimmer of a magic lamp. He reproached the ghost severely, and appointed a willow in a lonely glen as the place of its abode, with an injunction for it immediately to repair thither, never more to return. The ghost disappeared; but in the same instant a storm and whirlwind arose; which was dispelled by a procession of twelve pious men in the town, who rode on horseback, singing a penitential psalm, according to their usual custom. After this the spirit was never more seen.

The beautiful Frederic recovered his spirits and repaired again to the field under Wallenstein, where he fought many successful campaigns, in which he conducted himself so nobly that on his return to Bohemia he was honoured with the command of a regiment. He took his journey through Vogtland, and, upon perceiving the castle of Lauenstein, his heart beat with doubt whether his Emily had been faithful or not. He called, as an old friend, at the castle where he met with a reception suitable to the name. The dismay of Emily was inconceivable when her supposed faithless Frederic entered the room.

A mixture of joy and sorrow overwhelmed her. She could not resolve to deign him a tender look, and yet this constraint cost her many severe struggles. She had been reasoning herself for three years out of a passion which she thought beneath a person in her rank of life; but still she could never completely erase the plebeian lover from her thoughts. In this state of mind, fluctuating between resentment and affection, was the tender Emily when Frederic addressed her, and by his insinuating manners procured an opportunity of relating the whole affair; to which she in return informed him of her suspicions and resentment. The joy and affection of the two lovers redoubled upon these mutual confessions. They agreed to extend their secret a little farther, and include her mother in the circle of their confidence.

The good lady was struck with as much astonishment at the art of her daughter in carrying on an intrigue, as at the circumstance of her elopement in so extraordinary a manner. She thought it just, however, that an affection which had experienced so severe a trial should be rewarded by an union of the persons. And though this idea militated against the prospects she had formed for her daughter; yet, since no prince or count was in view, she gave her consent, after which the beautiful Frederic embraced his charming bride, and his marriage concluded happily, without meeting any farther opposition from the ghostly nun.

THE WARNING
An Adventure, as Related by the Late Hofrath E****, Merchant in B*****

by Gottfried Peter Rauschnick

IT happened in the autumn of the year 1799, that I found myself obliged to make a journey of considerable length, for which I had completed the necessary arrangements, and packed my *sac de nuit*, when my wife, on account of an extraordinary dream, begged most earnestly that I would give up my intention and stay at home. Having important business on hand, and being now in great haste, I could not patiently bear with her obstinate resistance, but answered at last so harshly, that she burst into tears. At this, I was much distressed. I durst not leave her in that unhappy mood, but began to expostulate, and to explain the absolute necessity for my journey. We tried to compromise the matter, and, instead of setting out early in the morning, I agreed to stay till after dinner, though even that change in my plan was exceedingly awkward and inconvenient.

By this means, however, my wife gained time to narrate her dream at full length, and it was no doubt sufficiently alarming. She had imagined that I was attacked in a gloomy forest by robbers, who had dragged me from my horse, and brought me into a cave, there to be instantly murdered. The ground was covered with horribly mangled carcasses, that seemed to stretch out their skeleton arms to grasp at the newcomer, and yet there was one hideous white figure in a shroud, that rather strove to protect me from the assassins. Whether or not he succeeded in these attempts she could not tell, for "a change came o'er the spirit of her dream;" and these phantoms made way for others which were less vivid and significant, but no less terrible.

As no one in the world despised dreams more than I did, I took this opportunity of telling my Sophia how truly absurd and ridiculous it was to dwell seriously on such fancies; adding, however, that, if superstitious fears were entertained and persevered in, this conduct might actually bring on those evil consequences which we sought to avert. For if she had not vexed me so much by her inopportune anxiety, I might have that day, according to my intentions, reached the country residence of an old friend, where I should have been comfortably quartered for the night, instead of which I must now either ride in the dark, or be forced to lodge in a wretched village alehouse.

Notwithstanding my arguments, Sophia's disquietude continued unabated; but this did not hinder me from setting out after dinner, for my business could not be delayed. Want of ready money obliged me, at that time, to visit several small towns, where I had accounts unpaid, and expected to obtain further orders. I might certainly have availed myself of my wife's carriage for the journey, but my physician had of late enjoined me to ride as much as possible on horseback, and I took the opportunity to put his advice into practice, for which I could otherwise spare little or no time from my engagements in the counting-house.

On my route, I could not deny myself the pleasure of visiting my old friend Nicholas Waldheim, (knowing that I must, at all events, pass near his house,) for we had been schoolfellows and play-mates; we had been brought up as merchants in the same town, and commenced business at the same time. His affairs, however, did not seem to prosper like mine; he retired early, and now lived on a small estate, which he had saved enough to purchase. As he never came to town we had not met for many years, and although I had often proposed to visit him, one melancholy occurrence after another had always come in the way, (for example, the death of my former wife, and of several beloved children,) so that I could never fulfil my intentions. By dint of time I had almost ceased to think of him; but now the impressions of old friendship were forcibly renewed, and I was resolved that I would, at all risks, find out his residence. This happened accordingly. Waldheim received me with great kindness. I was entertained with the best fare which his house afforded, and he insisted that I should by no means think of travelling farther that day. However, I could not decide on remaining with him through the night, this being the second day of my journey, but, at his earnest entreaty, promised that I would certainly make a longer stay on my return homewards.

To say the truth, I had been much disappointed in this visit. I had delighted myself with the thoughts of our meeting, had dreamed of old times, when, with glad hearts, in all the vivacity of youth, we had formed gigantic plans, and our future prospects appeared in the brightest, most dazzling colours. I wished to excite in my friend's mind the same visionary recollections which had taken possession of my own, but I soon found that this was with him quite out of the question. Whenever I touched on those subjects, Waldheim instantly broke off the conversation—inquiring particularly, however, as to my present employments and purposes, affecting the most cordial interest in my welfare, though it was but too easy to perceive that all the while his manners were constrained, and his kindness pretended. This could not arise from any special dislike to me; I gave him no farther trouble than that of a short visit; it only proved that he must have encountered misfortunes of which I was not aware, and that sorrow had brought on him this coldness of heart, which it was not possible for the presence, even of a very old and intimate friend to subdue. His brow was indeed furrowed by so many wrinkles, his eyes shone with such a dark mysterious fire, and their movements were so wayward and suspicious, that I could scarce bear to look at him. His wife, who might now be about fifty years of age, kept up a constant grin on her visage, which was intended for an expression of good humour, and yet, being evidently forced, gave her more the appearance of a malevolent sorceress than a kind hostess. She had two sons—to the younger of whom I had stood godfather. One was now twenty-three, the other twenty-two years of age; but, notwithstanding their youth, and features decidedly handsome, both wanted altogether that cheerfulness—that expression of candour and confidence which should have belonged to their time of life.

On inquiring what was to be their future destination in the world, I was informed that they preferred agriculture to every other employment. I could not approve of this, as I saw plainly that retirement in the country had by no means contributed to Waldheim's welfare; his house was indeed tolerably well-furnished and supplied; but his own gloomy looks betrayed the toil and care which this had cost him. I gave it as my opinion, therefore, that they would succeed better as merchants, and made a proposal to take the younger brother as a clerk into my own house. The young man appeared well pleased with my offer but his father's vexation was so evident, that he could scarcely answer in his usual tone of voice,—"he had been himself sufficiently unfortunate in trade, and would never consent to his son's engaging in any such speculations." As the conversation now seemed painful to him, I broke it off abruptly, and, recollecting my own urgent avocations, took my departure, having renewed my promise, that I would, on no account, forget to visit them on my return, and remain for at least one night.

During this brief interview, I had collected materials enough for after-reflection, and continued to perplex myself on the sub-

ject all the way to my next halting-place. Our moralists and po-
ets describe the pleasures of a country life, and the contentment
of the husbandman, in such brilliant colours, that, according to
them, it is to be wondered at if any mortal who can leave town
should confine himself within its gloomy prison-walls. On the
other hand, they assure us that cheerfulness, tranquillity, and
health, are to be found with never-failing certainty among the
fields and woods, while the townsman must always be a miserable and care-worn animal. How different, on the other hand,
is reality—of which my friends fate was a notable example!
In town he had uniformly been active and cheerful—seemed
to be quite contented in his domestic circumstances; in short,
was in all respects prosperous and happy. One glance, however,
was now sufficient to ascertain that he was in the last degree
dissatisfied with his lot—his former merriment had completely
declined; nor between him and his wife did there appear to exist any cordial union of spirit. His sons, young as they were, had
acquired already their father's gloom and perplexity of aspect;
and if on their parts this could not be the result of worldly cares,
it might have other causes—perhaps low libertinism and sensual indulgence. As to the sloth and inactivity of all the family,
this was, alas! proved beyond a doubt by the state of the garden,
which was an absolute wilderness, and by the miserable corn-
fields where the scanty straggling crop showed an utter want of
management and attention. The house and farm-offices were
half ruinous; the roads almost impassable; besides, the district
in which Waldheim's farm lay was gloomy and repulsive. The
lands were flat and sandy, surrounded on every side by dark fir-
woods, that shut out every pleasant prospect. No verdant mead-
ows refreshed the wearied eyes—no clear lively streams varied
the landscape; only, not far from the dwelling-house, there was
a desolate stagnant lake, which any good husbandman would
have drained and got rid of. "Thither," said I to myself, "one
should send the romantic panegyrists of a country life—there

they would find the most complete and incontrovertible refutation of their pastoral and Arcadian theories!"

I was glad when I came into the woods, which at least afforded me protection from the sun's heat; but the road, with its everlasting sameness of scenery and lonely silence, broken only by the screams of rooks and ravens, became insupportably tiresome, so that I felt again rejoiced on emerging into the open country. The district in which I now found myself seemed at first by no means attractive;—however, when I had ascended a steep eminence, a landscape truly beautiful was once more spread before me. The rich corn-fields gleamed in the golden light of the now setting sun. I saw the husbandmen returning from their labours; the herds and flocks; the white sails of the merchant-vessels on the noble winding river; while in the background rose the church-towers of a pleasant town, where I intended to pass the night. I could now have retracted all that I had said against rural life, and even become its panegyrist in my turn.

In this town, however, my commercial transactions first began; and in consequence the good spirits with which I had entered its gates were soon put to flight. The accounts of a wholesale merchant in a large city, with petty retailers in the country, are generally rather confused; and, as I now proved by experience, their adjustment is attended with no little trouble. These people have, in their confined circle, so many trifling stratagems, and their intellects are so narrow, that one must absolutely have new weights and scales, and a new measuring-rod, in order to deal with them! Their sphere is so limited, that, in comparing accounts, they set to work with a tediousness and circumstantiality that drive any opulent merchant beyond all bounds of patience; and, notwithstanding this, they have no pretensions to punctuality or good order; for the domestic arrangements of every family, which, in a small town, are talked of by the whole inhabitants, give each householder more than enough to do. Besides, on account of their narrow range of business, every merchant must enter into different and unaccording branches of trade. Their activity wants the principle of unity and concentration; therefore order is also completely deficient.

Consequently I had the more reason to be satisfied that I had undertaken the journey, for I was convinced that my presence only could be a check on their impertinent delays, or prevent serious losses which I might have otherwise incurred. With a good deal of trouble, I was fortunate enough to obtain payment of several heavy accounts, which I insisted on receiving in ducats or Friedrich's d'or, silver being inconvenient for a traveller; after which I pursued my journey. The same troubles awaited me in other small towns; yet in all I was successful in combating such obstacles, and winding up my affairs within the space of time that I had prescribed to myself at setting out.

At one of the places which I was obliged to visit, it was not without great alarm that I found one of my household servants waiting for me with a letter. I opened it in trepidation, expecting some disastrous news from home; but in this I was mistaken. My wife wrote to me, that, since my departure, she had been tormented by the most frightful apprehensions, which she had been enabled to quiet only by determining to send out a confidential servant, entreating that he might be allowed to continue his attendance for the rest of my journey. She had been again terrified by a spectral dream, which afforded her the most certain tokens that misfortune now hung over me. Vexed as I happened to be at the moment by a dispute that I had encountered with one of my troublesome debtors—startled too by the man's unexpected appearance—and provoked at my wife's childish superstition—I was in no humour to comply with her request. On the contrary, I expressed great displeasure that she should have sent the servant from home, where his assistance was always required in the ware-house; and turned him back with a letter, in which I begged that she would not trouble me anymore with such unpardonable folly—reminding her at the same time, that the personal safety of every traveller in that country was guarded by a most active and watchful police. On that day and the two following, my journey indeed led through a populous and flourishing district—one small town or another was always in view; the weather, too, was cheering and delightful; so that I felt no regret whatever at having sent away the servant.

My transactions being at last wound up, I thought of returning homewards by a new route, which was equally convenient with the former for a traveller on horseback, and was considerably shorter than the high road. But now, in truth, I had reason to think that it would have been better to retain my wife's courier, for I had with me a large sum of money, and its weight was too obvious to escape notice when the portmanteau was taken from my horse at an inn, and left often-times in the care of my host. It was hardly to be expected that the thoughts of robbery would not enter into the mind of some one or another, and, more than probable, that attempts would be made to put such plans into execution. I had, besides, to cross long tracts of forest scenery; and the autumnal weather began to break, so that, for the sake of expedition, I was obliged to travel a good way in the dark. I consoled myself with the thoughts that my horse was excellent, and that I was provided with a pair of doubly-loaded pistols, by which I trusted, that, in the hour of need, I should be able to defend my life and property.

The first day of my homeward journey I still kept on the high-road, but I had many a long mile betwixt me and the place where I intended to pass the night; so that I stopped for refreshment seldom, and as short a time as possible. My horse, therefore, shared in my sufferings from hunger and fatigue, when at last about nightfall I reached the appointed station. But here, what a strange reception awaited me! The host and hostess exhibited visages that were, without exception, the most repulsive I had ever beheld in my life. It is impossible to conceive a more determined concentration of savage wildness, gloom, and malicious discontent, than was betrayed by these people. At the same time, they tried as usual to appear courteous and friendly, but the effort that this obviously cost them rendered their aspect only more detestable. I would willingly have retired to rest, if hunger had not forced me to wait for supper, of which the preparations required unusual delay. Meanwhile they had shown me into a room, but, growing tired of its solitude, I only stayed to examine whether there were any concealed trap-stairs or tapestry-doors, and, being satisfied on this point, betook myself to the landlord's apartment, where I entered into conversation with his daughter, a girl of remarkable beauty. I was surprised at the proofs of good education which she displayed in this dialogue, and felt the more interested by an appearance of reserve and melancholy which seemed to have taken deep root in her young and innocent heart. I was afraid to give her pain by rash questions, but prolonged the discourse in hopes of learning the cause of this grief, or being able to guess at her misfortunes, till her mother came and called me to supper. Then, too, as in the preceding dialogue, my desires were left ungratified, for the dishes, produced at last, were so abominably bad, that I was unable to eat a single morsel. Want of sleep soon drove me to my bedroom, which was on the second floor. The frightful rushing of the wind through the neighbouring fir-trees—the beating of the rain on the casements, and gloomy *tout ensemble* of this vile habitation—brought my mind into a strange mood, which, though I am no coward, was nearly allied to terror. That my host and hostess were not to be numbered among good people I was thoroughly persuaded, but if they were so very wicked as to rob and murder their guest, was a question which I could not determine. The longer I thought on this subject, the more I was inclined to believe that my life was by no means safe under their care, and many stories crowded on my remembrance of secret murders, from which the best organized police in the world cannot afford protection.

At length I heard the outward doors of the house groaning on their hinges, and violently closing for the night. It seemed to me, thereupon, as if I were quite shut out from all the world, and thrown into a den of murderers. I even went to the window to examine whether, in case of need, I might not venture to leap from it, which expedient, on account of the height, I found quite out of the question. Now I remembered the dreams and forebodings of my wife, which increased my agitation. I carefully shut the door, piled up some chairs against it, that in the event of any one entering, I might be awakened by their fall; laid my pistols within reach, and betook myself to rest.

Weariness soon overpowered all other sensations, and I fell fast asleep. I might have slumbered about an hour, when a noise awoke me, that seemed to be in my chamber. I raised myself from the pillow;—but what language can describe my horror, when, by the glimmering star-light, I actually beheld a figure robed in white, a phantom as it seemed—wrapt in a shroud—that stationed itself opposite my bed!

My hair now stood on end, my teeth chattered, and for a while I lost all self-possession. At length I summoned up resolution and grasped one of my pistols, by which the figure did not seem in the slightest degree discomposed or intimidated; but, raising one arm in a threatening attitude, exclaimed in a hollow tone, "Be not afraid, for I come only to warn you. Go not again to the house of Waldheim, if you value your existence, for you will never come alive from under his roof." For a few moments the spectre stood motionless—then added, "Hast thou understood me?" and when, in a trembling voice, I answered "yes," he instantly disappeared.

I remained for a long while as if petrified, and stared at the place where the apparition had been, without being able to alter my position;—at last, I rubbed the cold sweat from my forehead, and, by a vehement effort, roused myself from this trance, but I was perfectly convinced that what I had witnessed had been *no dream*! I had never believed in ghosts, nor indeed troubled myself much with speculations as to their existence or non-existence; now, however, I had ocular and auricular demonstration of their reality; for, as to the possibility of deception, that idea was removed not only by the inexplicable mode of appearing and vanishing, but by all other circumstances. The innkeeper could never have caused this scene by stratagem, nor would have thought of doing so, for he himself had advised me earnestly to take the road that led through Waldheim's farm, and to pass the night there. And who but the inn-keeper could know anything of my plans, or wish to interfere with them?

What danger I could possibly incur at my friend's house, was to me a new riddle; and I kept awake debating this point long after my terror of the apparition had subsided. I firmly resolved, however, to follow its admonitions, which were evidently connected with, and in harmony with my wife's dreams and anticipations. Not till towards morning did I fall asleep, and never awoke till a loud knocking at my door disturbed me. This noise was made by the innkeeper, who had been alarmed at my non-appearance, and inquired whether I were unwell. I started up, dressed myself in great haste, paid my chalked bill for refreshments, which I was unable to taste, for I found the breakfast as abominable as the supper had been, then rode away as fast as I could, to make up for the time that had been lost in sleep.

About mid-day I began of course to feel unusually hungry, and was fortunate enough to find a pleasant inn on the roadside, where I was supplied with an excellent dinner. As I must, according to the ghost's injunctions, choose a different route from that with which I was acquainted, I made inquiries of my host, and obtained from him the necessary directions. He was a good-humoured loquacious man, and seemed very willing to enter into conversation on whatever subject I started. I inquired, therefore, whether he was acquainted with my friend Nicholas

Waldheim, who lived in that neighbourhood. At this question the man's cheerful countenance became immediately clouded—he looked at me suspiciously—was silent a few moments—and then answered drily, that he certainly did know the man of whom I spoke. I wished to hear more, and begged him to say what was his opinion of Waldheim; what character he bore in the country, and whether he had been successful in his farming occupations? My host shook his head; assured me that he was quite unprepared to enter into those particulars; and, for a long while, I could not obtain from him any satisfactory reply. At last he said, that, from his own knowledge, he could not vouch for any action good nor bad of my friend Waldheim; however, that his mode of life was considered by almost everyone quite inexplicable; for the produce of the fields there always turned out so miserable a crop, that it could not pay the farm-servants' labour, yet, notwithstanding this, the man continued to maintain a numerous household, and it was said that they all lived well. For the rest, he did not associate with any person of his own rank, never appeared with his family at church, and the members of his establishment were so reserved and shy, even of the daylight, that scarcely any neighbour could boast of having spoken with one among them. This intelligence was to me very perplexing, it seemed so inconsistent with the former disposition of my friend, who could scarce ever have enough of society! At all events, the change proved nothing in his favour, and I was by this means the more confirmed in my determination of not going to his house. The inn-keeper, to whom I mentioned what had been my intentions, approved highly of this caution, and begged urgently that I would adhere to my present resolution, adding, "There are many strange stories of the forests in these parts;" but as to the ground of these allusions, I could not obtain from him any adequate explanation.

I was obliged to hasten onwards, that the night might not overtake me; for on that day I had still a long way to travel.

Besides, there were dark clouds on the horizon, and it was easy to foretell that ere long a formidable tempest must ensue. I rode, therefore, as hard as it was possible to do, without absolutely foundering my horse. The recollection of the nocturnal apparition—my wife's forebodings—the doubtful expressions of my landlord as to the character of Waldheim, by turns occupied my attention, and beguiled the way, though certainly not in a manner the most agreeable. Meanwhile, the night drew on apace, and it was evident that the darkness, aided by the gathering clouds, would be quite impenetrable. There was a distant rolling of thunder, which reverberated hollowly through the forest; pale lightning quivered at intervals through the clouds, and the gloom always increased. It seemed as if the woods never would have an end. I made my horse exert himself to the very utmost, in order to reach some place of shelter; but at length I was obliged to pull him up, for the road became gradually more narrow, and the branches of the trees gave me such striking illustrations of the propriety of riding cautiously, that I was obliged to yield to them. My situation was certainly in the utmost degree vexatious,—more especially as I knew not even whether or not I was on the right road. *Now* I sincerely lamented my rash conduct in dismissing the servant that my wife, in her loving kindness, had sent after me, and was obliged to acknowledge that my present difficulties were only a well-deserved punishment. The darkness, which had by this time grown quite opaque, obliged me to dismount, and lead my horse by the bridle, otherwise I had no chance of avoiding the branches, from which I had already received many severe blows. In such manner, my progress was of course very slow, and my hopes of reaching any habitation become always fainter. At last, however, I found myself once more on the clear level ground; I felt as if I had just then escaped from a prison; I could again mount my horse, and ride along without dreading every moment to have my head knocked off my shoulders by a tree.

The thunder clouds, however, had always come nearer and nearer; the lightning dazzled me with its quivering flashes; the wind rose through the neighbouring wood in strange fitful blasts, which were regularly followed by a mysterious stillness, augmenting the terrors of the hour. Yet now my hopes were revived by a light gleaming in the distance, although, in order to approach it, I durst not spur my horse, for the thunder startled him, and I was obliged to use every precaution to avoid being unseated by a sudden plunge.

I had by degrees come so near the light, that I could discern, by its aid, the building from which it emanated, but, to my great consternation, I perceived that I had gone quite astray, and was now on the property—close to the very threshold of Nicholas Waldheim. Good counsel rose above par with a vengeance! Should I enter his house, or leave it? My horse was tired—the storm raged unrelentingly,—and I felt myself so much in want of that repose to which the hospitable mansion of an old friend invited me; while, on the other hand, the most alarming, even supernatural warnings had announced that *here*, of all places in the world, I must not risk my personal safety. Perhaps, however, my extreme want of food and rest would have made me decide on braving all dangers, if my horse had not shown a violent disinclination to proceed any farther, and turned sharp round. This trifling circumstance put an end to my debate, and I resolved that I would rather pass the night in the forest than trust myself with a man whose character and mode of life were so very questionable.

Accordingly, I took my way back towards the woods, leaving it to chance to bring me on the high-road; or, if that might not be, I hoped to find some cottage, or other place, where I could at least obtain shelter from the rain, which now began to fall in large drops. I was glad when I reached the trees, which would afford me some protection; but new difficulties awaited me, for,

on the outskirts of the forest, I did not think myself sufficiently secure against Waldheim's people, and the thickets were so
dense and entangled, that my horse could not be led through
them. I forced a passage through the branches, however, but
at every step these became more closely interwoven, and the
ground was more uneven. Several times I had fallen over the
roots of trees, my face and hands bled from the scratches I had
received, and my strength was nearly exhausted. At last, I heard
a rushing noise of water as from a mill race, whence I concluded
that I was near to some habitation, and redoubled my exertions
to reach it if possible; but as it was in vain to think of bringing
my horse any farther, I tied him by the bridle to a tree, took
off the portmanteau, which I threw across my shoulders, and
fastened by the straps round my neck. My route was now very
hazardous. I had to clamber over great trunks of trees and frag-
ments of rock—had to struggle through deep places, where I
was often so hemmed in by thickets of brushwood that I could
neither get backwards nor forwards—till I nearly lost all courage. Add to these hindrances the frightful thunderstorm, and
the terror that I might be struck down by lightning, attracted
by the steel clasps of my portmanteau. My condition was indeed
most grievous, but after long persevering labour, I came to the
edge of a declivity under which the rivulet rushed. I followed its
course, not without imminent danger of tumbling in headlong,
and found my conjectures confirmed that there was a mill there.
A gleam of lightning showed me a large building of that description, but the ruinous sluice, over which the water now played
idly, proved that it was in disuse; therefore, probably, there were
no inhabitants. On further search, I discovered an old tottering
bridge, leading across the mill-race; which I passed, and ran
towards the building for shelter, while the rain fell in torrents.
Suddenly it occurred to me that this place might be the resort
of robbers, in which case I should absolutely throw myself into
their hands; but my fatigue was so great that it overbalanced my

apprehension. I found the door open—(a sign that no one lived there)—I groped about with great caution in the darkness, and advanced till I touched the platform of the inner mill-wheel. Quite worn out, yet terrified by the thoughts of falling perhaps through a hole in the floor, or stumbling over some murdered victim, I seated myself at last in a corner, and resolved to wait there for daylight.

Scarcely had I composed myself for rest, when a most over-powering sense of horror came over me. What could be the real history of this building, which stood so desolate and forsaken—If robbers, as it seemed probable, haunted the place, would I not certainly be found out and murdered?—What if the mid-night spectre should again appear to me?—These, and other harassing thoughts, forced themselves on my mind; and I was the less able to combat them, when, reclining on the floor, I became aware of a most detestable atmosphere, as if from a charnel-house, which became so insupportable, that I would have left my hiding-place, if my fears had not rendered me powerless. After I had remained for about an hour in this torment, voices were audible at the door; and as I had no doubt that the newcomers were banditti, my death seemed now irrevocably decreed. I could hear that there was some wrangling among them as to the cause of the door being found open, after which four men came in with a lantern, and bearing a sack that was filled evidently with some cumbrous and heavy load.—They drew near without observing me, lifted up some boards in the flooring, and opened the sack. It contained the bloody corpse of a man, which they threw down under the floor, then closed up the aperture as before.

My hair now stood on end. I shook as in an ague fit, and nearly fainted; for, in addition to the other terrors of this scene, I recognised Waldheim's eldest son among the murderers. "So much for that fellow!" said he, when they had thrown down the body; "if we had met with E*****," (here he mentioned my name,) "and disposed of him in like manner, it would have been better worth our trouble."

"I am afraid,"' said another, "we have no chance of seeing him tonight."

"Well," answered a third, "if he comes not tonight, he will tomorrow—at all events, he shall not escape us."

Perhaps I had unconsciously made some noise; for the ruffian Waldheim remarked—"The door was left open; let us search the house, that we may be sure no one is watching us." The rest, however, were afraid; they alleged that it was no place to remain in longer than necessity required; and it was impossible that anyone would venture to watch there, unless it were some revengeful ghost. This cowardice saved my life; for if, in reality, they had searched the building, I must have been discovered, and my death was certain. At last they quitted this den of murder, and carefully locked the door.

My feelings at that moment baffle every attempt to describe them. How near I had been to destruction! I had just seen one murdered victim secreted, and heard that a like fate was destined for me. Even now I was by no means safe, for if by chance they discovered my horse, this would doubtless excite their suspicions—they would then come back and make a resolute search. If I could escape on the return of daylight was also uncertain; but these miserable apprehensions were increased to a nameless horror, when I heard the murdered man beneath me groaning hideously, and rattling in his throat. I am certain that I heard him—he was murdered, indeed, for his wounds must have been mortal, but life was not yet extinct. The cold sweat stood on my forehead—my heart beat audibly—I had almost died; indeed, it seemed as if the night would never have an end. My senses were confused in delirium, and I almost doubted if I yet lived.

At last the grey light of morning began to gleam through the broken roof, and hopes revived that I might make my escape. As soon as I could clearly distinguish objects, I went to the door, but it was so thoroughly secured that all my efforts to force it open were in vain. In searching through the building for some other outlet, I stumbled on the entrance to the pit-fall, into which the last victim had been thrown; I lifted up the boards, and, with indescribable abhorrence, beheld eleven dead bodies, many of them already in the most frightful stages of corruption—among these I was to have been deposited, and might be so still, if I did not succeed in gaining my liberty. After much trouble I found another door, which yielded to a vehement effort; it led into a room in which there were many bloody dresses hung up against the wall. This apartment was lighted by a small window, of which I instantly broke the casement, and, though at the risk of my neck, leapt out.

Now then I was at liberty; but still I had not my horse, nor, if he were found, did I know in what direction I should ride in order to escape from those assassins. I retraced, as nearly as I could guess at it, my course of the preceding night, and having now the advantage of daylight to guide me through the thickets, discovered my faithful steed sooner than I could have expected.

A beaten cart-road also presented itself; I mounted and trotted away with the utmost expedition.

Though the scenes were quite new to me, and I could not tell whither I went, yet chance, for this time, favoured my purpose; for, after riding about two miles, I reached a post-station. Here, as soon as I had obtained some refreshment, I took a carriage with extra horses, and drove as rapidly as possible towards B****. I reached home the same day, and, on my arrival, had recourse to the director of police, before whom I made a circumstantial declaration of my adventures, whereupon he ordered a proper legal inquiry to be commenced, and the same evening dispatched one of his officers with a band of soldiers to Waldheim's residence.

My wife was overjoyed at my safe return, having felt the most unconquerable anxiety during the whole time of my absence; but my sufferings from that terrible night were not yet complete. I was attacked by a fever, which ended in very serious illness. My strength had been so severely tried by the excitement I had undergone, that extreme weakness and relaxation followed, and I must have perished, but for the constant attention of a skilful physician, under whose management, after being six weeks confined, I felt myself once more in a condition to leave my room.

As soon as my health allowed of any exertion, I made a visit to the prison in which Waldheim was now secured. Notwithstanding his crimes, and the attack which he would doubtless have made on my life, I could not help looking on him with some degree of compassion, and wished to alleviate his sufferings as far as the law would permit. However, no sooner had I made my appearance, than he began to rave like a madman, and broke out into the most horrible imprecations, as if he were determined to prove how undeserving he was of that interest which I took in his fate. In a few minutes I was obliged to leave him with aversion and disgust, but I begged the gaoler to obtain for me an interview with Waldheim's younger son, from whom I hoped to extract some information as to his father's crimes. The young man, when he saw me, was moved even to tears, and answered my inquiries with such candour, that, on my return home, I was able to set on paper what here follows, and which corresponds exactly with the records of the criminal court.

Nicholas Waldheim, at his commencement in trade, was exceedingly active and prosperous. His income was competent; he lived within it, so that his fortune augmented slowly indeed, but securely, and his credit rose every year. By some unexpected windfalls, however, my capital increased so much that I was able to extend my business to an extraordinary degree, and this excited his envy. Till then, we had always advanced on an equal footing, both as to our gains and our expenditure; our credit and influence on Change were the same, and there was, in truth, no difference between our respective fortunes; but now these circumstances were completely changed. Never having been inclined to avarice, I did not deny myself any elegance or luxury which my resources now warranted; at length, I considered a handsome carriage and horses allowable, therefore indulged in the purchase of both. My first wife was perhaps more partial to fine dresses than was altogether commendable, but as we lived very happily together, I did not choose to run the risk of involving myself in domestic quarrels, by crossing her harshly in this humour. Meanwhile, the wife of Waldheim wished to be attired exactly like mine; and as he could not afford such expense, she overwhelmed him with reproaches for his bad management. He would indeed willingly have competed with me in all respects, but feeling this to be out of his power, he tried passionately every method, however hazardous, to become quickly opulent. He strained his credit to the utmost, and entered into speculations, which brought with them a tumult and whirl of business, quite beyond his strength to support. In the confusion thus induced, he overlooked the necessary precautions; his reputation for punctuality was impaired, and the fall of his house seemed inevitable.

The thought of being reduced to poverty through those very exertions which were intended to make him rich, were to Waldheim so insupportable, that he took the resolution of ending his sufferings by suicide. With this weight on his mind, he wandered about restlessly for some time, till the very day had arrived which he had fixed on for the execution of his purpose; and he was traversing the fields near a country house which he then rented in the environs of B****. Quite absorbed in his own gloom and despondency, he was insensible to all that passed around him, till he felt himself pulled by the sleeve, and saw a fine artless boy about sixteen years of age, who inquired of him the way to the house of a merchant, who was said to live in that neighbourhood, and for whom he had a packet of letters. This merchant was no other than Waldheim himself; and on inquiry, he found that the boy was a son of one of his own country correspondents, who sent not letters only, but a considerable sum of ready money, which was to be appropriated to certain specified purposes. The boy had come with the diligence, but had left it at the last station, in order to enjoy a walk in fine weather through the pleasant gardens that surround the city. Waldheim, as if the devil had been there present in *propria persona*, was seized with a horrid and overpowering impulse, which he was the less disposed to combat, as his whole soul had just before been possessed by the idea of self-murder. He led the boy by circuitous paths, where he would escape observation, and said that he was going himself to town, where the merchant then was, with whom he was well acquainted, but must first call at his own country house. He brought his unsuspecting victim into a retired apartment, without being seen by any mortal;—there put him to death, and thus became possessed of a large sum, partly in paper, but mostly in ducats, which the unfortunate lad had carried in a huntsman's leather bag.

He had just completed this atrocious deed, when the door unexpectedly opened, and his wife with her two sons entered the room. At first their astonishment and abhorrence were unbounded; however, when he had explained his desperate circumstances, from which only this crime could have relieved him, their detestation of his guilt was gradually lost in terror of the consequences which might else have awaited him and the whole family. Thus he threw the disastrous load of his own wickedness on the conscience of his wife and of his children; after which disclosure they became gradually more and more accustomed to a life of suspense, misery, and deception. They were obliged to assist him in that first adventure, to conceal the body of his murdered victim, and, in order more effectually to avoid all suspicion, he appeared with his wife and sons at a large party, to which they had been invited for that day. Aided by the money thus obtained, he upheld his sinking credit, but the conscious guilt which weighed on his heart left him not a moment's peace of mind. He could not endure the ordinary restraints of society; therefore by degrees he withdrew himself from trade, and purchased that landed property on which I found him.

Being quite ignorant of husbandry, he soon discovered that it would be impossible for him to live by this farm, which, even under the best management, would have yielded but a very narrow income, and was on the point of being reduced to abject poverty, when one stormy night a traveller made his appearance, and begged earnestly for shelter and refreshment. The stranger's dress and *tout ensemble* betokened opulent circumstances; his heavy saddle-bags (for he was on horseback) seemed full of money, so that the demon of Waldheim's avarice was once more roused. He received his guest with the most specious courtesy; and within the next hour he had entered into an agreement with his wife and sons that the man should be murdered, and his property seized.

The deed soon followed; and, with a view to concealment in this instance, he prepared a deep grave in a thicket of the neighbouring forest, to which, with the help of his eldest son, he carried the body. Now, however, it was the will of Providence that he should be discovered. A passenger, who had watched him occupied in this abominable task, came up boldly and questioned him what was the matter. Waldheim, in order to screen himself effectually, would instantly have murdered this intruder, but the latter, being well armed, was provided against any such attack. He assured the criminal, nevertheless, that, if allowed to share in the booty, he would henceforth preserve inviolable secrecy as to what he had then witnessed. Waldheim was of course under the necessity of assenting, and the bribed villain soon made it known that he also was by no means disinclined to such exploits, if only the spoils were sufficient to counterbalance the risk and trouble. This person was the detestable landlord of that inn where the ghost appeared to me. In a short time, the two miscreants were on confidential terms with each other; and not only did the innkeeper assist Waldheim with servants, who were bound on oath, and on pain of death, to conceal whatever might occur, but came personally on the field when the *corps* of his worthy partner was not sufficiently effective. To prevent discovery, he took special care never to make his own inn the scene of action, but for the most part served as a watchful spy, and gave notice to Waldheim when travellers were on the road who had with them any large sum of money. The innkeeper's wife was also an accomplice, but his daughter, who had been educated in the family of a worthy and conscientious aunt, was wholly ignorant of these atrocities.

It was proved that, in a course of eight or ten years, more than fifty people had been assassinated by these outlaws. The ruinous building in which I spent the night had been possessed and occupied by a certain miller; a man of good character, of whose voluntary connivance at such transactions there was no hope,—he was therefore looked on by this gang as a very troublesome neighbour, and, in order to be rid of him, they contrived, by various stratagems, to make it appear that his house was haunted. The loneliness of its situation favoured this undertaking, and by degrees they terrified the superstitious man so much, that, being completely tired of this residence, he sold his lease of the mill to Waldheim for a mere trifle; and the stories of ghosts were henceforth so industriously spread through the neighbourhood, that it was never wondered at if the building was left deserted and in disuse. It served the assassins thereafter as a regular place of rendezvous and concealment.

For my escape from the fate that otherwise awaited me, I was indebted to Waldheim's younger son. This youth had never taken any active share in his father's crimes, though he had been bound by a solemn oath, like the others, to preserve secrecy. Towards me as his godfather, he cherished, from earliest youth, some feelings of attachment and respect, which were increased by my well-intended offer to take him into my house as a clerk. He had been aware of the plot laid against my life, but could not, without betraying his father, give me any direct information. With the innkeeper's house, however, he was well acquainted;

and as there existed a love affair betwixt him and the girl whom I have already mentioned, he happened to be there at the time of my arrival, and afterwards made use of a private door, which I had not discovered, in order to appear like a ghost, and warn me against trusting again to Waldheim's hospitality. With the same view, also, he had made use of the opportunity, when I was in the landlord's room, to enter mine, and draw the slugs from my pistols, so that, if I had fired at the intruder, he would not have sustained any injury. Thus he was my protector from otherwise inevitable destruction; and became, in consequence, the cause of his father's guilt being duly punished.

It was impossible that Waldheim could deny or extenuate the many proofs that were brought against him; and circumstances came to light of a description so new and horrible, that everyone shuddered at the bare idea of such enormities. On account of many additional witnesses, and other instances of persons who had mysteriously disappeared in the forest, the trial was lengthened out, and it was not till a year had passed over, that judgment was pronounced, which was afterwards duly ratified by our sovereign. Waldheim and the innkeeper, with their wives, were broken on the wheel; Waldheim's elder son was punished in like manner; the servants and other accomplices were beheaded with the sword, and their bodies nailed to the wheel. As for the young girl, she was of course pronounced innocent; but her lover, though by silence only he had rendered himself an accomplice, was awarded ten years' imprisonment in the house of correction. Even that decree, in consideration of his having saved my life, was changed into a sentence of two years' confinement only. The fortunes of this youth and his wife (for he was at length married to the innkeeper's daughter) will one day fill another story.

THE COLD BRIDE AND THE RING
Legends of the Rhine

by Alois Wilhelm Schreiber

The Cold Bride

MANY years prior to the destruction of the castle Lauf, or more properly called Newwindeck, it had been totally forsaken, in consequence of the report that it was haunted.

Just about this period a young knight to whom the neighbourhood was strange, sought one night the shelter of its roof from a threatening tempest. In the courtyard of the castle, luxuriant grew the grass, rearing its green head amid the withered blade of many a summer past. The sound of his horse's hooves echoed along the castle-walls, and his oft repeated call received no other answer. At length he espied a solitary light in one of the castle-windows, and he ascended the mossy staircase to find the seemingly only habitable room. At a table, her head reclining on her hand, and seemingly so sunk in meditation as not to observe the knight's approach, sat a lovely maiden, whom, in her beauty, one might likened to an angel, one of another world; but it was beauty of a pensive cast, for the rose that should have mantled her cheek, seemed as if from sorrow to have fled its home. As he greeted her, she raised her languid eyes and with an inclination of the head alone replied. In answer to his entreaty that she would afford him shelter for the night—again her head bent forward. He was hungry, and ventured again to speak. She rose and placed before him venison and fragrant wine, but bread and salt the fair one had forgot, and for these the young knight dared not ask, for the scene brought him unease, especially as not a sound had yet passed the lips of his hostess.

At length, warmed by the wine he'd drank, Rhinish, of a favourite vintage too, he ventured to address the enigmatic fair one.

"You are doubtless, fair one, daughter of the knight who"—again her head cut short his speech.

"And your honoured father?"

She pointed to the portrait of a knight against the wall, that in costume bespoke ten generations back at least and in a hollow voice replied—"Of my race I am the last; this fair domain is mine; you're welcome."

"This fair domain is mine" rung in his greedy ear. The knight was poor. He looked at the fair maiden again: he thought her prettier than at first, nay were she not so pale, even beautiful.

The wine was good, and as he drank another cup or two, he argued 'twere no bad speculation. Grown bold at last—what will not mighty Hock effect?—he gently took her not unwilling hand—though cold he thought it pretty, and wondered if his lips would not impart some warmth to fingers, such as hers—he tried—then too essayed to press them against his heart—he had almost drunk too much to ascertain. Quite valiant now from wine he boldly asked, not as the timid lover often does, was the fair maid in her affections free, and might he hope? In affirmation of the fact she bent her ever bending head. He offered her his hand—his heart. Instantly she rose. A smile played round her lovely mouth, and on her lips, before so ashen in their hue, vermilion tints appeared—but for a moment though. From out of a casket which on the table stood she took two rings, and in her hair she placed two sprigs—the one of cypress, and the other of rosemary. She beckoned him to follow. Should he retract his plighted faith, and instantly fly the spot, or should he advance? Time was not left for thought. Two holy friars, clad for the service of the church, appeared as if from a hidden door, took the bridal pair between them, speaking not, and lead them to castle chapel. Here there were several tombs—on one of which reclined a bishop in grand ecclesiastical vestments, cast and cunningly wrought from metal. The strange bride lay a white hand upon his head and slowly the brazen figure rose and stepped in front of the altar, on which the candles had come alight by themselves. The rigid features of the bishop seemed to grow animated, his eyes flamed like stars through a light mist and he addressed the youth in a deep, hollow voice: "Kurt von Stein art thou willing to take Bertha von Windeck as thy affianced bride?"

As the aspen trembles in the breeze, so shook the fainting knight and the dread word died on his quivering lips . . .

The harbinger of morn, bright chanticleer, proclaimed from a neighbouring farm the reign of terror over. The whole assemblage melted into air, the knight sank senseless onto one of the tombs and when he recovered from his fit, he found himself stretched out in the long grass of the castle-court, while near him grazed his favourite steed. He fled the desolate ruins as fast as he could, and moons passed until he recovered from the horrors of that adventurous wedding night.

The Ring

Few are the castles now remaining on Germania's heights which in their pristine grandeur rear their embattled turrets over her smiling plains or mighty streams; but now the tottering fort, where many a brave one fell, the mouldering wall, the half-filled moat, the defenceless, portal and the moss grown arch, alone proclaim how great the giant strength of former days, and how her sons were brave. Of some no vestige now remains, and save in history no record of their tenant Lords is known.

Such was the fate of Berenburg; but as tradition told, beneath her vaulted church much treasure was concealed, a youth from Rosenstein resolved to explore the chambers of the dead, and seek the hidden wealth. It cost him small pains to clear a passage to the mansion of the dead. As he surveyed the costly trappings of the great now mouldering into dust, he took a skull of more than common size, and as he examined it, he said—"That you were, what the world called great, is certain, or you were not in this mausoleum; but whether good or bad, wise or a fool, a tyrant or a friend to man, where is thy fellow-man can tell!" and as he dropped the vestige he repeated to himself:

"When Adam delved, and Eve 'span,
Where was then the nobleman?"

In vain he searched the various coffins for wealth; in trinkets or in gold. At length he opened one, in which he beheld a corpse so fair, that he could scarce believe the remnants of mortality had slumbered ages there. A wreath of bridal florets yet fresh entwined the virgin's brow, and on her finger, delighted he beheld a brilliant ring. "Wert thou alive I'd willing call thee bride; thou art so fair a maid, would I could wed thee with this ring," and straight away plucked the diamond from her hand.

With joy he hurried homeward, and being before so poor, his treasure seemed of so great value that he wisely said all that he ever desired was now within his grasp, and he should never sigh for more. Beneath his head he placed his ring; he fastened well the door, looked over each nook and crevice of his room, and then retired to rest. He could not rest; sleep, formerly so sweet, had left his pillow, a thousand noises in his room he heard, felt for his ring, as though he feared it lost, and more than once he wished his treasure in the vault again, for he felt it as the nightmare of repose, and he vowed tomorrow he'd replace it there, for he'd discovered (what others too have done) that instead of a blessing wealth is too often a curse.

Our best resolves at night are often overturned by avarice come morning; for 'tis true the youth went to the vault again— not to replace that which was the nightmare of his rest, but in the hope of finding other treasures there; and as the story goes, his bride had left her narrow home, and stood at the threshold to receive him. He made a motion to retreat, her bony fingers grasped his trembling hand, and as she bore him to the vault, she whispered in his ear, "Man oft finds the phantom, when by avarice urged he seeks the substance; wealth is thy bride; thou hast her, now enjoy thy bliss!"—a cold, close embrace—a groan—and his life was gone.

THE PROSCRIBED KNIGHT

by Louise Brachmann

THE moon stood high above the distant mountains and poured her dim and sickly rays on the dark and silent wood, which lay stretched at the foot of the fallen castle of Waldburg. It was midnight when two travellers, whose appearance and dress bespoke them of another country, issued from amongst the trees, and urged their jaded steeds along the rough and perilous road. They came from the wars, and were hastening homeward. On arriving at a sudden bend in the road, the crumbling walls of the once stately castle lay before them, and the younger of the travellers instantly halted, to take a more accurate view of the scene, which so strikingly obtruded itself on their notice.

"Rudolph," said he to his companion, as he gazed earnestly at the ruined castle, "those old walls, thou seest yonder, recall to my mind events long since passed. Many scenes of joy and sorrow have they witnessed."

"Trouble not thyself about the past, Wilhelm," said the other, "but hasten onward, man. Come; I wish I was as near my home as to these old owl-inhabited walls here."

"I care not for home," answered Wilhelm with a sigh; "but if I could have again met my father there, then——"

"Nay, be not sad, my friend," said his companion, as he observed him brush a tear from his eye; "thou hast well portionied

94

every duty towards him, even unto death, and thy conduct deserves to be rewarded with the estate which your brother yet enjoys."

"Ah! that I gave to my brother as he was pining under sickness, and had a wife and children. As for myself, young and lusty as I was, I was determined to carve out my own fortune in the honourable profession of arms."

"But, methinks, thou hast not much profited by the favours of fortune, Wilhelm, during thy military service; for while others were heaping together a store of gold, you were dissipating it with the most lavish hands.—For my part, I have a snug little sum, and shan't be at a loss for a goldstich when at home."

"But are they not besmeared with blood?" asked Wilhelm. "No, Rudolph, my little patrimony will amply satisfy my necessities."

"Ha! ha! ha! hear him for a conscientious warrior," laughed Rudolph. "Good luck to everyone of his opinion!"

The words of the light-hearted young soldier were scarcely uttered, when the attention of both was arrested by the sudden appearance of a pale and ghastly figure, which arose from amongst the rushes of an old ditch. It issued from the moist clay in a half-reclining posture, and appeared to be the shadow of a knight. As he supported himself on one arm, he cast a wild yet mournful look around him, in which the strangers imagined they discovered the traces of deep sorrow rather than of anger or ferocity. His hair, which hung in long and clustering curls around his shoulders, was matted with blood, with which his short cloak was likewise stained.

The two travellers stood opposite the bloody knight, both motionless and half petrified with fear. In a moment after, however, they saw advancing down the narrow path which led from the castle, the white and ghost-like form of a young and beautiful woman. Her features were extremely lovely, but an expression of sorrow over-clouded her brow, which excited an irresistible feeling of pity in the mind of the beholder; but there was with-al—her light veil floating fitfully in the midnight air, and her snow-white drapery gleaming in the pale and sickly light of the waning moon—something so chilling and unearthly in her presence, that the very blood of the young soldiers almost curdled in their veins. She still kept the path, and proceeded with quickening step towards the shadow of the knight, who looked wistfully towards her. She bent over him, and affectionately entwined her fair arms around his bloody form, after which, locked in each other's embrace, they sunk into the watery ditch.

The travellers, after their surprise and terror had somewhat subsided, continued their journey. On arriving at the small town on that side of the mountain, they made many enquiries respecting the strange and fearful sight they had witnessed. "That," said the people, "is the ghost of the Knight Udo, the robber-knight, who pillaged the country for leagues round, but at last fell in this state by the steel of the avenger. The forest is uninhabited, and no one is bold enough to pass that way by night."

"And who is the female shadow," asked Wilhelm, "who so affectionately embraces the troubled ghost of the knight?"

"Holy mother!" exclaimed a young girl, at the same time devoutly making the sign of the cross, "what *she* was to the knight, God alone knows."

"Brother," said Wilhelm to his companion, "I feel myself moved with the deepest compassion for these poor spirits, and am resolved to give them rest."

"But hast thou not now heard that their enormous crimes have called down the just vengeance of Heaven upon all them; and wilt thou presume to interfere with its decrees? Be not rash, Wilhelm," continued Rudolph, "and keep thy compassion to be exercised on a more worthy object, for who can pity such hell-begotten crimes?"

"Rudolph," exclaimed he "ask rather if it be not a crime to condemn so harshly the actions of another, without just proof?

Can we, weak and erring creatures as we are—our best actions meriting reprehension—undertake to thread the inexplicable mazes of the human breast, and trace its dark and devious paths to the secret spring of thought? Do not external circumstances, over which we have no control, often exert a powerful and unforeseen influence in determining us to good or evil, when the mind is so nicely balanced between duty and temptation, that the slightest weight destroys its equilibrium? Are we not *made* what we are by the filthy contact of the world? O Rudolph, be not so hasty to condemn; for, as the fairest flower in nature droops its lovely head and falls, dried up and withered, before the scorching blast, so does the sacred fount, from which proceed the purest and holiest of man's thoughts, lose its sparkling brightness, and become as a stagnant pool, before the pestiferous breath of the defamer!

> ——e'en virtue
> Will sometimes bear away her outward robes
> Soiled in the wrestle with iniquity.

And surely we can lay no such claim to god-like purity, as to set ourselves above our fellows, and judge them as if we were gods! Say as thou wilt," he continued, "it is my determined purpose to remain here, for one night at least, to see it these poor spirits may not be quieted."

"I must then wish thee farewell, my good Wilhelm, for I am burning with desire to reach my home. See, the very stars that twinkle yonder appear to beckon me there." With these words the gay young soldier once more pursued his journey, which had been so unexpectedly interrupted; and, full of delight at the idea of again seeing his friends after so long an absence, perhaps within the short space of a few hours, the companion of his journey and the strange event which had detained him were alike soon forgotten.

Wilhelm remained in the neighbourhood, true to the resolution he had taken; and on the following night, when the moon appeared above the roof, he issued forth, and bent his steps to the same cross-road in which the adventure of the preceding night had occurred, and there watched anxiously until the fearful hour arrived. As it approaches, however, his enthusiasm and courage began to abate, and his failing strength at once assured him that he had thrown himself in the way of an adventure with which he was unable to contend. His heated imagination and disturbed fancy brought a thousand frightful spectacles before his eyes, and converted every bush and tree by which he was surrounded into some unearthly phantom, which threatened his immediate destruction. The mind of the boldest man shrinks at the idea of contending with the spiritual occupants of another world, and of wrestling with those incorporeal forms whose nature places them beyond the reach of mortals. With feelings such as these had Wilhelm contemplated the awful moment—rendered doubly so by long anticipation—and determined with one effort to renounce all further attempt at the enterprise, and flee the unholy spot forever. He roused all his powers, and was preparing for a hasty retreat; but hark the deep-toned clock now proclaims the witching hour of midnight from the time-worn tower of Waldburg, and as the last stroke vibrates on the ear, and gradually dies away in the still and silent night, the bloody figure of the knight rises from his ditch, and the white veiled shadow appears, gliding as before down path which led from the ruined castle.

A violent shudder ran through the ice-cold limbs of the young adventurer, but his courage and his compassion for the tormented souls in some measure overcame his terror. With determined mind he advanced towards the female shadow as she arrived at the cross-road, and addressed her with a sympathising voice as follows: "Alas! poor wandering ghost, who art thou, so cruelly deprived of the repose of the grave? And who is yonder blood-stained knight? Speak! thy misfortunes have excited my compassion."

The shadow halted at the words of the young man, and spoke with a melancholy but subdued voice:—"My name, when in life, was Una; *his* name was Udo; *then* much unjustly defamed, but *now* more worthy of pity."

"He was then, your betrothed, as you embrace him with such tender yet silent devotion?" asked Wilhelm; "or perhaps your noble and beloved husband?"

The shadow, with an expression of grief, shook her head.

"Then tell me, lovely woman, what relationship existed between you?"

The ghost was silent for some moments, as if afraid to reply: she then said with a tremulous voice, "He was my brother. If you desire to know more of our destiny, go tomorrow at noon into the vault under the western tower of the castle, and raise the broad stone which covers the rude table there; under it, you will find the history of our lives, which I wrote during my wretched confinement. If you can then pity us, and still feel a desire to assist us, hasten to give rest to our wandering souls. Surely a heart that possesses so much courage and compassion is destined to deliver us!"

Having concluded these words, the shadow glided from the young stranger, to again bury herself, as on the preceding night, in the waters of the ditch, clasped in the embrace of her beloved brother.

On the following morning, when the mid-day sun shone forth in all his splendour, Wilhelm set out with quick steps towards the ruined castle of Waldburg. He ascended the rocky heights and reached the deserted and frowning walls, now covered with moss and lichen, and from whose massive sides here and there flourished in wild luxuriance fern, bramble, and tufts of long waving grass, which fluttered with a rustling noise in the gentle breeze, and save which not a sound broke upon the deathlike stillness which reigned around. He tarried for a moment to take a hurried survey of the lovely landscape spread out before him, which could scarcely fail to arrest the attention of one whose mind was at all times keenly sensible to the varied charms of nature. He entered the lofty portal, and after traversing the empty hall, where the heraldic insignia of nobility were still remaining in sad mockery at the gallant deeds they were designed to perpetuate, he proceeded across the silent court, which at length brought him to the entrance of the western tower. Descending a narrow winding staircase, here and there obstructed with heaps of rubbish, our traveller found himself in the dark and chill atmosphere of a vaulted subterranean cave, whose ponderous iron doors too truly indicated that it had been the abode of unfortunate prisoners. By the light of a lamp which he now kindled, the murky darkness of the cave was somewhat dispelled, and enabled him to discover the table of which the ghost had spoken. He removed the stone, and the parchment scroll which was to reveal the mystery lay before him. He eagerly seized it, and placing the lamp before him, seated himself at the table.

"Here, sitting in the deep solitude of this dungeon, I have commenced writing my life, as a means of alleviating the misery which now oppresses me; and also to implore compassion, from the mortal who peruses this sad tale, for my brother Udo and myself, when death perhaps may long have swept me from the earth. Perchance, it may meet the eye of one as unfortunate and as worthy of compassion as myself;—one who has experienced ingratitude and treachery, whose soul, pure, and uncontaminated with vice, has been driven to crime and misery, by the scoffs, the calumnies of an unfeeling and heartless world,—in short, one in the mirror of whose mind the entire load of my own misery and wretchedness may be truly reflected.

"The very commencement of our career was unfortunate. We had never known the fostering care and tenderness of a mother, her anxious solicitude, her devoted love and protection,—death's unerring shaft had removed her from this world, during our infancy. Our father, naturally of a harsh disposition, was unkind to us, especially to my brother Udo, who, as he grew up, exhibited a noble sort generous nature, which rendered it the more surprising.

"It so happened, that my brother, still in early manhood, had promised his support to his bosom friend and sworn brother, Otto, who was engaged in a serious dispute with a neighbouring knight. Shortly afterwards, however, the fathers of the two friends were at enmity, which caused my father to lay strict commands upon Udo to withdraw the assistance he had promised to his friend, in the approaching emergency. So contrary were these injunctions to the noble nature of my brother, that they induced him rather to adhere with greater firmness to his purpose. 'What!' exclaimed he, 'Shall I desert my friend, and sworn brother, in a crisis so doubtful? Have I not pledged my knightly word to him, and is not that pledge as sacred as your own? Yea, my father, I have sworn to be true to him in life and death, and will hold myself to it.'

"He in this manner half forced compliance and half drew it from his unwilling father, who shortly after his departure fell seriously ill, and despatched a messenger to his son, who was now in a distant country, that he might hasten back to attend him in his last hours. It unfortunately happened, that through the uncertainties of war the combatants had taken up another position, and that Udo could not return in time to close the eyes of his dying father. The old man was enraged, and vehemently cursed the disobedience which deprived him of his son's presence in his last moments. Udo, however, hastened home expecting to receive his father's blessing; but, alas! the curse of his departed parent awaited him. This unfortunate occurrence, trifling though it may appear, was the immediate fountain from which the many subsequent misfortunes of his life received their origin. The father's malediction presses heavily and constantly on Udo's soul, as he had, although too late, hastened home to perform the last duties for his deceased parent. Then did he bewail with burning tears his first and last act of disobedience, which had been caused by the great love and fidelity he bore his friend.

"The unsophisticated simplicity of his life was as much affected on account of this untoward event, as if he had been in a weak and childish old age. He attached himself, however, with still greater love for his friend; for the greater the sacrifice one makes for the attainment of an object, the higher its possession is commonly valued. With him Udo divided the dangers of battle and the thorns of adversity, and once, when Otto was taken prisoner, and the whole of whose small property proved insufficient to ransom him, he offered him freely everything that he possessed, and thus liberated his friend. Shortly after, Otto married, and lived a life of ease and enjoyment; but my brother, in whose breast the love of indolent tranquillity dwelt not, now sought consolation in a career of glory and renown. He went with the Emperor to the wars, and as he could not attach himself to anyone without devoting to him the sincere affection of his heart, he performed for the Emperor unheard of services, expended in his cause his blood and riches, and even, by a singular accident, saved his very life. As a reward for his many and important achievements, the sovereign promised him the neighbouring rich earldom, when by the death of its present possessor, who was old, and also the last heir, it reverted to the crown.

"He now returned for a short time to our castle, since peace had been proclaimed. So many misfortunes had he suffered, that he appeared at one time to be sinking under them. The Emperor had deserted him; his friend was far distant with his beloved spouse; and his heart overburdened with sorrow and disappointment seemed to draw upon him a premature old age, for he sunk into a low effeminate despondency from which it was difficult to arouse him. Alas! this was the only happy period of my existence, when I had it in my power to divert his thoughts from the melancholy channel in which they ran, and afford him the comfort he so much needed.

"As the ivy entwines its branches around the lofty elm, so had my every inclination and desire, from my earliest childhood, been wound around him. We stood alone in the world, and therefore lived but for each other. On arriving at the age of manhood, however, our course of mutual love was, for the time, checked in its progress, for he burned for glory and renown, and sought the 'bubble reputation' amidst the clash of arms, and fearful din of war, with the impetuous ardour natural to his character. But now, disappointed in his expectation, deprived of his sworn brother and friend, and deceived by those for whose sake he had lavished both blood and gold, returned to me with redoubled affection. Was it then so culpable that I should bend my whole soul to delight my beloved brother, that I should strive to merit that love—dearer to me than life itself—he hourly bestowed upon me? The guileless and uncontaminated heart may learn from our misfortunes that the best may, through an evil destiny, and a concatenation of unforeseen circumstances, be forced by degrees into the gulf of sin; and how dubious is the line of demarcation between good and evil!

"It is, indeed, true that my brother from this time appeared to me the model of all manly beauty and perfection; and many rich and gallant knights who aspired to my hand were unhesitatingly rejected. This was the first act of indulgence to the infatuated and burning passion that now consumed me. Udo, also, sought not the affection of the many noble and lovely ladies in whose society he was constantly thrown. A secret passion was festering the hearts of both—a passion, indeed, that neither dared to think on, but which circumstances gradually developed to the knowledge, not only of ourselves, but of the world.

"Shortly, after my positive refusal of the many nobles who sought an alliance with our house through me, the Emperor himself demanded my hand for one of the richest and most powerful of his courtiers, who stood high in his favour. This nobleman had recently seen me at the grand banquet, and professed the ardent and burning passion that consumed him in terms so eloquent and persuasive, that the most haughty dame could scarcely have resisted them. Notwithstanding, I could not induce myself to comply with his suit, and therefore I rejected the Emperor's demand. My brother rejoiced at my decision, thought the person in whose behalf the Emperor had interfered was not worthy of me, and replied to the royal message in terms of great haughtiness and defiance.

"This refusal, or some other cause, was displeasing to the Emperor; the possessor of the earldom was now dead, but the promise still remained unfulfilled. My brother wrote earnestly, yet respectfully, to him, asking him whether he had forgotten his royal word, which he had solemnly pledged to him, or whether, on deeper consideration, he deemed his services of too little importance to merit such a reward. At this the Emperor was greatly enraged; and, as is usually the custom with great people, forgot the important benefits he had rendered to the state, in order to punish a trifling fault. The earldom was thereupon given to a favourite courtier, and all further hope of receiving a just acknowledgment of his important claims perished forever in Udo's breast.

"My brother Udo was as a sword of well-tempered steel, which, in the cunning hand of the accomplished fencer, never breaks, but bends under its control, and with elastic spring regains its former shape. The Emperor would have taken his life, but, his base ingratitude had aroused his noble pride. Udo determined to be avenged, cost what it may. My entreaties, perhaps, at this awful juncture, might have had the effect of restraining his rage, but he was absent on a secret enterprise.

"The torch of rebellion was quickly lighted up in the breasts of many other malcontents, who had suffered from the tyranny and unjust oppression of the Emperor; who now, maddened by the numerous complaints and the increasing power of the rebels, determined to exterminate them by force.

"The die was now cast; my brother was named the Hauptmann of the rebel army, and the horrors of war instantly commenced. From this time misfortune abode under our roof. The royal army defeated the insurgents in a battle, and the whole of our property was confiscated, with the exception of our ancestral castle. Udo patiently submitted to all, until he heard to whom the Emperor had given his estates. The words struck an appalling chill on our hearts:—to Otto—to that false friend, for whom my brother had sacrificed wealth, blood, nay, even his father's blessing, and his own peace of mind! Then did his manly courage sink, the very 'tackle of his heart' appeared to snap, and tears rolled down his death-like cheeks. 'Una,' said he with a heavy sigh that shook his whole frame, 'I have now nothing left on in the whole world but you; will you also forsake me?'

"Overwhelmed with sorrow at beholding the excess of his mental agony, I threw my arms passionately round his neck, and wept bitter tears upon his breast. 'Never, never, my dearest brother!' I exclaimed, 'will I forsake thee: there exists nothing in heaven, or on earth, that I love more than thee!'

"A ray of consolation appeared to break in upon the gloomy darkness of his soul, when he heard these words; he threw his arms convulsively around me, and pressed me to him. At this moment, the prior of a neighbouring convent entered the hall, and presented a letter to my brother. It was in the hand-writing of our deceased mother, who, in a severe illness, had vowed me to the cloister. She recovered, and sought afterwards, by means of rich presents, to release me from the vow, but without effect. The pious abbess now saw the ruin of our house fast approaching, and my own unhappy condition; and thus, in order to save me, urged the demand that Heaven had upon me, that I should devote the remainder of my days to a state of monastic seclusion. Both Udo and myself were greatly agitated, as we perused the letter of our departed mother, containing in solemn words this awful vow. 'You see, madam,' said the venerable man, 'that the Holy Church opens her arms to you! A great and terrible calamity will speedily fall upon your house. Why do you longer remain with a man so desperate, then, whose life must shortly pay the forfeit, for the crimes he has committed.'

"'Una,' said my brother with an unutterable look, 'it rests with you! Decide!'

"But I burst into a flood of tears, and cried, 'I cannot, cannot leave you—with you I will share danger and death!'

"'Then by the God of heaven, I forsake you not!' exclaimed Udo, holding me on his left arm, and raising the right towards heaven.

"The prior then departed from us in anger, exclaiming, 'The Church has power to defend her own rights.'

"After this occurrence my brother made many warlike incursions, seeking forgetfulness in the noise of battle. He did the enemy mischief, whenever an opportunity offered itself, a small band of faithful and desperate followers still adhering to him. These men, enamoured of a life of unrestrained freedom and reckless pillage, enacted many enormities; for the once tender and harmless nature of my brother had given place, by means of grief and disappointment, to a fierce and revengeful courage. So far, however, from shedding the blood of those who were innocently oppressed, he frequently proved their avenger.

"On one occasion, when my brother was absent on an enterprise, which would detain him for some days, the principal of the monastery came with his people, seized me by force, and carried me back carefully guarded. The pious and noble abbess, a friend of our late mother's, resorted to every means in her power, in order to induce me to devote myself unreservedly to a religious life, and to renounce forever all worldly desires and cares. I could willingly have followed her advice, and would have endeavoured to persuade my brother to refrain from all attempt at revenge, had it not been for the passion that seemed to have increased since his absence. I therefore resolved to indulge the desire I had of being again re-united to him, and gave him secret intimation of the place of my confinement, and expressed to him my wish that he would immediately liberate me. Thereupon Udo came in the night with his followers, stormed the walls of the convent and carried me away with him, resolving never more to leave me.

"I was rejoiced, but yet not happy, in finding myself again in our solitary castle; so many conflicting ideas were constantly present to my mind, that I was as a frail bark upon the bosom of the troubled sea, lashed hither and thither by the merciless fury of the storm. It was midnight. I lay restlessly upon my couch, and many visions swept before my disturbed soul. The pale moon smiled her silvery rays on the silent landscape, as a fond mother who watches with delight the sweet repose of her darling offspring. Suddenly I was alarmed by three hollow knocks at the castle gate. I sprang up, hastened to the window, and saw in the doubtful light three dark muffled figures, which a sad presentiment assured me were the messengers of the Secret Tribunal. They cut three splinters from the door, and then warned my brother in a harsh voice to appear on the third night at the next cross-road. The messengers then disappeared.

"Udo heard their warning with a shudder for, alas! his accusing conscience told him that he was about to undergo a severe punishment for the many crimes he had committed. The certainty of punishment, and perhaps death, deterred him from exposing himself to the unrelenting vengeance of the Secret Tribunal, by obeying the summons and I myself did not hesitate to persuade him from keeping the fearful engagement. Twice had the nightly call been heard, and as Udo had not answered either, we found one morning a parchment scroll of the Freischöppen fastened to the castle gate, containing these words: 'Rebel, robber, unholy lover of thy sister! The Knight Udo, by not appearing at the call of the Secret Tribunal, has thereby acknowledged his guilt. He is sentenced. The steel of the avenger shall slay him wheresoever it finds him.'

"'Una,' said my brother, when he had read these words, 'my time is come. For you is still left safety; fly to a convent—save thyself! My body now belongs to the birds of heaven—fly, fly; why will you longer remain with a man proscribed by the Secret Tribunal?'

"But, O God! how could I have forsaken my brother *now* in his greatest extremity? My course was decided, and I wept no more. Necessity gave me courage, and I solemnly swore I would not leave him living. He answered me calmly, 'My Una! I have drawn you into ruin, but your faith is greater than I could have imagined.'

"We now fortified the castle, and made it secure against any hostile assault, but we dared not set a foot beyond the threshold of the door, as on that side hovered the arm of death in the unseen avengers, who were everywhere, and, like the Deity, executed in secret. We had sufficient food in the castle, and the days passed on as usual. I found a sorrowful, yet sweet employment, in assuaging the grief that weighed so heavily upon my brother's mind, and, notwithstanding the danger that threatened our lives, our love daily increased. Until this period we were innocent of the crime of which the world accused us.

"For some months we lived altogether apart from the rest of mankind; nor did we desire to again return to the former intercourse that had proved in every way so unfortunate to ourselves. To one unaccustomed to restraint, however, it is painful to exclude oneself forever from beholding the fair face of nature, and we therefore often felt ourselves induced to venture out, but dared not risk the dangerous experiment. But one night, when the moon was shedding her beautiful light over the landscape, we stood in the recess of a Gothic window, and my brother took the lute, and sung in sweet and melancholy tones, the following song:

> Sieh, Schwerterchen, seih! der versilberte Hain,
> Er winkt uns so lieblich im Mondenschein
> Die thanigten Wiesen und Fluren wie kell!
> Es winkt uns hinüder schimmernde Quell.
> Sie rufen; wir trinken die himmlische Luft,
> Wir Kinder der Erde, die liebend sie ruft;
> Ihr amen Verbannten, und sollt ihr allein
> Verstoszen vom Anblick der Mutter seyn?
> Ach, süsz wohl, mein Schwesterchen, wär' es und schön,
> Sich einmal rieselnden Quell zu ergeh'n
> Am Tage die Rache, die blutige, wacht
> Doch Frieden wohl beut uns die himmlische nacht!

"My inclination, as well as his, at once induced us to again enjoy the sweets of long lost freedom. With timid and noiseless step, we issued from the castle, and directed our course towards the beautiful valley. A still small voice seemed to whisper in my heart, 'Are ye not like shadows, ye poor proscribed wretches, who now glide as unearthly beings amongst things of life? Life is now but of little value to you, and perhaps in a short time it will be still less so!'

"We wandered like phantoms through the flowery meads, which now no longer belonged to us. My Udo, his heart overwhelmed with apprehensive fear, conducted me into the wood as far as the bank of the dry ditch. In a moment the fearful Avengers sprung out from a thicket hard by, and threw themselves upon my unhappy brother. Instantly three daggers were plunged into his breast, with this exclamation,—'Woe, woe unto him!'

"They tore me from his bloody corpse, which I had clasped to my breast, and cast it into the ditch. My life was spared. I was carried back to the castle, and lived in a state of mental agony, that for the time deprived me of reason. At length the Emperor, feeling perhaps that he had pursued a spirit of persecution against my unhappy brother, to an extent unwarranted by the slight provocation he had received, despatched to me one of the nobles of the court, for the purpose of again soliciting my hand in marriage. To have entertained the proposal would have been at once ungenerous towards him and dangerous to myself, as my only consolation was to weep over my beloved Udo's ignominious grave, and to utter prayers for the rest of his soul. But alas! alas! how ran the orisons of a sinner such as I reach the throne of mercy? His bloody figure still haunts me!—he is now before me!—Oh God!..."

Here terminated the manuscript of the lovely Una. A monk, however, had added the sequel of her unfortunate life, in the following words:—

"Whilst thou, pious wanderer, readest these melancholy words, the fair writer herself has long ceased to be numbered with the quick: death terminated her worldly cares and sufferings—but in what manner will be seen hereafter.

"The nobleman, who sought to gain her hand in marriage, used every inducement to win her affection and, in order to divert her mind from the melancholy that oppressed it, he proposed removing her from the scene of her calamities, and to conduct her to the gay assemblies of the court. But the torch of love that her deceased brother had lighted in her breast still burned vividly. She listened not to these flattering offers, and at once resolved to free herself from further importunity on a subject so repugnant to her feelings. Seizing the first suitable chance that presented itself, she escaped secretly from the castle, and wended her way, under the dark veil of night, to the silent wood; after threading its intricate and glooming mazes—long familiar to her—she arrived at the deep ditch in which her brother's body had been cast by the assassins of the Secret Tribunal, and, with desperate energy, threw herself headlong down into the very place where her brother's bones were mouldering. Truly, such determined love and devotion towards a brother must always be worthy of admiration; but Una, from the very excess and abundance of *her* affection, hast deeply sinned, because she set at nought the bonds of honour, and despised and contemned the glory of Heaven, in refusing to consecrate herself to its service. To what extent the love of these two proceeded, especially in the latter part of their career, when their unheard-of and almost unnatural faith bound the hearts of the proscribed pair in indissoluble union, must be left to the knowledge of One who errs not. But that Una augmented her sins, by committing the fearful act of self-destruction—departing from this world without any previous repentance, and without having received the holy Sacraments of the Church—her disturbed and wandering spirit will at once prove. Their souls will never rest, nor arrive at peace, and they will continue to affright the nightly traveller—he, by rising in the solemn midnight hour from his moist and bloody bed; she, by gliding down the path, embracing, and consoling, as she was wont to do when living, the sorrowful shadow of the knight, and at length sinking with him into the watery ditch—until a young man shall come who dare to speak to the tormented spirits, and to read in this very place the scroll of parchment here placed. To him who brings a pious heart, and offers a devout prayer, shall belong the reward of removing two souls from the pangs of torment."

The heart of Wilhelm, after having carefully perused the foregoing history, was filled with sorrow and compassion. The sins that he had never committed, appeared to him to be as mere weaknesses of human nature, when compared with their wonderful virtues; and he knelt down and prayed earnestly, with many tears, that the bonds of punishment might be unloosed, and that they might be received into ever-lasting peace.

Returning to the wood, to ask the poor shadows what more he could do for them to release their souls from suffering, he arrived at the spot where he had been accustomed to await their appearance. The midnight hour sounded. The pale figure of the bloody knight, no longer raised itself from its moist and noisome bed; nor did the female with white and floating drapery appear on the narrow foot-way: but two streams of pale light, agreeable to look upon, shot upwards, which shed a transient ray upon the objects beneath. It continued its course towards heaven, and instantly a flood of sweet and soul-captivating melody fell upon the ears of the young soldier, in which he distinctly heard the following chant:

> Segen, Segen dir! wir scheiden,
> Geh'n nun ein zur ew'gen Ruh;
> Du erlöstest uns vom Leiden
> Herz voll Mild' und Demuth du.
> Segen, Segen dir, und Dank!
> Nich verdammt im reinen Herzen
> Hast du, wo in Schuld und Schmerzen
> Dein verirrter Bruder sank.
> Ob der Segen sich bewähret?
> Fragt des dunkeln Schieksals Macht!
> Mild im Sternlicht verkläret
> Strahlt uns Antwort durch die Nacht.

VALERIE

by Baroness Caroline de La Motte Fouqué

FOR several years after the peace of 1763, there lived at Berlin the widow of a bookseller, of the name of Fonrobert, in a high, narrow, dark-looking house, situated at the end of "The Brothers' Street," adjoining St. Peter's Church Yard. The aged lady continued the business of her deceased husband with good success, by the aid of a skilful and honest assistant. Herr Etienne, like his principal, was of the French settlement, and, besides the bonds of nationality, was personally his relative; and being a poor, but useful member of the family in which he had been trained and brought up, he was, at last, as intermediate between confidant and servant, appointed head manager of the business.

During the agitations of the war-time, every species of commerce had suffered manifold shocks, but especially had the field been narrowed for intellectual productions. The spread of French literature, which occasioned such early success to the active, sharp-witted foreigner, must, under the hostile influences of the time, have experienced the most discouraging checks; so that speculation was at a stand, and only diligence and carefulness availed to extricate the business from its heavy and still increasing burdens. Here it was that the sprightly, joyous Fonrobert, ever more disposed to a rash forwardness than to a timid forbearance, especially needed the calmness of his companion. Gentle and even-tempered in all things, the latter took no useless step, made no ambitious movement, did not reach far forward; though, unperceived, he by small degrees provided for the future; and thus, by such measures, retrieved his temporarily embarrassed vocation.

At a later period, Madame Fonrobert had every reason to be thankful for such a procedure: she saw herself, after the sudden death of her only son, and that which quickly followed of her husband, supported by a friend, to whom she owed not only the assistance of the moment, but the comfort of a station which exactly corresponded to her modest and peaceful spirit. The mute sorrow of her gentle soul desired nothing more from life than quietness, and an unanxious resignation to the course of outward events. In her first terror she would have fled altogether from the cares of the domestic circle, for she had not the power actively to contend with them; she therefore blessed the hand of the faithful Etienne, who had so easily conducted her out of those days of darkest anguish to the old habits of her former life. Though all within her was as if dead and palsied, yet, without everything remained in place; and, from henceforth, that which one day brought might also be expected from the morrow. Gradually her sorrow subsided into the depths of her soul, and nothing thereof remained for the rest of her life but the need, from long habit, of an unchangeable tranquillity. Nowhere could more order and regularity be seen than prevailed in her house. She seldom left the little back room which immediately adjoined the shop. Herr Etienne spent the greatest part of the day in a small latticed apartment between the two, for the double purpose of being to both places—as circumstances might require—immediately at hand. Here he managed his correspondence, made his calculations, gave and received commissions, and was in all these occupations scarcely ever disturbed by the intrusion of her to whom he had devoted a whole life, full of labour and exertion. Exactly as during the life-time of her husband, did Madame Fonrobert now remain free from all participation in the affairs of business—as formerly, she only conversed with her kinsman at meal-times, and shewed herself fully content when, now and then, from the nearness of the solitary being, his dry, hectic cough convinced her that she was still connected, through benevolence and gratitude, with the living world.

At six o'clock, in the harvest and winter seasons, the shop was closed; in the longer days this happened an hour later. As soon as the closing doors had creaked into the corners, the bolts been driven, and the iron bars had rattled, the old servant maid arose from her comfortable seat on the chimney hearth, in order to prepare the light supper for her mistress. When she had served it, and placed a seat against the little table, Madame Fonrobert, taking a small hand-bell, gently rang it, which was the accustomed signal to the already waiting company. Immediately the door opened, when, almost unperceived, the quiet man entered, and having made his greeting, noiselessly took his seat; then laying aside his manuscripts and printing toils, he tasked himself to get up an enlivening conversation, which reminded both of better days, and especially of a journey into France, in which Madame Fonrobert had accompanied her husband. This brighter epoch of her existence recurred to her as with the early dawn of youth, and gave to its recalling images a surpassing warmth and liveliness. Involuntarily, the generally inactive fancy of the dull, sickly lady, was thus enlivened; and though she was far removed from encouraging the wish for similar enjoyments, yet she loved whatever might lead back her thoughts to the lighter materials of a harmless gaiety. The repeated requests to continue the conversation—which always began with the words, "You know, Monsieur Etienne"—were by him carefully regarded. He always knew what she wished to be told, and was only silent when, having wiped her fork, she laid it aside as a signal that the meal-time was over: then he left his seat, helped the good Anna to remove the cloth, opened for her the door, which she gently drew after her, filled the drink-cup of the little Bolognese dog, that was frisking and sniffing by his side, poured out for himself a glass of fresh water, which he held in one hand, whilst with the other he took down from the chimney-piece a little oblong chest, by which movement he could seldom prevent the dominoes which it contained from clattering, and Madame Fonrobert's exclamation, "Aha! our play!" which somewhat displeased him, as he really only contemplated devoting the little pastime to some useful purpose, but did not wish to be mindful of the thing itself. As, however, the same misluck befell him every evening, it came, at last, to belong to the established order of things, and was not to be omitted. For one short hour, then, the quiet play lasted, only interrupted by the short, husky cough of poor Etienne. After nine o'clock there was seldom a light seen in the widow's chamber.

Contrary to all custom, one rough and stormy evening in autumn, the domino game of the two friendly combatants had been prolonged, through various little stratagems and calculations of the complaisant kinsman, beyond the appointed hour. Madame Fonrobert was in her best humour: she amused herself in watching for the failure of her wary opponent, and laughed almost audibly whenever she had the good fortune to catch him. While she was considering her play, she was suddenly terrified by the growling of the little dog, which, from lying behind her on the sofa cushion, sprang up, and as if, from the approach of something strange, began, first in a low tone, then more briskly, to bark. She looked about after him in astonishment, and endeavoured to quiet him. But quick as lightning the little beast flew by her, into a side-chamber that stood open, and where the windows looked toward the street. Formerly the deceased Fonrobert had occupied this room; it was now empty, yet the affectionate spouse loved to have it opened and lighted of an evening. In the strangest emotion she followed the dog, which kept springing from chair and table on to the window-board, and barking out still more vehemently against the panes. Amidst the noise hereby occasioned, there was plainly distinguishable the moaning voice of a human being crying for help. At the same moment the house-bell was rung with such violence, that Madame Fonrobert, so accustomed to quietness, trembled in every limb, and sinking on a chair, could imagine nothing else than that, in the midst of peace, the enemy was breaking into the unguarded capital. The same terror again agitated her, as again it rang, and more vehemently. Herr Etienne had already a light, and the house-key in his hand, when his relative, with disturbed mien, stammered out, "Where are you going? to the robbers and incendiaries, who are storming the house? For God's sake stay here—stay here, Etienne!"

"Someone is calling for help," he replied softly, bowed, and in an instant was out at the door.

"Now it is all over with us!" exclaimed Madame Fonrobert, as Anna rushed into the room to inquire the cause of the unwonted tumult. "The Russians and Hungarians are here again! they will plunder all the houses! and whoever opposes them is doomed to death!"

"The Hungarians!" screamed Anna, as if demented, whilst she covered her head with her upraised apron. With hurried steps the book-keeper now approached them; he thrust his head in at the door, beheld the two frantic women, and in perplexity asked, in a low and uncertain tone, "Dare I, madam?—A helpless creature begs for your protection."

"What can I do?" replied Madame Fonrobert, starting back in terror.

"Protect grace and innocency," was the modest answer.

"Force their persecutors here to us; who will then escape from their revenge?" exclaimed the lady.

"Anguish and want are the persecutors," replied Etienne: "these will remain without, if we allow the persecuted to come in."

With these words he entered the room, dragging after him, almost by main-force, a sobbing, trembling young maiden.

"What!" exclaimed Madame Fonrobert, quite angry, "is it a child that has made all this alarm? and are you bringing the impetuous little creature into our quiet house?"

She said this and more, softly and hastily in her mother-tongue, partly because she was accustomed to use this to her relative, and partly not to be understood by the unwelcome guest. However, immediately after the first words the little maiden raised her head with an astonished air, and fixing upon her fine dark eyes, full of intelligent expression, replied quickly and passionately in the same language—

"Ah! do not fear, madam; I do not wish to be burdensome to anyone here. I only ask for a glass of water to moisten the tongue of a dying woman."

She could scarcely pass the last words over her quivering lips; whilst, at the same time, the beseeching and vehement motion of her uplifted hands showed how ardently she desired the accomplishment of that little wish. Herr Etienne hasted to do as she desired, whilst Madame Fonrobert, most deeply agitated by the strange expression of the beautiful child, repeated with every token of sympathy—

"A dying woman! For God's sake where, then? pray tell, my poor maiden. Who is dying, and where?"

Unable to repress her tears, she replied by pointing with up-raised arm toward the street; and Etienne, drawing on his coat, ran with her to the door.

"Go with them, Anna," said her mistress; "see what happens, and bring me word."

A murmuring and bustle in the street, occasioned by the concourse of a multitude, drew, at the same time, Madame

Fonrobert to the window. She opened it, and heard from several voices—

"Death on the spot! The thunder-clap must have struck her!"

"No one can know that, certainly," interposed a young man, who with difficulty had made his way through the crowd, and who added with officious confidence, "Only into the nearest house with the unfortunate! There must be means employed for her preservation."

Starting, and vainly contending with the aversion to such a strange and horrible sight, Madame Fonrobert beheld immediately the stiff corpse of a lifeless female drawn over her threshold, and into the very room where she was, as being the nearest to the house-door. The faithful Etienne hastened towards the painful object, and seizing with mute and pacifying gesture both the hands of his benefactress, he seemed to invoke, in the name of Providence, forgiveness for the misfortune which in so unforeseen a manner had befallen her. He gently urged her away from the place where she was standing, and tried to turn her look from that strange and startling countenance. But the terrified lady once aroused from the peaceful course of her gentler feelings, was riveted in fevered stupefaction on the object which infused into her soul the deadliest anguish. Meanwhile, could anything reconcile her to the involuntary cause of so great a disturbance of the household, it was the still, resigned features of the softly sleeping woman, whom no medical skill, no art of surgeon could awaken. Quite sunk from the weakness of age, there lay on a hand-barrow, in the middle of the room, surrounded by idlers and strangers, a small, slender female form, with a foreign physiognomy, now as unconscious as painless. Her glazed eye no longer regarded the stiff and motionless child, that seemed to ask herself and the men around her what had happened. A momentary silence, which even the rudest did not venture to interrupt, held in restraint all questions and surmises. Here, however, the unfortunate one could not remain. But who was she? and on whom was the burden and expense of the interment to fall? Was she a poor person of the town, or a nameless stranger of whom no one could give any account? All this passed with lightning-speed through the minds of the bystanders.

Most men think aloud, and, as the natural contemplations occurred to each one, there ran through the little apartment corresponding expressions to the ear of Madame Fonrobert, who, undecided and anxious, watched the entire procedure. As now, in the meantime, an officer of police entered, and made preparations for removing the dead body to the Town-hall, where it should remain exposed till some relative, or at least acquaintance, might recognise it, and tell the name and station of the deceased; as he fixed the space of two days for this purpose, and declared that in case of entire desertion, it would, as belonging to the class of the common poor, be buried as such, the magnanimous lady stepped forward with the assurance that "she would not suffer that any who as God's poor had passed her threshold, in order, in her peaceful little house, quietly to fall asleep, should thence be torn away to the rude gaze of starers, and at last, without kindness or sympathy, be put under the earth. Here shall the departed one remain undisturbed. Public notice can be given of the event. If any demand her who have a nearer claim, then indeed every stranger will be exempted from further obligation; but as the matter now stands, let that person be and remain her last protectress, to whose care Heaven has commended her."

Madame Fonrobert spoke this warmly and rapidly. She was in unwonted excitement; her self-denial had given her new courage. She was quite absorbed in the strange affair, and heeded nothing else. The police-officer bowed respectfully towards her; Herr Etienne occasionally kissed her hand with great emotion. The stranger child beheld all with an air of astonishment. Her striking appearance next excited the observation of those present. Clad in a short petticoat of variegated red silk, thickly quilted and in rich folds, she was leaning against the staves of the hand-barrow. Her black mantelet, drawn about her neck, hung loosely over only one shoulder, thus displaying a full-flowered bosom-dress, with short sleeves down to the elbows, and fringed with lace. Her wonderfully beautiful thick black hair, glittered with several hair-pins, with which it was fastened together; and this was surmounted by a raised circular gauze cap, such as was wont to be worn at that time by children of distinction. From this mixture of affluence and poverty gleamed a languid, half-opened eye, full of gloomy quiet and mute abstraction. The fine, delicate features were almost motionless, yet betrayed by their expression that sorrow which is too dignified to vent itself loudly. Short and slender, the singular little figure made it doubtful in other respects whether one should call her beautiful and attractive, or only strange and extraordinary. It was, besides, manifest that the poor maiden understood as good as nothing of what was spoken around her; this was clearly shewn when the police-officer, after a short, private conversation with Madame Fonrobert, stepped up to her and asked her whether the woman that had so suddenly died was her mother. The little girl looked embarrassed at Etienne, who complaisantly repeated to her the question in French; to which she replied—

"No, sir; but I never knew any other."

"Who art thou, then, and where is thy home?" he continued.

The child remained mute for some time, while from her fixed staring eyes ran two big tears, without the muscles of her countenance betraying any visible emotion. "Must I answer that?" she then said, firmly and steadfastly. "This one would once have answered for me," she added, softly, and with outstretched hand pointing towards the dead. "Now——" She stopped; her lips quivered, yet she did not weep.

"Confide in me," said the kind Etienne, while at the same time he led her backward a few steps, and urged her to sit down by his side. "Tell me all, my dear child," he whispered to her secretly. "I will then speak for thee; and to those who have a right to inquire more closely after the circumstances of thy life I will communicate what is necessary for them to know, not more—on that you may rely."

The child looked full at him. "I have nothing to conceal," she replied, proudly and drily; "it only troubles me to think on the past, and therefore I do so unwillingly."

Etienne, astonished at the cool and thoughtful answer, contemplated her more closely; and almost uncertain, as it seemed, whether so much earnestness could well abide in the child-like little creature, he asked her, "How old art thou, young maiden? I do not comprehend thee."

"I am going into my eleventh year," she replied, without regarding the flattering import of the question.

"And who art thou? may I further ask?" said Etienne, urgently. "Who were thy parents, and how earnest thou hither?"

She sighed, and then said plaintively: "I was born on the battle-field of Minden, where my father fell under the Duke de Broglio, and where my mother, in despair, had followed to look after his corpse. A market-woman brought me up, and has informed me that I am a Colonel's daughter, and that my mother was a German lady." With these words she felt in her pocket, which was skilfully hid beneath the folds of her dress, and drew forth a small packet, from which she carefully unfolded a fine handkerchief, and shewed to Etienne a name inscribed with a Count's coronet. After this she opened the little packet, and took out a bracelet, with the miniature of a fine, manly countenance; which having contemplated awhile, she handed with two descriptive papers to the good-natured man who had declared himself as her protector. Etienne glanced over the papers. One was the poor orphan's certificate of baptism, and contained the names of two families that seemed to forbid the notion of so young a creature living in want and misery. The second paper threw light upon the other. The unfortunate spouse of the handsome foreigner was, on his account, removed from the family; a secret marriage rendered their union equivocal before the world, and she was exiled from her native land. In the deepest anguish of soul, she wrote this to the author of her affliction, whom amid reproach and sorrow she had followed for some little distance, when the news of that disastrous battle overtook her. Concealing the letter in her bosom, she hastened to the battle-field. This and what follows was added in worse handwriting on the margin of the paper—probably the compassionate market-woman had undertaken this task. She had noted that the unfortunate lady had expired by the side of her husband, after giving birth to the child; that she had confided the latter to her, and that never should little Valerie be forsaken by her.

"Canst thou read?" asked Etienne, folding the papers together.

"Yes," was the short reply.

"And thou knowest—" he continued, hesitatingly. She nodded assent. "Forget it," said he, beseechingly. "It nought avails thee to remain in this condition wherein thou hast been nurtured." Valerie answered nothing. "But yet do tell me one thing," he said, already on the point of reverting to other matters—"Wert thou always in Germany? or how is it that I see thee here?"

"The good old woman," replied the child, smilingly, "begged for me in France and other parts, where she ought never to have led me. Now she wished to make trial of the great Frederic. The family of my mother belongs to his vassals; but death has destroyed this plan also."

"Forget this too," Etienne again besought her; "forget all!" She answered nothing. He led her back to Madame Fonrobert, to whom he made known the substance of his conversation with Valerie, and induced the compassionate lady to receive her into the house, which put a stop to the police inquiries; and after the interment of the French mendicant, as the deceased woman was called, the occurrence soon came to be forgotten.

✳

The feverish excitement which, that evening, had set the even-tempered Madame Fonrobert into an almost passionate condition, left a languor which preyed in a distressing manner upon her spirit. That readiness with which she had joined her first act of benevolence to a second, and so added one self-conquest to another, belonged obviously to a strange energy, which, with the incident that produced it, also passed away. The following morning, therefore, brought her a troop of disturbing contemplations, of which one half sufficed to poison the life of the quiet-loving woman. She was ashamed indeed to make known her feelings: it seemed to her mean and ungenerous to betray untimely regrets over an act of benevolence; yet, scarcely mistress of her inward anguish, she poured forth a flood of bitter tears without revealing the ground of her sorrow. So long as the careful Etienne was occupied with the preparations for the funeral, and for the reception of the new guest, he could pass over her discordant humour; but, with the return of the quiet belonging to his ordinary way of life, it was impossible for him to look silently on such a change. He ventured therefore, one lonely evening-hour, when Valerie was sleeping in Anna's little chamber—he ventured the timid question, "Oh, madam, has any bad news arrived, or has any loss been sustained, to cause you sorrow?" She silently shook her head. "It is doubtless very bold," he continued, "that I should wish to intrude myself into your confidence, but impute it somewhat to the fear that, through some failure, I may have deserved your displeasure; and at least deem me worthy of the favour of some explanation."

"It is not that, my dear Etienne," replied Madame Fonrobert, with weak and tremulous voice, "it is not that; but, as you speak of it, and we are now without burdensome affairs—which, alas! will henceforth seldom be the case—I will venture to tell you. I have feared that we have been too hasty. Yes, I fear that we have imposed upon ourselves a family-cross that will grievously oppress us; and which, Herr Etienne, will crush me to death."

While she spoke, he several times changed colour; and as, at last, tears stifled her voice, he was obliged hastily to take two or three pinches from his box, to refrain himself from weeping with her. "How then," he at length said, "does madam think that little Valerie can wish to be burdensome to her?"

"Burdensome!" she exclaimed. "Ah! that is not the question; that she will and must be by her mere presence. But if that were all——" She ceased. Perhaps she herself knew not further what lay darkly within her mind. Yet suddenly there rose involuntarily to her lips, "See you, Herr Etienne, I have the feeling that this child brings unhappiness to us. I become so anxious when near her, that I know not how to express it. In her large eyes there is something presaging sorrow. Only once contemplate her more closely; hers is surely no child's look. She was born in an evil hour, upon a bloody bed, amongst the dying. Think only, how many souls must there have fluttered about in unrest, and been by angels and devils snatched away; and, in the midst of the confusion, hers wound its way into the light."

The perplexed book-keeper rose from his chair, in inexpressible embarrassment, and paced up and down, twisting and rubbing his hands. The strange words had excited in him a feeling of aversion and indignation towards the innocent object of his inmost compassion; and yet the more this feeling overpowered him the more he was ashamed of it, and strove against it, which occasioned him infinite suffering. "Besides," Madame Fonrobert continued, "the little unfortunate is, in her singular position, more matured than other children at her age. It is only her form that is undeveloped; and by what a hand has she been cultivated? What principles may she not have imbibed from vulgar associations? Think only what she could learn from such a creature, with what else become acquainted than with what is immodest and untractable. Herr Etienne! Herr Etienne! believe me, this good old house has lost its peace."

"Then we will get rid of the stranger," he exclaimed, over-powered with disquiet and anxiety, yet shocked at the hasty word which consigned to so unhappy a fate one who was quite forlorn.

"That we cannot do without injuring ourselves," she observed thoughtfully. "What would the world judge of such an unjust procedure? And how we should lower the poor maiden in the opinion of others!" Etienne felt more calm. "No," continued his old friend, "the matter no longer concerns others. We have been too precipitate, and must now await the end."

This *we* really meant *you*, and was a disguised reproach which the too sensitive Etienne took very pleasantly, but was much vexed therewith in secret. Therefore he kept silence, whilst he once more thought over the matter. Many opposing considerations now hastily occurred to him, which he seemed not before to have sufficiently regarded. What if he really through a single evening should have entailed on the house, which owed to his management its prosperity and peace, a lasting disadvantage, and on his benefactress anxiety and vexation. "I will take the entire burden on myself," said he resolutely. "Valerie shall find in me a father, a teacher, and a protector; she shall have the little room above on the third floor, which I have so long occupied; the little chamber beside the shop will do for me. The homeless wanderer does not need waiting upon; she has been early schooled by want. By day she shall work with me in the counting-house, and only during the short meal-time need Madame Fonrobert be near her." He immediately made the latter acquainted with his plan, released her from all obligation, and declared himself as ready as he was bound to take it all upon himself. But, to his great astonishment, this did not at all satisfy her. The deadening impression which had fallen upon her had deprived her dull imagination of all its quickening power.

"What will all that avail?" she replied. "What has been, has been: the child will never again be absent from my thoughts."

At the same time she was not unwilling that Valerie should occupy the little upper room, while Etienne should have possession of Herr Fonrobert's, from which since the terror of that evening, the delusive breath of earlier recollections had passed away. A waiting-girl, who now and then attended upon Anna, agreed to have her sleeping-room next to Valerie's chamber. And thus the stranger child was accommodated with the least possible disturbance to the customs of the household. For this she thanked her benefactor from her heart. A stranger to everything, she had no longing for the world; besides, her disturbed frame needed rest. She slept much, and even when awake dreamt of that with which her deceased nurse had filled her childish mind. At table she appeared reserved and distant towards Madame Fonrobert, who to her was almost painfully kind and solicitous; and who, the more she felt discommoded by the approach of her little guest, the more redoubled her attentions towards her. They remained, however, unknown to each other; their intercourse was only kept alive by that which had first originated it, namely, their language.

Valerie long desired to learn German; she had a fine and agreeable manner of expressing herself; the lighter tones of thought glided so smoothly over her lips, and found in the harmonious play of her features an accompaniment that seemed to render both inseparable. Etienne at all times avoided imposing any strange and disturbing notions on the unintelligible child; he therefore let her take her own way, and be as she was, quiet as to herself, buried in her own feelings, sparing in their expression. What course her education took it would have been difficult to estimate: outwardly, she appeared unchanged; thus she lived for years. She had no play-mates, nor wished for any; nor could she attain any taste for female occupations. Proper hours of study eluded her; yet she knew the most of what is usually taught to girls domestically educated. The habit of sitting the greatest part of the day by the side of Etienne, turning over the stores of the book-shop, and reading historical and poetical works of a religious and moral tendency, raised her above the mechanical condition of a common elementary development. And if, in the confusion of accidental impressions, her notions and judgments lay sometimes disordered, they yet struck out upon a path in which it was very difficult to accompany her. Least could the modest Etienne here follow her, who could only proceed step by step, when he would understand any direction, and whose sensitive mind was sickened by the slightest ebullition of feeling; and therefore he often sought Madame Fonrobert's forgiveness for the haste with which he had recommended the stranger to her generosity. It is true that his attachment daily increased for the lovely and highly-born maiden, in whom, much as he had contemplated her, he had not been able to discover any fault which could reproach him for this inclination; and yet the more his satisfaction arose from Valerie's society, the more ashamed he felt on that account, and the more carefully he measured and regulated his behaviour towards her. Indeed, he held himself aloof just in proportion as he realized the nearness of her presence. Madame Fonrobert, on her part, glad that matters went so favourably for the peace of her household, disturbed no one in ought that kept other considerations away from her. All these circumstances, combined together, caused the soul of Valerie, in the midst of the busy capital, to be as lonesome in the benevolent family, as had she been on a desolate island, where only the echo of her own voice from wild and uncultured nature had struck upon her ear. She might have been about the age of fifteen, when Etienne surprised her one day at a side book-case, containing only German authors; Valerie, a small volume in her hand, was reading without observing him, half aloud, with all the signs of excited attention, mingled with terror and astonishment, the following words:—

"Ah, see! ah, see! I suddenly
Behold a fearful wonder;
A horseman's raiment all despoil'd,
And torn, and worn asunder;
His manly head a skull become,
A naked skull! Ah, frightful doom!
His body, once so full and fair,
A shrivell'd skeleton lies there—"

Etienne interrupted her. "Do you understand what you are reading?" said he. "Since when have you learned German, Mademoiselle Valerie?"

She let fall her hand which held the book, and contemplating with dreamy look the images which then passed before her, she said, "Oh, a long time, Herr Etienne; the old servant always speaks it to me, and lets me read in her song-book; it is quite familiar to me in the hearing, but I express myself awkwardly in the strange language."

"And this frightful poem," continued he. "Who gave it you?"

"I took it myself," she drily replied, adding immediately, "I believe it was written for me. It makes my hair stand on end; my skin is cold as ice, but my heart, Herr Etienne, my heart never beat so warmly as at this moment."

His own heart felt strangely at these words. He perceived something inexplicable as his half-sunk eye met hers with its dark, quivering beam. He started back, as if he had suddenly seen a strange and unknown form stand before him, and endeavoured, under a forced smile, to conceal the aversion which only more strongly influenced him, as she now with passionate inspiration again took up the book, and repeated with an elevated tone:—

"Ah, see! ah, see! I suddenly—"

"Lay aside that wild stuff, Mademoiselle," said the agitated Etienne, beseechingly; "you will only bewilder your imagination with it."

"No," replied Valerie; "I can explain it to myself, only hear:—

"Loud wailings from the upper air,
And moanings from beneath;
Leonora's heart with trembling fear
Shook betwixt life and death."

"Say now," asked the agitated maiden; "is not that the history of my mother?" And then, she continued: "Was not thus the hour of my birth? —

"And now, amid the shadows pale,
Beneath the pale moon glance,
The spectres chant a fearful wail,
And whirl their horrid dance."

"I conjure you," Etienne interrupted her, "throw the book into the fire. It is madness that you are reading. Oh, the imprudent one," he sighed, "to impress on your weak brain such horrible images of the past!"

"Do not blame the old woman," said Valerie; "she has given me here a kind home. And were this only a chamber of death, it is a spot upon the earth," she added, with deep melancholy, "where I feel at peace."

She had, in the meanwhile, concealed the book, without Etienne venturing to hinder her; he only shook his head, and gazed after her as she went upstairs with it to her own chamber. He was obliged to confess that, since her coming into the house, she had not before so unreservedly disclosed her inward mind; but had ever avoided revealing it to a stranger's eye. But now astonished, and ravished by an overwhelming power, the true voice of a wounded and diseased soul had broken forth. Those hard, wild tones were they that had ever struck dumbly within her; at length she had found words for their utterance. The voice of the mother whispered them to her in the proper language.

Etienne involuntarily shuddered at this coincidence of strange occurrences. For the first time, he could not today feel right in his simple occupation. With a disturbed mind he took his place later at the dinner-table, opposite Madame Fonrobert. He almost felt thankful that Valerie did not make her customary appearance. She had excused herself from illness, but he could easily guess the true reason, which made him thoughtful and taciturn.

Madame Fonrobert observed the change in him. She probably ascribed it to Valerie's absence, for what fluttered convulsively on her lips, and was betrayed by an inward smile, that seldom came out openly, as she generally kept her thoughts to herself. Therefore she only slightly hinted that her table companion had not become more sprightly, and seemed to be pre-occupied by one exclusive idea.

"It will be agreeable to her," she added, "when she can learn to communicate her thoughts."

At these words he looked at her with astonishment; not understanding her meaning.

"I would," she continued, "that you told me plainly what plans you are projecting. Besides, it were better at once to take the first step, and so spare me the trouble of further inquiries."

"Good God!" exclaimed Etienne, seized with anxious foreboding; "what plans could I form, which in the least could concern my personal interest? And how have I deserved, madam, that you should think me guilty of a secret intention?"

"Gently, my friend, gently," she softly replied; "the zeal which you show for your justification could almost make me mistrustful of your integrity. But I will not disquiet you. The simple question now is, whether you think of occupying, in a short time, the middle story, which since the deceased Herr Fonrobert's time has remained shut up."

"I make a change in your house?" asked the affrighted Etienne, who did not comprehend what she intended.

"I thought," she replied, "if you should marry."

The words died upon his ear; he thought himself dreaming, when she added—

"See! Valerie is grown fully to the age of fifteen; after my death you are my heir. What will you that you delay the period when you may be happy? What I see in the future, I can also endure at the present. And then, at least, I shall have the consolation of knowing that matters will be hereafter as I have directed, and that nothing new will subvert the ancient order."

"Is it possible?" stammered the bookkeeper, in a perplexity which half arose from astonishment, half from inexpressible embarrassment; "is it possible that you deem me guilty, at my age, of so great a folly? Ay, Heaven forbid me from harbouring wishes for which I should only blush! How ungenerous, willingly to consign the blooming young maiden to a sickly, consumptive husband, whose infirm health more weds him to death than to life. No, no, Madame Fonrobert, no more of this, I beg," he added quickly, as if he could not with sufficient haste dismiss an imagination to whose impression he could pay no regard.

Madame Fonrobert was silent awhile, without showing any signs of surprise at his answer. After a long pause, during which Etienne endeavoured to collect himself, she said calmly—

"Very good, my dear Etienne; but what then will, in the end, become of Valerie? She has appeared to me for some time past more melancholy and reserved than before; she is too lonely here with us."

"Indeed!" responded Etienne, hesitatingly.

"It will then be well," she continued, "for me to accept the offer of my brother-in-law the surgeon, who, with his only daughter is coming to Berlin from Cleves, and who wishes to lodge with me. I would at once have agreed to this, but I wished first to know your intentions; for had you——"

"I am not at all worth considering in any of your arrangements," said he, hastily interrupting her, that he might not again be disquieted with the proposal.

"My niece, Philline, is about the same age as Valerie," observed Madame Fonrobert; "they will teach each other what they mutually require to learn. Much can be regulated in our foster-child, through intercourse with persons of her own age; besides," added she, "the new guests will be welcome to you, my friend, as age is ever taciturn, and Valerie is a dreamer."

He could not but grant this; and as he was glad to see her busied with another object, he obtained leave to write immediately to the surgeon, and to make the necessary preparations for his arrival. The many particulars which the precise lady prescribed for this purpose, and for the security of her own repose, gave her active assistant abundant occupation. He thereby lost sight of the lonely young dreamer, who kept apart in her own little chamber. To his joy, however, he next morning found in its place in the bookcase, the dangerous poem, which he had so unwillingly seen in the hands of the excited maiden; he immediately took it away, and locked it up. Valerie smiled, when afterwards she observed this, but forbore from any remark.

After several weeks, the surgeon arrived with his daughter. He was an earnest, learned man, quite devoted to his studies, of stirring industry, and untiring investigation. As soon as he had unpacked and arranged his books, his chemical and surgical apparatus, everything stood in its place; he found his own occupation in a spacious room in the midst of embryos in spirits, skulls, skeletons, and other scientific indispensables, so that his presence in the house was but little noticed.

It was otherwise with Philline. Sprightly as a roe, communicative, sportful, and ever ready to sacrifice herself and friends for a joke; now she pursued her pranks with the old tedious Anna, now with her aunt's Bolognese dog; with her aunt herself, and the pale, coughing, house-spectre, as she was wont to call Etienne, while she spared Valerie, whose coldness affrighted her, and towards whom, therefore, she felt more reluctance than confidence. Their mutual intercourse remained a long time sufficiently restrained. Wearisomeness, at last, induced Philline to seek her young companion in her own little chamber. She found her sitting idly in a corner, and repeating in a loud voice some verses, which her visitor did not at all understand. The thought to play a comedy arose immediately from this incident in the mind of the sportive Philline. She communicated her notion to the other, but as they were entirely without the necessary means and characters, they contented themselves with learning scenes from tragedies (for Valerie liked only the tragical), and reciting them with much pathos before the deaf and silent walls. The scanty pleasure, enlivened neither by the sympathy nor admiration of beholding friends, could be of no long entertainment for the social, sprightly Philline; she was at all times restless and ill at ease in Valerie's little room, and it was only not to disturb her father that she had hitherto resorted thither to unfold her dramatic talent.

Fully content with her accomplishments in the art, she resolved to give both her father and the other members of the household an astonishing proof of it. Valerie was not to be wanting. During the hours when the surgeon took his circuit in the city, the daughter desired to make all preparations for the little festival in her apartment, and for this purpose invited Valerie to accompany her there, which the latter had with singular anxiety avoided; nor could she today subdue her reluctance. Alternately becoming red and pale, she stammered out excuses, not one of which was comprehended by the other, who almost forcibly drew the trembling maiden after her. But scarcely had they approached the door, which was standing open, and which led to the surgeon's room, and scarcely had Valerie cast a single glance therein, then, with distorted countenance, she uttered a terrific cry, and rushed breathless from the spot. Philline, first frightened, then angry, followed her, scolding and blaming, and overwhelmed her with such bitter reproaches, that the former in excited vehemency revealed the reason of her conduct, which she had rather have kept secret, saying, with bewildered look—

"Do with me what you will, but never can I pass the skeletons which grin at me from your father's glass case."

Philline burst out into loud laughter. Familiar with the objects of so great terror, she was as deficient in the notion of it, as in sympathy with the emotion, and she knew not the sad circumstances of Valerie's birth in the field of carnage.

"Is it possible," she exclaimed, "that you are so little above the prejudices of the lower classes as to be overcome in this manner by the impression of what you are not accustomed to?"

"Do not mock me," replied Valerie, deathly pale, and trembling as an aspen leaf; "I cannot help it. Once before, I stood at the same spot, as your father was coming out. I had not time fully to recollect myself. Quick as thought my eye had strayed towards those horrid forms. I carried about with me the sensation of them for days together."

At this Philline again openly laughed in her face. She understood her so little, that she sported in the most heartless manner with the most pitiable of all weaknesses, as she termed the poor maiden's unconquerable aversion, and exposed her to the like blame from all who had any regard to her tale of the laughable incident. Etienne's tender soul suffered much from the strokes of the inexhaustible raillery which befell the object of his protection, yet he ventured not to defend her as his sympathy desired, from fear that the fine texture of her mind might in another way be discomposed by unpleasant emotions. Especially since his last conversation with Madame Fonrobert, had his demeanour towards the young girl been far more circumspect than before. She also but seldom now came into the shop to look for a book. When on one occasion Etienne remarked this to her, referring at the same time to that poem which had once so much inflamed her, she seemed vexed, and answered him shortly—"that she did not want the volume anymore."

This, and similar answers, had quite turned Etienne from his former custom of being her defender on all occasions. He now, therefore, took no part against Philline's attacks, which induced her father to interpose. He felt deeply interested in the extraordinary young creature, through a strange impression which she had made upon him. He said he thought he saw something like a shadow upon her brow, as if by accident a dark body were sportively hovering over her; a phenomenon he had often observed in persons strangely organized, or who were destined by Providence to violent events. With this opinion regarding her, he declared the jestings of his daughter to be ungenerous, indeed, even silly, inasmuch as the peculiar seat of innate aversions can as little be ascertained as that of many secret diseases; and, therefore, such manifestations are rightly no more to be laughed at than are the contortions of spasm.

This medical judgment, far from restraining Philline, only stimulated her spirit of contradiction; and whether it was to revenge herself for the spoiling of her comedy, or by a bold joke, in defiance of opposite counsel, to bring the laugh upon her own side, she resolved, at all hazards, to cure Valerie of her imaginary fears. One Sunday evening, when the old servant slept out at her daughter's, who dwelt outside the gate, Philline contrived during supper, with the help of her own maid, to remove one of the skeletons from her father's closet, and conceal it under Valerie's bed-clothes. Full of the expected result, her merriment rose above all restraint; even Valerie was infected by it, who therefore later than usual retired to her own chamber.

Madame Fonrobert detained her friend Etienne a while longer. She was agreeably excited by the favourable alteration which she thought she saw in her foster-child, and communicated to her good kinsman her observations thereupon.

"Philline works very well upon Valerie, Herr Etienne," said she, with an air of self-satisfaction; "very well. Did you see, to-day, how unconstrainedly she fell in with the other's wit, and returned it? I think we may congratulate ourselves upon my resolution of inviting here these pleasant people."

She looked smilingly over to Etienne, who, silent, and listening with the greatest attention to an obscure noise, was standing aside with his face toward the door.

"You do not understand me well?" she abruptly asked; at the same moment, however, starting up from the sofa, and seizing his hands with the words—

"God! my God! what is the matter? You are pale as death!"

"Nothing—nothing!" whispered Etienne; "it is surely nothing; but I thought I heard someone screaming in anguish."

He had scarcely said this, when Philline rushed wildly into the room, with a staring look, shrieking vehemently—

"She has lost her senses! Help, Heaven! she is caressing the skeleton, and speaking words of madness to it!"

More was not necessary to drive Etienne to Valerie's chamber.

Already before he entered, he heard her in quite an altered tone, more scream than speech. She was repeating in a breath, the horrible ballad, and at the place,

"Ah, see! ah, see! I suddenly
Behold a fearful wonder"—

she fell into such a wild ecstasy, that Etienne burst open the door, thinking she would not survive the next moment. He found the unfortunate one erect in bed, and embracing the skeleton in her arms with a joy as if she had now found the happiness of her life.

The surgeon, who was present, and who ascertained the particulars from Philline's painful confession, found that, after the ill-
planned joke, she had stood before the door to observe Valerie;
and seeing her, when undressed, quietly approach her bed, and
express no terror nor reluctance, she foreboded some misfortune. Full of anxiety she then entered, and found her pitiably
deprived of her senses, softly whispering and playing with the
object of her former horror. The surgeon immediately gave up
hope; and Etienne soon perceived that she had imagined herself to be her mother, who had again found the long-lamented
object of her love. Madame Fonrobert's forebodings were now
fully realized. The peace of her house had departed. She herself
did not long survive the last blow. The surgeon also in a short
time left the dwelling, in order to rescue his daughter from entire ruin; for, since that evening, health and cheerfulness had
both forsaken her. Her father was often heard to repeat, that he
had never thought that the bones of a dead warrior, which he
had once brought from the battle-field of Minden, could have
prevailed over the reason of two maidens.

Etienne was vividly penetrated with these words.
Involuntarily, unanswerable questions pressed his spirit, yet he
avoided the wish vainly to inquire after the hidden cause of such
mysterious connections. He bore his lot quietly and patiently.
For long years he remained the possessor of the little house,
the lonely supporter of the unhappy Valerie. Her gloomy lamp
was every evening seen glimmering from the bow-window. The
passer-by sent up to heaven a short prayer for her salvation. She
herself sang and toyed with her phantom, till once the moon
shone in at the open window, and lightened upon the coffin, in
which her bones by the side of those that had been disturbed,
found rest and peace.

THE JOURNEY TO BRCZWEZMCISL

by Johann Heinrich Zschokke

I had but just quitted the university, and was a mere stripling, when I received the appointment of judge-commissary at a little town in New East Prussia, as the part of Poland was termed which, during the partition of that country, had fallen to the share of Prussia.

I will not weary the reader by giving any lengthened account of my journey; the country was but one flat throughout, the men mere boors, the officials uncouth, the accommodation execrable. Yet the people all seemed happy enough. Man and beast have each their allotted elements. The fish perishes when out of water—the elegance of a boudoir would prove fatal to a Polish Jew.

Well, to make my story short, I arrived one evening, a little before sunset, at a place called, I believe (but should be sorry to vouch for my accuracy), Brczwezmcisl, a pleasant little town enough. When I say pleasant, to be sure I own that the streets were unpaved, the houses begrimed with soot, and the natives not over refined either in manners or person; but a man who works in a coal-mine is pleasant, after his fashion, even as the pet *figurante* of the day after hers.

I had pictured to myself Brczwezmcisl, the place where I was to enter upon my functions, as far more formidable than I in fact found it, and perhaps on that account I was now prepared to term it pleasant. I remember that the first time I tried to pronounce the name of the place I very nearly brought on lock-jaw. Hence, no doubt, my gloomy anticipations as to its appearance. Names certainly do influence our ideas to a most marvellous extent. Moreover, what mainly contributed to enhance my secret misgivings as to the town destined to enjoy the benefit of my talents was the fact that I had never yet been so far from home as to lose sight of its church steeple. I had a tolerable idea that my way did not lead me in the vicinity of the Cannibal Islands, or of the lands where men's heads "do grow beneath their shoulders;" but I was not without some apprehension, as I journeyed on, of receiving an occasional pistol-shot, or feeling the cold steel of a stiletto between my ribs.

My heart throbbed violently as I caught the first glimpse of Brczwezmcisl. It appeared, at a distance, a vast plain, covered with mud-heaps. But what mattered that to one of my imaginative powers? There was my goal, there my entering scene in life. Not a soul did I know there, with the exception of an old college acquaintance, named Burkhardt, who had been but recently appointed collector of taxes at Brczwezmcisl. I had apprised him of my near advent, and requested him to provide me with temporary lodgings. The nearer I approached the town, the keener waxed my esteem and friendship for Burkhardt, with whom I had never been on terms of intimacy; indeed, my mother enjoined me always to shun his society, seeing that his reputation for steadiness was not of the highest. But now I was his till death. He was my only rallying point in this wild Polish town; he was the sole plank to which I could cling.

I am not of a superstitious character, but I own to a certain belief in omens; and I had settled in my mind that it would be a lucky sign if the first person we met coming out of the town gates should prove a young woman, and the reverse if one of the other sex. As we were about to enter the town a girl, to all ap-

140

pearance comely and well-made, issued from the gate. Damsel of happy augury! Fain could I have quitted the cumbrous vehicle, and cast my travel-worn frame prostrate at your feet. I wiped my eye-glass that I might not lose one of her features, but grave them forever in the tablets of my memory.

As she came nearer, I discovered to my dismay that my Brczwezmcisl Venus was a bit hideous. Slim she was, good sooth, but it was the slimness of one wasted by disease! shape and figure had she none. Her face was a perfect surface, for some untoward accident had deprived her of her nose; and had it not been for the merest apology for lips, her head might have been taken for the skull of a skeleton. As we came yet nearer, I remarked that the fair Pole was a warm patriot; for she put out her tongue at me in derision of her nation's oppressors, whose countryman I was.

Under these happy auspices we entered the town, and halted at the Post-office, newly decorated with the Prussian eagle, which would have shown to much greater advantage, in all the glories of fresh paint, had not some patriotic little street blackguards adorned it with a thick coating of mud.

I asked the postmaster very politely where I could find Mr. Tax-collector Burkhardt. In order, I suppose, to convince me that even in that remote corner of the globe officials were true to those habits of courtesy and attention for which they are so eminently distinguished, he suffered me to repeat my question six times ere he vouchsafed to inquire, in his gruffest tones, what I wanted; a seventh time did I reiterate my inquiry, and that, I flatter myself with a degree of politeness that would have done honour to the most finished courtier.

"In the old Starosty," he growled out.

"Might I be permitted most respectfully to inquire whereabouts this same old Starosty may be located?"

"I have no time. Peter, show this person the way."

And away went Peter and I, while the postmaster, who had no time to answer me, lolled out of the window, with his pipe in his mouth, watching us. Aha, my fine fellow, thought I, just let me catch you in the hands of justice—whose unworthy representative I have here the honour to be—and I'll make you rue the day you dared sport your churlishness upon me.

Peter, the Polish tatterdemalion, who escorted me, understood and spoke so little German that our conversation was extremely limited. His sallow face and sharp features rendered him particularly unprepossessing.

"Tell me, my worthy friend," I asked, as we waded side by side through the mud, "do you know Mr. Tax-collector Burkhardt?"

"The old Starosty."

"Good; but what can I do in your old Starosty?"

"Die!"

"God forbid! that does not at all chime in with my arrangements."

"Stone-dead; die!"

"Why, what have I done?"

"Prussian—no Pole."

"I am a Prussian, certainly."

"Know that."

"What do you mean by dying then?"

"So, and so, and so;" and the fellow thrust the air as though he clenched a dagger. He then pointed to his heart, groaned, and rolled his eyes in a manner awful to behold. I began to feel rather uncomfortable, for Peter had by no means the look of one beside himself; besides, the understrappers at the post-office are seldom recruited from a lunatic asylum.

"I think we are at cross purposes, my excellent friend," I at length resumed. "What do you mean by die?"

"Kill!" and he gave me a wild sidelong glance.

"How, kill?"

"When night comes."

"When night comes—this very night? Your wits are wool-gathering, sirrah!"

"Pole, yes; but no Prussian."

I shook my head, and desisted from any further attempt at conversation. We evidently could not make each other out. And yet there was fearful meaning in the scoundrel's words. I was well aware of the inveterate hatred felt by the Poles toward the Prussians, and how it had already led to fatal collisions between them. What if the dunder-headed fellow had meant to convey a warning to me? or perhaps he had involuntarily betrayed the secret of a plot for the general massacre of every Prussian. I mentally resolved to divulge the whole to my friend and fellow-countryman Burkhardt, as we arrived at the so-termed Starosty. It was constructed of stone, evidently of some antiquity, and situated in a dull remote street. Ere we reached it I observed how each passer-by cast a sly furtive glance up at its time-worn walls. My guide did the same; and pointing to the door, he shuffled off without word or gesture of salutation.

It must be owned that my arrival and reception at Brczwezmcisl were none of the most flattering. The discourteous damsel at the gate, the surly New East Prussian postmaster, and the Pole, with his unintelligible jargon, had put me on the very worst terms with my new place of sojourn and office of judge-commissary. How I congratulated myself to think that I was about to meet one who had, at least, breathed the same air as myself! To be sure, Mr. Burkhardt was not held in the best repute at home; but a man's character varies according to the circumstances of his position, even were he still the same as of old. Better far a jovial tippler than a sickly skeleton with her projected tongue; better far a hare-brained gambler than the postmaster with his studied coarseness; ay, better the company of a vaporing hector than that of a Polish malcontent. The latter phase in Burkhardt's character even served to elevate him in my eyes; for, between ourselves be it observed, my gentleness and love of quiet, my steadiness and reserve, so oft the theme of praise with mamma, would stand me but in sorry stead should any rising of the people take place. Some virtues become vices in certain positions.

As I entered the old Starosty I was puzzled to know where to find my dear and long-cherished friend Burkhardt. The house was very spacious. The creaking of the rusty door-hinges resounded through the whole building, yet without bringing any one to ascertain who might be there.

I discovered an apartment on my left, and knocked gently at the door. As my signal was unanswered by any friendly "Come in," I knocked more loudly than before: still no answer. My knocks re-echoed through the house. I waxed impatient, and yearned to clasp Burkhardt, the friend of my soul, to my heart. I opened the door and went in. In the middle of the room was a coffin.

If I be always polite to the living, still more so am I to the dead. I was about to retire as gently as I could, when a parting glance at the coffin showed me that its hapless occupant was no other than the tax-collector, Burkhardt, who had been called on, poor fellow, in his turn, to discharge that great tax so peremptorily demanded of us by that grim collector Death. There he lay regardless alike of flagon or dice box, calm and composed as though he had never shared in the joys or cares of this life.

Indescribably shocked, I rushed from the chamber of death, and sought relief in the long gloomy corridor. What on earth was to become of me now? Here I was, hundreds of miles from my native home and the maternal mansion, in a town whose very name I never had heard until I was sent to un-Pole-ify it as judge-commissary! My sole acquaintance, the friend of my heart, had shuffled off this mortal coil. What was I to do, where lay my head, or how find the lodgings engaged for me by the dear departed?

My gloomy reflections were here disturbed by the creaking of the door on its rusty hinges, whose harsh grating jarred strangely on my nerves.

A pert, flippant-looking livery-servant rushed up the stairs, contemplated me with a broad stare of astonishment, and at length addressed me. My knees shook beneath me. I suffered the fellow to talk to me to his heart's delight, but for the first few moments fright deprived me of all power of reply; and even had my state of mind permitted me to speak, it would have amounted to much the same thing, seeing that the man was speaking Polish.

Perceiving that he remained without reply, he proceeded to address me in German, which he spoke very fluently. I at length mustered up sufficient courage to tell him my whole story, and the various adventures I had met with since my arrival at the accursed town whose name it still dislocated my jaws to pronounce. As he heard my name he assumed a more respectful mien, took off his hat, and proceeded to give me the following details, which, for the reader's benefit, I have compressed into the smallest possible space.

He informed me, to begin with, that his name was Lebrecht; that he had served as interpreter and most faithful of domestics to Mr. Tax-collector, of pious memory, until the preceding night, when it had pleased Heaven to remove the excellent and ever to be lamented tax-collector to another and a better world. The manner of his death was perfectly in keeping with the tenor of his life. He had been passing the evening at wine and cards with some Polish gentlemen. The fumes of the wine aroused the Prussian pride of my friend, while it kindled to a yet fiercer pitch the old Sarmatian patriotism of his companions. Words grew high, blows were exchanged, and one of the party dealt my late friend three or four blows with a knife, any one of which was of itself sufficient to have extinguished life. In order to avoid incurring the penalties of New East Prussian justice, the guilty parties had taken themselves off—whither none could tell. My ever-to-be-regretted friend had, shortly before his death, made all the requisite arrangements for me, and hired a very experienced German cook, who would wait upon me at a moment's notice. In the course of his narrative, Lebrecht led me to infer, from several hints that he gave me, how the Poles were sworn foes to the Prussians, and how I must expect to meet with such delicate attentions as those lavished on me by the damsel at the gate. He explained to me, moreover, that my friend Peter was a muddle-headed jackass, and that his pantomimic gestures referred, in all probability, to the fate of my hapless friend. He warned me to be constantly on my guard, as the infuriated Poles were evidently hatching some plot; as for himself, he was fully determined to quit the town immediately after the funeral of his late master.

This narrative terminated, he conducted me up the broad stone staircase to the apartments provided for me. Passing through a suite of lofty rooms, very spacious, but very dreary to behold, we came to an apartment of large dimensions, wherein was a press bedstead, with curtains of faded yellow damask, an old table, whose feet had once been gilded, and half a dozen dusty chairs. Suspended from the wall was an enormous looking-glass, almost bereft of its reflecting powers, in a quaint, old-fashioned frame, while the wall itself was garnished by parti-coloured tapestry, representing scenes from the Old Testament. Time and the moth had done their work upon it, for it hung in tatters, and waved to and fro at the slightest motion. King Solomon sat headless on his throne of judgment, and the hands of the wicked elders had long since mouldered away. I felt by no means at my ease in this my lonely dwelling; far rather would I have taken up my quarters at the inn, and, oh that I had done so! But I kept my own counsel, partly from sheer nervousness, and partly because I did not wish to appear at all daunted at being in such immediate vicinity with a corpse. Moreover, I entertained no doubt but that Lebrecht and the experienced cook would bear me company during the night. The former lost no time in lighting the two candles that stood on the table, for it was fast getting dusk, and then took his departure for the purpose of procuring me the means of subsistence, and such like, to fetch my luggage, and to apprise the aforesaid experienced cook that the time had arrived for her to enter upon her functions. My luggage arrived in due time, likewise every requisite for my meal; but no sooner had I re-imbursed Lebrecht the money he had laid out for me than he wished me good-night, and went his way forthwith.

I misdoubted the fellow at once, for the moment he had swept up his money he was off. I was on the point of rushing after him, to entreat him not to leave me, but I held back for very shame. Why should I make the wretch the confidant of my timidity? I had no doubt but that he would spend the night in some room or other, to keep watch over the body of his slaughtered master. The sound of the banging of the street-door undeceived me at once; and that sound thrilled through my very marrow. I hurried to the window, and beheld him scampering across the street, as though the foul fiend were at his heels. He was soon out of sight, leaving myself and the corpse sole tenants of the old Starosty.

I do not believe in ghosts, but yet at night-time I own to being somewhat apprehensive of their appearance. This may seem to involve a paradox, but I only state the fact. The death-like stillness of all around, the time-worn tapestry that clung in fluttering shreds around that dreary chamber, the consciousness of the body of a murdered man in the room above, the deadly feud between the Prussian and the Pole, all conspired to fill my soul with awe and apprehension. I hungered, but could not eat. I wearied for repose, but could find none. I examined the window, to ascertain if it could afford me egress in case of need, for I should have been utterly lost in the labyrinth of chambers and corridors necessary to traverse ere I could gain the door. To my dismay strong iron bars forbade all hope of escape in that quarter.

Suddenly the old Starosty seemed awakening to life. I heard doors open and close, steps at some little distance, and the sound of voices in animated conversation. I was at a loss how to account for this rapid change in the state of affairs, but I felt that it boded me but little good. It seemed as though I heard a warning voice saying, "'Tis thou they seek! Did not that blundering Peter betray the secret of the intended massacre? Save thyself ere it be too late." I shuddered in every limb. Methought I saw the murderous band, how they thirsted for my blood, and were concerting the method of my death. I heard their footsteps approaching nearer and more near. Already had they reached the ante-chamber leading to my apartment. They were muttering together in low whispers. I sprang up, and bolted and barred the door, and, as I did so, became aware that someone was endeavouring to open it on the other side. I scarce dared breathe, lest my very breath should betray me. I heard by their voices that they were Poles. As my unlucky stars would have it, I must needs study a little Polish, by way of qualifying myself for my official duties; and I could detect the words "blood," "death," and "Prussians." My knees quaked, cold drops started to my brow. Again was the attempt to open the door repeated, but it seemed as though the intruders wished to avoid confusion, for I heard them depart, or rather glide, from thence.

Whether it were that the Poles had aimed at my life, or my property, or whether they had determined upon another mode of attack, I resolved to extinguish my candles, in order that their light might not betray me from without. How could I tell but that one of the ruffians might not fancy taking a shot at me through the windows?

Night is friend to no man, and man has an instinctive dread of darkness, else whence the terror of children, even before they have been scared by the tale of goblin grim and spectre dire?

No sooner was I in utter obscurity than all manner of horrors, possible and impossible, crowded upon me. I flung myself upon my bed, in the hopes of sleeping, but the clothes seemed tainted with the foul odour of dead men's graves. If I sat up it was worse; forever and anon a rustling sound, as of someone near me, caused me to shudder afresh. The form of the murdered man, with his livid brow and half-glazed eye, seemed to stalk before me. What prospects would I not have sacrificed but to be once more free! And now the bells tolled the

> "Witching hour of night,
> when church-yards yawn, and hell itself looks out."

Each stroke vibrated upon my soul. In vain I called myself a superstitious fool, a faint-hearted dastard: it availed me nothing. Unable at length to bear up any longer, and nerved either by daring or despair, I sprang from my seat, groped my way to the door, unbolted and unbarred it, and resolved, albeit at the risk of my life, to gain the street.

Merciful heavens! what did I behold as I opened the door! I started and staggered back. Little had I looked for such a grisly sentinel.

By the dim flickering of an old lamp placed on a side-table, I saw before me the murdered Tax-collector, lying in his bier, even as I had seen him in the room above. But now I could perceive how his shirt, which had previously been concealed by a pall, was dyed with the big black gouts of blood. I strove to rally my senses, to persuade myself that the whole was the mere phantom of my over-heated imagination; but as I stirred the coffin with my foot, till the corpse seemed as though about to move and unclose its eyes, I could no longer doubt the fearful reality of the spectacle before me. Almost paralyzed by fear, I rushed to my room, and fell backward on my bed.

And now a confused noise proceeded from the bier. Was the dead alive? for the sound that I heard was of one raising himself with difficulty. A low and suppressed moan thrilled in my ears, and I saw before me the form of the murdered one; it strode through the door, entered my room, then stalked awhile to and fro, and disappeared. As I again summoned up my reason to my aid, the spectre, or the corpse, or the living dead, gave my reason the lie by depositing its long, lank, livid length upon my bed and across my body, its icy shoulders resting upon my neck, and nearly depriving me of breath.

How I escaped with life I cannot explain to this present hour. Mortal dread was upon me, and I must have remained a long while in a state of unconsciousness; for as I heard from beneath my grisly burden the clock sound, instead of its striking one—the signal for spirits to vanish—it was striking two.

I leave the horrors of my situation to the reader's imagination. The smell of the charnel-house in my nostrils, and a yet warm corpse struggling for breath, as though the death-rattle were upon him; while I was benumbed by terror, and the hellish weight of the burden I bore. The scenes in Dante's Hell fall far short of anguish such as was then mine. I was too weak or terror-stricken to disengage myself from the corpse, which seemed as if expiring a second time; for I conjectured that, while senseless from loss of blood, the wretched man had been taken for dead, and thrust forthwith, Polish fashion, into a coffin, and now lay dying in good earnest. He seemed powerless alike for life and death, and I was doomed to be the couch whereon the fearful struggle would terminate.

I strove to fancy that all my adventures in Brczwezmcisl were but a dream, and that I was labouring under an attack of nightmare, but circumstances and surrounding objects were too strong to admit of any such conclusion; still, I verily believe I should have finally succeeded in convincing myself that it was all a vision, and nothing but a vision, had not an incident more striking than any that hitherto preceded, established, beyond the shadow of a doubt, the fact of my being broad awake.

It was day-break; not that I could perceive the light of heaven, for the shoulders of my expiring friend impeded my view, but I inferred so from the bustle in the street below. I heard the footsteps and voices of men in the room; I could not make out the subject of their conversation, as they talked in Polish, but I remarked that they were busy about the coffin. Now, beyond a doubt, thought I, they are looking for the dead man, and my deliverance is at hand; and so it proved, although it happened after a fashion for which I was but little prepared.

One of the exploring party smote so lustily with a stout bamboo upon the extended form of the dead or dying, that he started up, and stood erect. Some of the blows lighted upon my hapless person with such effect as to make me yell out most vigorously, and take up a position directly in the rear of the defunct. This old Polish and New East Prussian method of restoring the dead to life proved, certainly, so efficacious in the present instance, that I doubt whether the impassibility of death were not preferable to the acute perceptions of the living.

I now perceived that the room was filled by men, for the most part Poles. The timely castigation had been administered by a police-officer appointed to superintend the funeral. The Tax-collector still slept the sleep of death in his coffin, which stood in the ante-chamber, whither it had been transported by the drunken Poles, who had been ordered to convey it to what had been formerly the porter's lodge. They had, however, been pleased to select my ante-chamber as a fitting resting-place for their charge, whom they confided to the watch of one of their besotted comrades, who had slumbered at his post, and, awakened probably by my entrance, had groped his way, with all the instinct of one far gone in liquor, to my bed, and there slept off the fumes of his potations.

The preceding incidents had so thoroughly unmanned me as to bring on a severe attack of fever, and for seven long weeks did I lie raving about the horrors of that fearful night; and even now, albeit, thanks to the Polish insurrection, I am no longer judge-commissary at Brczwezmcisl, I can scarce think on my adventure in New East Prussia without a shudder. However, I am always glad to relate it, as it contains a sort of moral—to wit, that we ought not to fear that which we profess to disbelieve.

THE CASTLE SPECTRE OF SCHARZFELD

by Friedrich Gottschalck

SITUATED upon one of the foremost hills of the Hartz, not far from Osterode, lie the ruins of Castle Scharzfeld. There about sixty years back there was still one of the high round towers to be seen, in the front of one of the angles without any roof, and too dilapidated to bear anything upon it. When more recently there was attempt to rebuild it, the castle spectre regularly destroyed in the night what was executed in the day, by throwing all the materials down a precipice.

For a deed had been perpetrated of old within its precincts: a wanton outrage, by the Emperor Henry himself, (Henry IV.) and hence arose the vengeance of the Castle Ghost, who to the eternal discredit of the place would never permit another roof to be raised.

The Emperor had beheld at Goslar the consort of one of his lords, who ranked among his heroes, and had the superintendance of his works upon the Hartz mountains. The lady pleased him, and the Emperor sought to win her to his pleasure. With this view he despatched her husband to a distance, upon an embassy; and when he had ascertained that his beautiful consort was now left alone at the castle, he set out upon a stormy day, and under the pretence of hunting, he rode in the direction of the lady's dwelling. As the tempest increased, and the heavens grew darker, while the vivid lighting-bolts glanced athwart the sky, he suddenly rode up to the castle gates, and demanded shelter from the storm. The young hostess, rejoiced to shew him all honour and hospitality, hasted to bid him welcome, and ordered the richest fare to be set before him, as Sovereign Lord of the Empire, that her castle would afford. She indulged not the least kind of suspicion; but after he had well regaled himself, the Emperor basely resolved to give full loose to his passions, ensue what would. With this most unworthy and unchristian feeling, and with the assistance of the still more base and wicked Priest of Pohlde, he broke through all the sacred bonds of a prince, a guest, and a man of honour, to effect his purpose by force.

The offenders flattered themselves that the whole would remain a secret, for secret was the scene: but scarcely had the Emperor on the ensuing morning taken his departure, when the spirit of vengeance spoke. It was the Castle Spectre that betrayed the deed. For centuries before he had traversed the neighbouring hills of Scharzfeld, and been heard in various places, besides the ancient tower. But as he had never been known to do any injury, he was suffered to range at large, nor had he ever by holy word been laid. From this time forth, however, he raised a frightful gibbering and lamentation, rattled horribly through the halls and chambers, and often shook the whole castle to its very foundations. Then first the household began to make sign of the cross, and number their beads to the Virgin, while the unhappy lady shrunk weeping and praying from the sight and sound. Still the Spectre did no mischief nor injured any one; he merely wished to proclaim the Emperor's shame, and to abandon his ancient haunt, where such a woeful deed had been committed. Shortly he betook himself to the round tower, where a noise of crashing and falling denoted that he was hard at work. In fact he took the roof, and cast it with unearthly force, and tremendous noise into the precipice at some distance below. This done, he burst loose, and stalked with angry voice

154

and gesture over Scharzfeld, crying aloud, that the parish priest was a still more monstrous villain than the Emperor: and then he disappeared.

From that time forth no art of man could succeed in fixing a roof upon the fated tower; for as fast as the masons completed the work, the castle sprite made his appearance, and destroyed it again at night. The parish priest ran crazed, deserted by all about the country, carefully and avoided by every honest eye.

The whole of these events took place as they were thus recounted in the year of our blessed Lord one thousand, one hundred and ten.

THE DEATH WATCH

by Luise Mühlbach

COUNT MANFRED knelt, deeply affected, by the bed of his poor friend—now destined to be his death-bed. Silence and gloom were in the narrow room, which was only dimly lighted by a night-lamp.

The moon shone, large and cold, through the one window, illuminating the wretched couch of the invalid. Soon loud groaning alone interrupted the melancholy stillness. Manfred felt a chill shudder in all his limbs, a sensation of horror came over him, and the bed of his slowly expiring friend, and he felt as if he must perforce go out among mankind, hear the breath of a living person instead of this death-rattle, and press a warm hand instead of the cold damp one of the dying man. He softly raised himself from his knees, and crept to the chimney to stir the almost extinct fire, that something bright and cheering might surround him. But the sick man raised himself up, and looked at him with fixed glassy eyes, while his heart rose higher and quicker with a breathless groaning.

The flame crackled and flew upwards, casting a harsh gleam through the room. Suddenly a coal flew out with a loud noise, and fell into the middle of the apartment upon the wooden floor. At the same time a terribly piercing cry arose from the bed, and Manfred, who looked towards it with alarm, saw that the invalid was sitting up, and with eyes widely opened and out-stretched arms, was staring at the spot where the coal was lying. It was a frightful spectacle that of the dying man, who seemed to be struggling with a deep feeling of horror; on whose features death had already imprinted his seal; and whose short night-gown was insufficient to conceal the dry and earth-grey arms and legs, which had already assumed a deathlike hue. Frightful was the loud rattle that proceeded from the heart of one who could scarcely be called alive or dead, and dull as from the grave sounded the isolated words which he uttered, still gazing upon the coal on the floor. "Away—away with thee! why will thou remain there, spectre? Leave me, I say."

Manfred stood overpowered with horror, his trembling feet refused to support him, and he leaned against the wall contem-plating the actions of his friend, the sight of whom created the deepest terror. The voice of the invalid became louder and more shrill: "Away with thee, I say! why dost thou cleave so fast to my heart? I say, leave me!"

Then striking out with his arms he sprung out of the bed with unnatural force, and darting to the spot where the coal was lying, stooped down, grasped it in his hand, and flung it back upon the hearth. He then burst into a loud, wild laugh, which made poor Manfred's heart quail within him, and returned back to the bed.

But the coal had burned its very dross into the floor, and had left a black mark.

The room was again quiet. Manfred now breathed freely, and calmly crept to the couch of his friend, whose quiet, regular breathing and closed eyes showed that he had fallen into a re-posing sleep. Thus passed one hour, the slow progress of which Manfred observed on his friend's large watch, which lay upon the bed, and the regular ticking of which was the only interrup-tion of the stillness of the night, except the still, quiet breathing of his friend.

The steeple clock in the vicinity announced by its striking that another hour had passed. Manfred counted the strokes. It was twelve o'clock—midnight. He involuntarily shuddered, the thoughts of the legends and tales of his childhood darted through him like lightning, and he owned to himself that he had always felt a mysterious terror at the midnight hour. At the same moment, his friend opened his eyes, and softly pronounced his name.

Manfred leant down to him, "Here I am, Karl."

"I thank you," said the sick man, in a faint voice, "for remaining by me thus faithfully. I am dying, Manfred."

"Do not speak so," replied the other, affectionately grasping the hand of his friend.

"I cease to see you," said Karl, more and more faintly and slowly; "dark clouds are before my eyes."

Suddenly he raised himself, took the watch which was lying by him, and placed it in Manfred's hand.

"I thank you," he said, "for all the love you have shown me; for all your kindness and consolation. Take this watch, it is the only thing which now belongs to me. Wear it in remembrance of me. If it is permitted me, by this watch I will give you warning when I am near. Farewell!"

He sunk back—his breath stopped—he was no more.

Manfred bent over him, called his name, laid his hand on the forehead, which was covered with perspiration; he felt it grow colder and colder. Tears of the deepest sympathy filled his eyes, and dropped upon the pale face of the dead man.

"Sleep softly," whispered Manfred, "and may the grave afford you that repose which you sought in vain upon earth!"

Once more he pressed to his bosom the hand of his deceased friend, wrapped himself in his cloak, put up the watch which Karl had bequeathed him, and retired to his residence.

The sun was already high when he awoke from an uneasy sleep. With feelings of pain he thought of the past night, and of his departed friend. In remembrance of him he drew out the watch, which pointed to the half hour, and held it to his ear. It had stopped; he tried to wind it up, but all in vain—it had not run down.

"Is it possible," murmured Manfred to himself, "that there was really some spiritual connexion between the deceased and this his favourite watch, which he constantly carried?"

He sunk down upon a chair, and strange thoughts and forebodings passed through his excited mind.

"What is time?" he asked himself; "what is an hour? A machine artificially produced by human hands determines it, regulates it, and gives to life its significance, and to the mind its warnings. The awe which accompanies the midnight hour does not affect us if the hand of our watch goes wrong. The clock is the despot of man; regulating the actions both of kings and beggars. Nay, it is the ruler of time, which has subjected itself to its authority. The clock determines the very thoughts as well as the actions of man; is the propelling wheel of the human species. The maiden who reposes delighted in the arms of her lover trembles when the ruthless clock strikes the hour which tears him from her. Her grief, her entreaties, are all in vain. He must away, for the clock has ordered it. The murderer trembles in the full enjoyment of his fortune, for his eye fails on the hands of the clock, and they denote the hour when the already broken eye of the man he murdered looked upon him for the last time. In vain he endeavoured to smile; it is beyond his power; for the clock has spoken, and his conscience awakes when he thinks of the horror of that hour. Shuddering with the feverish chill of mental anguish, the condemned culprit looks upon the clock, the hand of which, slowly moving, brings nearer and nearer the hour of his death. It is not the rising and setting of the sun, it is not the light of day, that determines destruction; but the clock. When the hand, with cruel indifference, moves on and touches the figure of the hour which the judge has appointed for his death, the doors of the dungeon open, and he has ceased to live. As long as we live we are governed by the hour, and death alone frees us from the hour and the clock! Perhaps the whole of eternity, with its bliss, is nothing but an hourless, clockless existence; eternal, because without measure; blissful, because not bound to a measured time."

Manfred had once more entered the desolate residence of his deceased friend, and stood mourning by the corpse, the face of which bore, in its stiffened features, the peace which Karl had never known in life.

He thought of the life of the deceased—how poor it was in joy, and how, during the four years he had known him, he had never seen him smile. Tears came into his eyes, and he turned away from the corpse. Then his glance fell upon the black spot on the floor. The whole frightful scene of the preceding day revived in his soul, and the thought suddenly struck him, whether there might not be some connexion between that particular spot and the strange excitement of Karl. Fearful suspicions crossed his mind; he thought how often conscience had unmasked the criminal, in the hour of death; he remembered the frequent mysterious gloom of his friend; he remembered the wife with whom he had long lived unhappily, from whom he had been separated, and after whose residence Manfred had often inquired. On this subject Karl had always preserved silence, and often broke out into an unusual warmth. He reflected with what obstinacy Karl remained in this room, although Manfred had often and earnestly entreated him, as a friend and near relative, to go into his house. Nay, he now recollected quite clearly, that in the newspaper in which, years before, he had read the arrival of Count Karl Manfred, it was stated that he had arrived with his wife. A few weeks after he had read of the arrival of his relative, Manfred had gone to him, and found him alone; and when Karl had told him of his separation from his wife, had inquired no further.

All this now passed before his mind. He looked timidly back at the corpse, and it seemed to him as if this were scornfully nodding at him confirmation of his thoughts.

"I must have certainty," he cried aloud, and stooped down to the floor. He now plainly perceived that the middle boards, upon which was the burn, were looser than the others, and that the nails, which must have been there firmly, and the marks of which were still plainly to be seen, were wanting. He tried to raise the middle board, which at first resisted, but at last gave way a little. With a piece of wood he knocked the thick knife deeper into the floor; the nails became more and more unfastened, and he lifted and pulled with all the might of anxiety and curiosity. With a loud crack the board gave way entirely; he raised it, and—sight of horror!—saw that a skeleton lay stretched out beneath. Manfred at first almost fainted; then feeling how necessary were calmness and presence of mind, he collected himself with a strong effort, and looked hard at the skeleton. It held a paper between its teeth, which Manfred, with averted face, drew forth. Opening it, he soon recognised the hand-writing of Karl. The words were as follows:

"That no innocent person may be exposed to suspicion, I hereby declare that I, Karl Manfred, am the murderer of this woman. This declaration can never injure me, as I am determined never to quit this room before my death. The small, wretched house is my own property, and as I inhabit it alone, I am secure from discovery. When I am no more the secret will be unveiled, and for the finder of these lines I add, for nearer explanation, a short portion of the history of my life.

"I am the son of a collateral branch of the rich Count Manfred. My father was tolerably rich, and loved me; but he was haughty even to excess, and quite capable of sacrificing the happiness of his child to the pride he took in his ancestors. One day I went to the shop of a clock-maker to buy a watch. The clockmaker's daughter stood at the counter in the place of her father; her beauty excited my admiration, her innocent air attracted me: I talked with her for a long time, and at last bought a valuable watch set with brilliants. I then departed, but returned in a few days, and again, and again; in short, we were enamoured of each other. I told my father that I had resolved to marry the clockmaker's daughter; he cursed me and disinherited me. But I persuaded my beloved to fly with me, and one night she robbed her father of his money and jewels, and effected her escape. We went far enough to remain undiscovered, and sold our brilliants, which, with the money we had taken, was sufficient to afford a considerable, nay, rather abundant fortune. As for the clock, which had been the cause of my acquaintance with my beloved Ulrica, I kept that constantly by me.

"Ulrica told me that her father had made it with his own hands. One day it stopped; I tried to wind it up, but all in vain, for it would not go. I laid it aside peevishly, and when, after some hours, I again took it in hand, it went. With a feeling of foreboding, inexplicable even to myself, I observed the hour, and some days afterwards read in the paper the announcement that Ulrica's father had died a beggar. We, however, continued happy in our mutual love. Years had passed away, when, one evening, I received an invitation from one of my friends. I was on the point of going, when Ulrica asked me when I should return. I named a time; 'Leave me your watch then,' said she, 'that I may know exactly the hour at which I am to expect you, and delight myself with the prospect of your return.' I gave her the watch, and departed. When the appointed hour had arrived, I hastened back to my dwelling, entered Ulrica's chamber, and—found her in the arms of one of my friends. She screamed with fright, while I stood petrified, and consequently unable to prevent the flight of the seducer. We remained opposite to each other, perfectly silent. 'You must be more cautious,' I said at last, and tried to smile; 'you could have told by your watch when I was coming back, and when it was time to dismiss your other lover.' At these words, I took the watch, and pointed at it scornfully. 'It has stopped,' said Ulrica, turning away. The watch had indeed stopped, and had thus deceived the deceiver, and caused the discovery of her crime. With unspeakable horror, I looked upon the watch, which I still held, when the hands slowly moved, and the watch was going. I swore to be revenged on the faithless woman, but preserved a bland exterior, and, with her, quitted the city. When, after a long journey, we arrived here, I enquired, whether it would be possible to purchase a small house, in which my wife and I might dwell alone. I soon found one, paid almost the entire remains of my ready money, and entered it with Ulrica. At night, when she was asleep, I tied a handkerchief about her mouth, that her cries might not alarm the neighbourhood, and called her by her name. She awoke, and when she saw my ferocious countenance, stooping over her, knew my intention at once. She lay motionless, and I whispered into her ear, 'I have awakened you, because I would not murder you in your sleep, and because I felt compelled to tell you why I kill you: it is because you have betrayed me.' It is enough to say that I slew her. I had already turned the board from the floor, and now placed her in the cavity. I then took out the watch, as if, having betrayed the false one, it had a right to see how I revenged my wrong. It stood still, the unmoved hand pointing to the half-hour after midnight—the time when I murdered Ulrica. I laughed aloud, and sat down to write these lines. Tomorrow morning I shall lock up my house, and travel for a time. When I return, the body will have decayed."

Manfred had read the manuscript, shuddering, and having finished it, looked again on the corpse of his friend. It had changed frightfully. The features, which before had been so calm and so clearly marked, now bore an aspect of despair, and were distorted by convulsions. At this moment the mysterious watch, which Count Manfred had put into his breast pocket, began its regular sound, but so very loudly, that Manfred could hear plainly, without taking it out, that the watch was going. An irresistible feeling of horror came over poor Manfred. He darted out of the room, and hurried into his own residence, in which he locked himself for the entire day. He had laid the watch before him, stared at it, and fearful thoughts crossed his mind. On the following day he was calm, but could not summon resolution to see the corpse again. He caused it to be quietly buried. The house he had already bought off poor Karl for the sake of contributing something towards his support.

Some nights after the burial, the stillness of night was broken by an alarm of fire, and at the very house in which Count Karl had lived. At first, as the house was uninhabited, the opinion prevailed that it had been purposely set on fire, but, as it had not been insured, this opinion gained no credence.

Count Manfred set out on his travels, that with the various scenes of a wanderer's life he might get rid of the gloomy mind that troubled him. The watch he took with him. He fancied that some great misfortune would befall him, if he did not attend to it; he considered it as a sort of demon, always wore it, and regularly wound it up.

For years it went well. Count Manfred had recovered his former cheerfulness, and indeed was happier than ever, for he loved and was beloved in return. Dreaming of a happy future, he arose from his bed on the day appointed for his wedding. "I have slept long, perhaps too long," he said to himself. He caught up his watch to see how late it was, but the watch had stopped. A loud cry of anguish arose from his heart, he hurried on his clothes, and hastened to his bride. She was well and cheerful, and Manfred laughed at himself for his foolish superstition. However, when the wedding was over, he could not refrain from looking at his watch once more. It was going. After some weeks, Count Manfred discovered that the ill-omened watch had spoken truly after all. He had been deceived in his wife, and found that she would bring him nothing but unhappiness.

A melancholy gloom took possession of the poor Count. For whole days he would stare at the watch, and grinning spectres seemed to rise from the dial-plate and to dance round him in derision. In the morning, when he arose from his bed, he looked trembling at his watch, always expecting that it would stop, and thus indicate some new calamity. He felt revived, and breathed again when the hands moved on, but yet, from hour to hour, he would cast anxious glances at the watch.

His wife bore him a son, and the feeling of parental joy seemed to dissipate his gloom. In an unusually cheerful mood he was seen to play with his child, sitting for half the day at the cradle, and by his own smile teaching the little one to smile also. The very watch, which had been the torment of his soul, must now serve to amuse the child, who laughed when it was held to his ear, and he could hear the soft ticking.

One day, however, as Manfred approached the cradle, he found the child uncommonly pale. His heart trembled with anxiety, and following a momentary impulse, he drew out the watch—which stood still. With a fearful cry Manfred flung it from him, so that it sounded on the ground, and, scarcely in a state of consciousness, buried his face in his hands. The child fell into convulsions, and died in a few hours. Manfred was, at first, beside himself with grief; then had became still, and walked calm and uncomplaining around the room in which the corpse lay. Having struck his fist against something, he looked down, and saw that it was his watch, which was still on the floor. He picked it up and held it to his ear—it was going. Manfred laughed aloud, till he made the silent room echo frightfully with the sound. "Good! good!" he cried, with an insane look, "You will not leave me, devil! stop with me then!"

From this time, it was his serious conviction that the spirit of Karl the murderer, whom he had called his friend, had found no rest in the grave, but had been placed in the watch, that it might hover round him as a messenger of evil. He ceased to think of, feel, hear anything but his watch; he wound it up, trembling every evening, he held it in his hand throughout the night, and kept awake, gazing upon it. Some months afterwards his wife bore him a daughter, and died in childbed. The news made no further impression upon Manfred than that he looked at his watch, and whispered, "It has not stopped." When his new-born daughter was brought to him, he looked at her with indifference, and glancing at the watch said, "It will stop soon!" His bodily strength soon gave way under this ceaseless anguish of mind. He fell into a violent fever, and, in a few weeks, was buried by the side of his son.

THE SORCERERS

by Ludwig von Baczko

IN those regions in which, when the snow has dissolved upon the Carpathian Mountains, where, after heavy showers, rapid torrents rush down into the valleys, and the swollen Vistula suddenly overflows its banks, there stood upon a height, which commanded the whole country, a stately castle (built in the times of the Jegellons) which, together with the surrounding territory, belonged to the Vayvod Zochanowski. This prince had, at various periods, served his country by his influence at the Diet, and he had rendered her even greater service, by the valour which distinguished his arms, in protecting her against the inroads of the Turks and Tartars. He had now retired, with his beautiful and accomplished lady, to a favourite country domain he inherited from his fore-fathers. That tranquillity and contentment, however, which he promised himself, in this retreat from the cabals of court, were clouded by the death of his children. Antonia was the only surviving child of nine boys and girls. Her lovely features, and personal charms, combined with a lively imagination, increased the love her parents naturally bore her; whilst, at the same time, they created painful apprehensions, that, from the delicate state of her health, and her tender frame, she might shortly share the fate of their departed children. The amiable parents might therefore look for some allowance, if the excessive indulgence they showed her, somewhat spoilt her, as they granted her inconsiderately every wish which her puerile fancy suggested to her. Antonia never knew what contradiction was; it consequently became irksome to her; every youthful error she committed was ascribed to her lively character, and was the more readily excused; nay, even her goodness of heart was highly extolled, when she requited her companions for the severity and ill-treatment she had shown towards them in the ebullitions of her anger.

The pious Damasus was the only person who considered this rash indulgence in another point of view, and was bold enough, particularly in the confessional, to give his advice upon it. But whenever the parents, who wished to bring up their child for the inheritance of heaven, were made to reflect upon their injudicious conduct by the exhortations of the confessor, all the good they had effected, was again frustrated by the flattery of the courtiers who surrounded them, and who extolled Antonia's merits, even in her presence, that, instead of coming to any fixed resolution, to counteract the evils of her education, they only ridiculed the old monk, for the troubles which his scruples of conscience gave him. Nay, when the latter was one day speaking earnestly upon the subject, the sister of the Vayvod's lady, who was *dame d'honneur* at the court of Warsaw, and was at this period upon a visit to the castle, answered him in a petulant manner:

"Make yourself happy, venerable father! what signifies it that Antonia suffers a little purgatory in the other world, so that she passes her time gay and merrily in this."

The anxious countenance, however, which Damasus turned towards heaven, was not observed in the general laugh which this occasioned. Agreeably with the advice of Mary (the Vayvod's sister-in-law) a Parisian lady was written to, through a mercantile house at Warsaw, to repair to the castle, in order to finish Antonia's education. Elegance of manners, a graceful deportment, with the facility in the French language, which she soon acquired, only served to increase Antonia's vanity by the unqualified encomiums which were bestowed upon her.

The parents, at the first sight of Demoiselle Marie, were by no means prepossessed by her personal appearance, which exhibited a picked chin, a crooked nose, a toothless mouth, catlike eyes, black bushy hair, and a certain yellowish brown complexion, which mark the old French women. But, observing the improvement which their daughter made under her superintendency, they began to consider her in the light of a benefactress and friend; and her influence over them daily increased. The indifference towards all the duties of religion, which at first surprised them in Marie, was now overlooked. They first ridiculed the old shivering Damasus; then brought the priesthood into contempt, and, finally, proceeded to mock even religion itself. Marie interceded, that the court Jew, Ezekiel, who had been turned away, from having been convicted of various frauds and all kinds of scandalous practices might be once more received into favour. The Jew was therefore allowed to make his reappearance at the castle, and he came with fresh articles of dress every day, which were immediately purchased for Antonia. The vain young lady was provided with sumptuous apparel, without regard to economy, as she never expressed a wish for anything that was not immediately granted her. She disdained to associate with any of her juvenile friends and playmates, who had once shared her confidence; and the latter were probably as anxious to abandon her society that they might no longer be exposed to her caprices and ill humour.

Agnes alone, whose father was a country gentleman of very small fortune, renting his farm from the Vayvod, faithfully adhered to her young friend. She was only two years older than Antonia, although she assisted her mother in carrying on her household affairs, on which account her parents declined the offer made to them by the Vayvod to have Agnes educated at the same time with Antonia, representing to him, "that a poor girl, whose fortune depended entirely upon her industry and good behaviour, did not require such an education as would fit her only for the society of the opulent and persons of quality, and which, for that reason, would fill their daughter with lofty ideas and expectations, incompatible with her fortune". They adhered to this decision; although the Vayvod frequently pressed the offer at the instigation of Marie, who, disappointed at not gaining Agnes over to her purposes, viewed her only with supercilious contempt. Marie found means to assure the parents of Antonia, that the rustic and uncultivated manners of Agnes would be prejudicial to their daughter's education, and thus endeavoured to break off the intercourse between the two young girls, whose early habits had closely attached them to each other. The ridicule passed upon Agnes, who bent her knee as often as she went by a crucifix, or a picture of the Virgin Mary, the contempt which her simple attire, for the most part the work of her own hands, excited, her blushes and bashfulness represented as awkwardness, gradually lessened the warmth of attachment towards the friend of her early youth. Agnes and her parents perceiving the charge wrought upon Antonia's mind by Marie's address, modestly withdrew; and Agnes henceforward presented herself only on birthdays and other anniversaries, either to express her humble congratulations or to offer some trifling present to Antonia.

It happened on one of these mornings, that she came when Antonia was at her toilet, at which two waiting maids, under Marie's superintendence, were busied about her person. Antonia exchanged a few friendly words with Agnes, whilst her hair was arranging and adorning with costly jewels; when, suddenly turning to the glass, to which, in her conversation with Agnes, she paid no attention, her cheeks began to flash with anger, and she exclaimed: "Hey! what stupidity!" addressing herself to her waiting women, "How ugly I look! You stupid creatures."

One of the poor girls endeavouring to exculpate herself, when Antonia, in a rage, threw the glass at her head; the poor girl was severely hurt by the breaking of the glass, and some drops of blood ran down her cheeks. Agnes trembled with fear: Antonia too seemed to repent of what she had done, but upon Marie calling out to her in the French language, that the greatest fault a person of quality could commit was to acknowledge herself in error, she then ordered the girl, in an angry voice, to go on with dressing her, but if she committed any other mistake, she should be punished more severely.

Agnes, shocked at Antonia's intemperate conduct, looked out of the window without uttering a word; and, as soon as the toilet was finished, and that Marie and the maids had retired, Antonia came up to her, and observing a tear in her eye, asked Agnes what was the matter with her? "Oh, my dear lady," said she, "I am praying for you." Antonia felt some emotion, but Marie's quick return prevented the favourable impression having any effect; and Marie now endeavoured the more to keep Agnes out of Antonia's company.

Antonia had now completed her thirteenth year. Her beauty, together with the hope of becoming the possessor with her hand of her father's splendid estates, attracted the first young noblemen of the country to the Vayvod's castle, when one festivity was followed rapidly by another. Antonia, the heroine of all these fetes, thought of nothing but entertainments and of herself, when she was taken ill; and, during the many cheerless nights which the pain she endured occasioned her, she recalled to her recollection how Agnes had sat by her bedside in similar circumstances when they were children together; and, by the tender anxiety she evinced for her, afforded her every alleviation of her sufferings. Antonia had no sooner made this known to the mother of Agnes, when she was ordered to the castle to take care of her sick friend. With a willing heart she undertook the task. It was not merely the recovery of her friend's health, but the care of her soul that engaged her attention. Upon her touching lightly, however, for the first time, upon the idea of death, Antonia trembled with fear. Agnes threw herself on her knees before the bed, bedewed her hands with tears, and conjured her to have regard for her soul. She then began to pray; but Antonia assured her she was not in a state to accompany her in prayer, as the dread of death deprived her of the use of her intellectual faculties.

Agnes knew that Damasus was accustomed to leave his abode at sunrise, and go to prayers in the chapel of the castle. She went to him and found him kneeling before the altar, at which Agnes also fell down, and prayed for Antonia. Damasus, as he rose up, observed her. Agnes explained to him the motive that had brought her in search of him. The venerable old man highly commended her, promised forthwith to say mass for Antonia, to implore the Holy Angels to come to her protection, and to visit Antonia himself. Agnes begged of him to pay his visit early in the morning, before Marie, who would hear nothing of Antonia being reminded of death, could prevent their meeting. Agnes returned to her sick friend, prepared her for a visit from the venerable Damasus, who soon after tottered into the room, supporting himself upon his staff. The old man, who, from her earliest infancy, had participated in all her little sorrows, who had endeavoured to warm her heart for everything that was holy, and to make her acquainted with God and the duties she owed him, failed not, in the present instance, in producing a right impression. When he sat himself down at her sick bedside, and spoke like an inspired person, of the probability of the approaching hour of death, of the goodness of the All-merciful, of the great hopes which were held out beyond the grave, of the joys of eternity; when his sanctified features and his eye became more animated, tears began to trickle down the cheeks of Antonia. She repented of her childish errors, and felt sufficient strength to pray. She begged the further assistance of the venerable father, and every sentiment of early friendship, of sisterly love for Agnes, again awakened in her breast. She ordered a picture of our Saviour on the cross to be taken down from an adjoining room, to be placed by her bedside forbidding the astonished Marie to have it removed. The latter now loaded poor Agnes with the bitterest reproaches, telling her that she endeavoured only to increase Antonia's malady, by holding before her the fear of death. But when the physician declared that Antonia's pulse had abated since the preceding day, and she never found herself more happy than when Damasus and Agnes were about her, Marie found herself compelled to yield, although her choked rage was depictured in every trait of her countenance.

As Antonia gradually grew better, entertainments were given to celebrate her recovery. Ezekiel made his appearance with fresh articles of apparel and jewellery: the surrounding gentry returned the festivities that had been given them; the time was filled up with music, dance and pleasure; and the promises made to God and the holy angels were soon forgotten. The pious Damasus moreover, who had long been in a bad state of health, was found one morning lying dead in his room before a cross; and a young priest, who adapted his ideas entirely to the tone prevalent in the house, obtained his situation upon Marie's intercession. Every effort was now made to keep Agnes out of the way; and all the good impressions which had been made on the mind of Antonia, were soon obliterated. The good Agnes was deeply sensible of this. The expectation of being once with Antonia, in the presence of God and all that was holy, had taken such strong possession of her heart, that she had seized every opportunity of bringing her back to the path of righteousness. At times, Antonia appeared somewhat irritable at this assiduity; but the sincere cordiality with which her friend treated her, the amiable language and manner she adopted towards her, brought her always back to her. Marie observed this with malignity. "My Lady," said she one day to Antonia, "since you are now grown up, I allow myself no further influence over you than you yourself grant me, but is this miserable Agnes, who is so greatly your inferior in talent, in understanding, and polite education, to become your tutoress? She ought to know of herself that the daughter of a little country gentleman is not at all adapted to be the companion of the daughter of a Vayvod." Thus she poisoned the friendship of youth. The more Agnes observed the coolness with which she was treated by Antonia, the more she redoubled her efforts to regain possession of Antonia's heart by the most zealous attention, and giving her constant proofs of the warmth of her affection. Marie considered this nothing more than troublesome impertinence; and instigated Antonia to make use of bitter words towards Agnes; until, finally, by evincing towards her the greatest indifference, she succeeded in lessening the close familiarity which had existed between these young friends.

Agnes had reared two little doves, as white as snow, and taught them to eat out of her hand. These, together with a rose-tree, which she had taken care of in her own room for several months, and other flowers, she intended to present to Antonia on her birthday. She set out early one morning with a superb nosegay and her two little doves, and again found Antonia at her toilet. She handed her the nosegay and the doves. "May every day of your life," said she, "be productive of a fine flower for eternity, and may your spirit one day ascend in mildness, innocence, and purity, to the mansions of eternal peace." While she was laying the nosegay upon Antonia's dressing table, and placing the two little doves by the side of it, Marie cast a significant look at Antonia, who, as she was reaching for a dressing pin, pushed from the table the nosegay, which was immediately seized by the lap-dog. "Oh!" said Antonia, as Agnes was about to take it away from him, "let the playful little animal have the nosegay, see how pleased he is with it, and how he pulls it about." Agnes stood as if petrified.

"Gertrude," said Marie to one of her chambermaids with a malicious sneer, "take these doves to the cook, to be killed and dressed."

"What?" said Agnes, stroking her doves, and casting an anxious look at Antonia.

"Well," said the latter, "what other purpose are they good for?"

"I did not bring my doves hither, to be killed," said Agnes.

"Oh then, take them back," replied Antonia, "for they can be of no other use to me."

Agnes took up her doves, and left the room deeply affected. She heard Marie laughing and sneering at her upon the stairs, and resolved never more to appear at the castle.

Antonia's guardian angel appeared now to have taken his final leave of her. She loved and valued nothing but herself. She gave herself up to the violence of her passions, without restraint; and the high wages she paid her waiting maids, together with frequent presents, indemnified them only, in some measure, for the overbearing ill-treatment they were obliged almost daily to put up with. Upon one or two of these occasions, when their tears and complaints appeared to have re-kindled some feeling of compassion in Antonia's breast, Marie said to her in French: "Oh, such creatures neither feel nor understand such sentiments! throw them only a piece of money, now and then, and their pain is immediately paid for." By this and other means, Antonia conceived an opinion that money did everything. She saw gambling continually going on in her father's house, and observed that many of the visitors made money by it. She now made a trial herself; fortune was favourable to her. This encouraged her to go on; and thus arose the passion for gambling, which now became a daily necessity. At first without disguise, she betrayed her feelings whenever she either won or lost; but Marie having warned her that this was not becoming a person of quality, she accustomed herself to conceal her passions, and, although she was inwardly consumed by rage whenever she lost, she gave the money over to the winner, with an affected smile—Antonia was going on in this manner, when her mother was taken ill and died. On other mournful occasions, respect to propriety had put some bridle upon her passions; but now even the death of her mother was only dissolving a troublesome tie of parental influence; and her manifestation of grief was consequently nothing but hypocrisy. She availed herself, however, of this opportunity, to induce her father, who was deeply affected, to further expense, and to give many an entertainment, under the plea that diversion was become indispensable. A diet that was held at Warsaw, furnished a pretext for a journey to that capital, and the Vayvod was the more willing to correspond with Antonia's wishes to take her with him, as he hoped he might probably meet with some wealthy young nobleman of the country to marry her to, and thus to mitigate, in some measure, the pain arising from the loss of his dear consort, by the happiness which a good son-in-law might afford him. Antonia, under the superintendence of Marie, was totally left to herself, and the weak father rejoiced when he saw Antonia's charms produce an impression far beyond his own expectation. She was the heroine of every fete, the theme of every poet's ode; and all the young men, who could at all approach her, or obtain the favour of her hand at a dance, considered themselves truly happy. Among the rest there were two, Count Ignatius Dembinski, who possessed vast estates, and Count Stanislaus Rogowski, the only heir to an immense property. Both of these young noblemen were superior to all their contemporaries in personal elegance, and refinement of education, and were consequently treated even in an indulgent manner by many of the fair sex. These were the two young men who riveted Antonia's attention. Not that she felt any inclination for one or the other, for she was only capable of loving herself; nor had she at all made up her mind whether she would take either of them for her husband: the fame which the vain

Antonia wished to carry on, with the hearts of her lovers, was to chain them both to her triumphant chariot, to receive their homages and assurances of respect with apparent indifference; sometimes, to favour the one, and, when the other, in consequence thereof, modestly withdrew, to regain them over to her by some apparent testimony of favourable consideration. In this manner she maintained her influence over both, and even increased the crowd of her adorers. The most distinguished beauties were now deserted, on account of Antonia, who became an object of envy of all the fair, and gained the most bitter hatred of many of them.

A masked ball was given. Antonia entered in a magnificent Turkish dress, and was not unperceived by the enquiring eyes of her lovers. As soon as she took off the mask "What a beautiful, what a divine girl!" was everywhere whispered about the room. Surrounded by her lovers, she cast a pleasing smile upon all around her. A fresh dance was led off, and the fine figure, displayed by a Spanish lady in the first couple, attracted universal attention. Nobody knew who she was; but no sooner had she taken off the mask, when she excited only one impression of pleasure and astonishment throughout the whole assembly. She was the Countess Constance, who, in company with her mother, a very rich widow, had arrived in Warsaw a few days since from their estates in Volhynia. All eyes were now directed towards Constance, and Count Ignatius, who was at that moment engaged in a conversation with Antonia, became absent, broke off the discourse and drew near the beautiful stranger. Antonia, in order to punish him, went in search of Count Stanislaus, and painful indeed was the sensation she experienced, when she saw him getting up to dance with Constance. In a few days Antonia saw herself unnoticed and deserted, and, what still more increased her anguish, she became the laugh and ridicule of everybody. She tried another method to recaptivate her lovers, by appearing at the next masked ball that was given, in a Romish dress; and, availing herself of the license granted by a mask, she endeavoured to fix their attention in various ways. She observed Count Ignatius writing down a word in the hand of a lady who was standing next to her. She offered him her hand to do the same. He surveyed her with a penetrating look, and, smiling at her, wrote down the name of Dido, Antonia felt the severity of this allusion; and vengeance became, from that moment, the predominant passion of her breast.

There was another of her talents, which she had not hitherto called into action: this was singing. She happened to meet her rival the following day at a fete. An instrument was in the room. She sat herself down to it. Only a few old gentlemen, however, paid her some attention, and begged of her to favour them with letting them hear her voice. She used her utmost efforts, and attracted general notice, which awakened another flattering hope in her breast. When she had quitted the instrument, Constance was conducted to it by Count Stanislaus; her play was admirable; her voice charmed everyone. Antonia felt herself far surpassed, and was hardly able to conceal her rage. Marie, into whose bosom she poured out all her griefs, shrugged her shoulders.

"If we were in Italy," said she, "I would soon take the trouble to find a quieting draught for Miss Constance, and a couple of stilettos for the faithless Counts; but here in cold Poland, I suppose, we must patiently bear all this ignominy."

Ezekiel now entered the room. He came from the estates, and brought the information that miss Agnes had obtained a very handsome and accomplished young gentleman for her husband; and, upon being asked what other news he brought, he added, Gertrude, who had been in the service of her ladyship Antonia, was grown quite lame, and contracted together; that she cried out day and night, that she was bewitched by another girl, who had alienated from her the affections of her intended husband; and that some *white people* were fixed upon her neck[1].

"How is that possible?" said Marie laughing.

"In the name of God," cried the Jew, "the ladies will not deny the existence of such a thing as sorcery! I could give you thousands of instances of both men and cattle tormented by it."

"Now," said Antonia, turning herself to Marie, "I wish Ezekiel may be in the right, and such a sorcerer were at my commands."

"What do you say, Ezekiel," asked Marie, "do you know of any?"

Ezekiel shook his head in a dubious manner.

"We must not," said he, "even mention it; for no sooner does a bishop, an officer, or even a monk hear of it, then the burning pile is immediately prepared. But that such things exist as witches, I will swear to be as true, as I am an honest Jew; and one half of Warsaw knows well enough that more than one witch inhabits Praga."

The conversation was broken off; but the seed of the poisonous plant was now sown; and consequently Antonia, as soon as she found herself alone with Marie, renewed the discourse. Marie now told her a number of stories of persons having taken revenge by means of witchcraft, and having affected marvellous things. "What is the most strange of all," added she, "there is nothing baneful in the whole doctrine of witchcraft, for it is nothing more than certain secret words, some plants and such things which have it in their power, to force the world of spirits to act according to the pleasure of the person, who is in possession of this secret science." Antonia, with her head filled with these tales, went into another company, where she overheard it

---

1 The Prussians of old believed in the assistance of little men, whom they called *Bastukai*, who sucked the blood of men. Hence appears to have arisen the popular superstition, which still prevails in Poland and Prussia, that there existed sorcerers, who fix certain bad creatures, whom they call white people, (*biali cuderi*) by couples both on men and cattle, or send them even into their bodies, whereby the bewitched became tortured in the most dreadful manner, and finally died.

said, immediately as she entered, that the two young noblemen were of one opinion that Constance was the first female dancer in all Warsaw. She was now in an ill humour, and determined she would not dance, but repaired to the gambling table. Ill luck, however, persecuted her even here; Count Stanislaus held the bank. She lost as often as she staked a card, and came off in his debt a considerable sum, which she promised to send him the day following. Shame prevented her discovering her situation to her father; and Ezekiel was applied to, to sell a great part of her jewels, the following morning. He could only dispose of them for a trifling sum. Count Ignatius was the purchaser. Antonia lost all command of herself when she saw Constance adorned with them, the very same evening, and learnt that Count Ignatius was engaged to her. She now determined upon giving her hand to Stanislaus. She expected he would throw himself at her feet in repentance; but her adversaries knew how to play their cards; and the answer, which Count Stanislaus had given to one of his friends (who anticipated his union with Antonia) namely, that it was far from his intention to make his life unhappy, by a marriage with a proud fool, and determined gambler, soon reached the ears of Antonia.

Antonia burst into tears of rage, and flung her arms about Marie's neck. "Vengeance," cried she, gnashing her teeth, "vengeance upon these horrid men."

"How willingly, my dear child," said the crafty old French woman, "would I have vengeance for thee, would that witchcraft were in my power." Thus the opinion that witchcraft alone could give consolation by affording the means of vengeance daily gained ground in Antonia's mind. A few days afterwards appeared a ludicrous caricature, in which Antonia was held up to the most bitter shafts of ridicule. Antonia now almost lost her senses; and Marie promised her, if it were possible, to find out the sorceress which Ezekiel had confidently spoken of as existing in Praga. Antonia, overcome by mortification, now feigned illness, to avoid going into any society. Marie went out daily, and returned three times in a sorrowful mood. Antonia's rage continually increased; whosoever came near her felt proofs of it. At length the fourth evening, when Marie returned, Antonia thought she could read something consolatory in her countenance. Marie gave her to understand by a wink, that, when all the house were asleep, and they were both together in their own room, she would impart to her the wished for information; and she then signified to her that she had found what she had been in search of.

"There lives at Praga," said she, "a woman well known by the name of the doctress. She removes, in a few days, all diseases, which physicians declare to be incurable. The general opinion is that she understands something more; but she does everything with the greatest secrecy. I have finally, however, so far prevailed upon her, as to unfold to me the nature of her connexion with the supernatural world."

"What is that?" said Antonia, "and will she be serviceable to our purposes?"

"Perhaps" rejoined Marie, "you will soon carry these purposes yourself into execution. Listen to what Zarowka has confided to me, under the seal of secrecy. The Supreme being, which has created so many thousand worlds, cannot possibly occupy himself with looking after and controlling all the little minutiae which he has created. On that account, spirits were placed over our world, who partly act out of their own planets, partly upon the earth itself, each in the respective sphere allotted to it. The ancients called them deities. As they have a kind of corporeal substance, and are subject to wants and passions, the fragrance of sacrifices, and proofs of reverence, are by no means unacceptable to them. Whoever is acquainted with the manner of acquiring a connexion with them, and gaining their favour, obtains, by his influence over the world of spirits, that indescribably wonderful power, of which I have already read to you in fairy tales."

"And of what avail is all this prattle to me?" cried Antonia in an angry voice.

"For the present it is of no avail," replied Marie, "but for the future it is everything. For, Zarowka declares that she will not expose herself to the risk of perishing on the burning pile, on account of services which she renders you in any fit of piety and repentance, which you may please to take into your head. But I have prevailed upon her, by my own entreaties, to make you privy to those secrets, which subject the whole supernatural world to your control!"

"What?" said Antonia shuddering, "must I then become a witch?!"

"Change this name," replied Marie, "for that of a good fairy, and every prejudice becomes removed. But I am weary from walking; I cannot keep my eyes open; therefore, goodnight, dear Antonia!"

Antonia combated violently with herself. Everything that had been told her of witches and fairies, floated before her imagination; she lay in the height of a fever until morning dawned. She then fell into a gentle slumber; and during this, it appeared as if her protecting genius whispered in a dream to her soul. She saw herself upon a narrow tottering board, which conducted over a deep abyss. On one side thereof stood Damasus, as she had beheld him in the last days of his life, scarcely able to keep himself on his feet with his staff, reaching to her a cross with a trembling hand, accompanied with the words: "Hold fast thereon." She was about to take hold of it, when Marie appeared on the other side of the abyss, holding a costly fillet in her hand, worked with gold and purple, and decorated with whimsical characters, one end of which she threw to her, and ordered her to hold fast by it. Antonia stretched her hand to the fillet; a dreadful clap of thunder followed; the board gave way under her feet, and she awoke.

"You are mistress," said Marie, as Antonia related this dream to her, "of a lively poetical imagination, but do not give way to anguish; not a step has yet been taken in the business, and, as it occasions you such painful sensations, we will say no more about the matter."

Marie never touched further upon the subject. Antonia, however, who could not get rid of the idea, returned into society, where she saw Constance upon the arm of her beloved, and herself deserted by her former adorers. She took her seat accidentally by the side of an old lady, who had passed in her youth, for the first beauty at court; a woman who was endowed with a good understanding, had received an excellent education, and was now leading a miserable life. She related this in confidence to her neighbour herself.—"My dear," said she, "our sex is very unhappy. Man gains, as his years increase, greater merit and respect; poor womankind loses everything, together with her outward charms, and therefore, I frequently wish I were carried back to those fabulous times, in which good fairies made beauty and youth imperishable gifts."

"You might then have taken advantage of these qualities", thought Antonia to herself; and Marie's proposal assumed thereby a favourable aspect. The indifference with which Marie appeared to treat the subject, was the occasion of Antonia brooding over it the more. She sat one day, thus immersed in thought, when Marie entered, and asked her if she had heard that Count Stanislaus had made his bethrothment to Constance publicly known.

"Why do you come to me," asked Antonia, "with such intelligence; why do you not rather remind me of the other subject?"

"I thought," replied Marie, "that you gave no further consideration, and it was my wish to avoid bringing to your recollection anything which may be obnoxious to your feelings."

Thus the matter was again brought upon the tapis. It was now agreed upon, that Antonia should represent herself as unwell the following day, and go to bed early; slip out with

Marie, at the back gate of the palace, and both of them were to make the best of their way to the old sorceress in a sledge, which Ezekiel was to have in readiness for them.

All this was carried into execution. Zarowka received her with a friendly welcome, and promised to summon the spirits for the occasion of making a solemn offering, at which Antonia had nothing farther to do than to hand over to the spirits a parchment, to be filled up by Zarowka. In all other matters, Antonia was to act according to Zarowka's instruction. Antonia enquired whether the preparations were alarming. Upon being assured that she would only have an interview with the beautiful and well-proportioned deities of the Greeks and Romans, and make a covenant with them, everything was approved of, after a few shudders, which Marie ridiculed, as arising from an irresolute state of mind. "Antonia is not yet accustomed to travel in our way," said Zarowka, "and therefore I would wish to transport her, whilst asleep, to the proper place." She touched Antonia's forehead with a little wand; and when the latter awoke, she found herself in a wood upon a crossway, by the side of a little altar, from which a flame issued. Marie, Zarowka, and Ezekiel, were standing by her in sumptuous oriental attire. First a lamb and a dove, and then a black goat, and a raven, were offered up as sacrifices. The blood was carefully preserved. Marie then laid hold of Antonia's hand; made a small incision in it with the offering knife; let a few drops of her blood fall into the bowl; cut a lock of her hair off, and threw it into the flame. Antonia trembled. At that moment a grand music resounded; and the deities of Greece and Rome, in far more charming shapes than either the pencils or chisels of the greatest artists could have represented them, came forward. All of them appeared to tarry a few moments, and refresh their senses with the fragrant odour which was produced by Antonia, so often as a form appeared, spouting something liquid into the flame, and throwing into it a handful of frankincense. At last appeared a superb triumphant chariot, upon which sat a man of dignified aspect, surrounded by a number of spirits. All that were present prostrated themselves upon the ground; and at their nod, Antonia, who held out the parchment did the same. A genie took this out of her hand, and gave it to the man upon the chariot. "You wish," said the latter to Antonia, throwing a look upon the parchment, "to be consecrated a priestess of the Gods, and made acquainted with the secrets of former ages?"

Antonia affirmed, she did.

"You are sureties for her," he asked again.

"We are sureties," cried Marie, Zarowka, and Ezekiel, steeping their fingers in the blood of sacrifice, and laying them upon Antonia's forehead.

"So I take thee," said the spirit, "for thirty years into my covenant, and mark thee with the sign of the same." He laid a finger upon Antonia's shoulder. She felt a pain which pierced every nerve, but which quickly left her. Two genies flitted by, who put a costly ancient garment upon Antonia, gave her a wand in her hand, and bound a fillet round her brow. One of the spirits asked her:

"In what form shall I henceforth appear?"

"Assume," replied Antonia, "that of a parrot."

"I will," said the genie, "fulfil thy commands, as often as thou beckonest to me, three times with the wand in thy hand."

"And ye three," said the man upon the chariot, "gradually inaugurate the new priestess into the secrets of former ages."

The music resounded again; and the triumphant chariot disappeared.

"We now salute thee as our sister," said Marie and Zarowka to Antonia, and they folded her in their arms. As Ezekiel was about to do the same, Antonia repulsed him.

"Why dost thou refuse the sister's kiss?" cried out Ezekiel simpering, "we are now all equals;" and he then encircled her in his arms, in spite of her resistance.

The lofty Antonia began now to feel to what a low ebb she was sunk. In the meantime, Ezekiel spread out his mantle, upon which all present sat themselves down, with Antonia in the midst of them. A wind took the mantle into the air, and left it, in a few seconds, in Zarowka's court yard. Antonia and Marie now wrapt themselves up in their cloaks, and hastened, in Ezekiel's sledge, to their dwelling. How thunderstruck was Antonia, upon taking the fillet from her brow for it was exactly such a one as she had beheld in her dream, of the colour of fire; worked with gold and black magic letters; and, upon undressing herself, she beheld upon her shoulder, a spot as red as fire, in the shape of a pitchfork! "Into what hands have I fallen," said Antonia, and looked at Marie.

"Into the hands of thy friends," replied Marie, "and thou wilt get an insight into everything, as thy inauguration proceeds."

Everything that she had brought with her was carefully concealed; Antonia's blood rolled wildly in her veins. "Wilt thou not invoke thy spirit?" asked Marie the following morning.

"What can the spirit do for me?" said Antonia anxiously.

"Hast thou forgotten Ignatius and Constance?" asked Marie, "this is their wedding day!"

"I will send them a wedding present," said Antonia. Thrice she waved her wand, when a beautiful parrot appeared upon her dressing table—"Revenge me to the height of vengeance," cried she.

"I obey thee, mistress," answered the parrot; and vanished.

Antonia now learnt that the count's horses had taken fright, as he was driving to see his bride; and that he himself had been seriously wounded by the overturning of his carriage. In this state, his servants had taken him into a small cottage, in which three children were then lying dangerously ill of the small pox. Ignatius, who had never had this disease, was immediately seized with it. It was therefore found necessary to postpone the nuptial festivals, which Constance consented to, as far as regarded the festivities; but the marriage was solemnized. The Count's illness increased every day, and the physicians declared his death to be inevitable, Antonia, much as she had at first panted for vengeance, now perceived that vengeance did not produce happiness.

At the instigation of Marie, many a nocturnal visit was paid to Zarowka. To prepare and employ the arts of witchcraft, to injure both man and beast by conjurations and spells, was what Antonia learnt; but she never derived real satisfaction from such pursuits.

"Are these," she would ask in a pettish manner, "are these your enjoyments?"

"Bring hither tomorrow in haste," replied Zarowka, "thy fairy clothes, and thou shalt then become acquainted with another part of our life."

Curiosity induced Antonia to be present.

The old witch, Marie and Antonia decked themselves out; and great was the astonishment of Antonia, when Marie and Zarowka laid the fillet of enchantment upon their brows, and appeared like two juvenile beauties. They struck the wainscoat with their wands, when a door, which had been hitherto concealed, flew open, and a small temple, beautifully decorated, from the sides of which rose-colored curtains hung down, received the three enchantresses. A table was covered with the most dainty meats, pine apples, and fruits from all quarters of the world, while the glass, filled with the choicest wines of Chios, of Schiras, and Cyprus, circulated freely.

"Antonia," observed the others, "has this life no charms for thee?"

"For me," replied Antonia, "who am no stranger to such enjoyments, far less certainly than for you."

Zarowka then waved her wand, when the rose-coloured curtains drew up, and paintings, as if from the hands of the greatest masters, representing the most wanton and unblushing scenes covered the walls. Antonia cast her eyes down to the ground; but the loud laughter set up by the two others, together with the effects of the exhilarating wine, annihilated all feeling of shame. Three young men, of rare personal accomplishments, dressed in a similar manner to themselves, entered the room. Two of them appeared to be friends of the old witch; the third paid homage and attention exclusively to Antonia.

"How dost thou like thy friend?" asked Marie.

"He is as handsome as Apollo," replied Antonia, who, being alike inflamed with wine and passion, imitated not the example of Daphne. These dissolute bacchanalian scenes, were continued every night. Antonia soon remarked in her glass that the ruddiness of youth had abandoned her fallen cheeks.

"What harm does that do thee?" said Marie smiling, "for, as soon as thou puttest on the fillet of enchantment round thy brow, thou immediately resemblest a goddess."

But no female soul was ever indifferent to the loss of beauty. Antonia too appeared to return somewhat to herself. Her father was taken ill. The physicians advised some change of scene, and the Vayvod went, in company with his daughter, to a neighbouring resort of pleasure, where, soon after their arrival, another carriage appeared. Constance alighted from it, and offered her hand to her husband, who had lost his eye-sight by the small-pox. "Oh, what a noble woman," said some of the bystanders. "She is a divinity," added others. She did not stay long, and soon returned, with her husband, to the city. There was only one voice in praise of her. Every person had something to say of her magnanimity, of her virtues, of her piety, in Antonia's bosom raged an hell fire. "Why am I sunk so low?" cried she, gnashing her teeth, when she was alone in her apartment, "and why is this detested Constance raised so much above me?"—She waved her wand three times, and the parrot appeared. "Take vengeance," cried she, "upon this Constance; she must not alone become miserable, but an object of universal contempt. Hasten, execute my orders, and bring me back an account."

Two days elapsed without his returning; on the third, he was summoned by the wand. "What hast thou executed?" said Antonia.

"Nothing," replied the parrot with a melancholy tone of voice, "for I have no power over pure and innocent souls."

Antonia, in a rage, had recourse to the sorcery with which she had been acquainted. Storms and hail, locusts and blight, destroyed the estates of Constance, who became only more firmly attached to heaven by all these evils. The Vayvod, who had been detained at Warsaw by illness, died about this time. Antonia, in order to avoid all further meeting with Constance, returned to her estates, accompanied by Marie. At the last bacchanalian scene which had taken place between Zarowka and the others, she had invited her Apollo (so she called her lover) to follow her thither; and he promised not to fail in being there.

The first person who welcomed her return to the castle, was Ezekiel. He was with her in the room alone, as the stewards were employed in unloading her luggage; he approached her in a confidential manner, and caught her in his arms.

"Thou madman," cried she, "how darest thou presume to do this?"

"Pardon me," said Ezekiel; "I forgot that I had not put on the enchanting fillet: I therefore appear before thee now as simple Ezekiel, and not as Apollo."

"What!" cried Antonia, "am I then sunk so low? Are deceit, disappointment, and shame all that I have gained by this infernal witchcraft?"

Agnes and her husband were now announced. She appeared with her son upon her arms, taking hold of her husband. They seemed as handsome and beautiful as an holy family of Raphael. "How do you do?" asked Antonia.

"Oh," replied Agnes, "I am unspeakably happy by the side of my husband, and this child," pressing her son to her breast, "still heightens my happiness."

"How far," said Antonia to herself, "is this stupid creature, to whom I am in every respect so superior, how far is she now above me!" Envy and rancour then took possession of her soul. She considered herself as the only unhappy mortal; and the chief occupation of her mind was how to do all possible injury to her fellow creatures.

Lipkowski, (this was the name of Agnes' husband), was a man of uncommon comely appearance. The sight of him excited Antonia's sensuality; and every art of seduction was called into action; but, as he felt only one sentiment for his Agnes, every magic endeavour failed. Even the parrot was ordered to attend.

"Hast thou, then, no power over these creatures?" asked Antonia in a rage.

"No," answered the spirit, "for their guardian angels protect the innocent."

Antonia became almost mad with rage, and Marie advised her to seek distraction. She travelled, engaged in amours, and indulged in every kind of excess; but her heart was always stung with reflection, and she detested herself. Thus seven years had elapsed, since the dreadful day on the cross way, represented in her dream. She returned to the castle. Agnes and Lipkowski were still in her neighbourhood: she again endeavoured to enchain him; but, everything failed. She therefore tried every means of destroying the happiness of this couple, and therein she fully succeeded. They were ruined by a series of untoward events, and a small cottage and garden were all that remained to them. A neighbouring proprietor, who possessed extensive forests, and knew Lipkowski to be an excellent huntsman, allowed him to sport upon his grounds, upon the condition that he would turn over to him half of the game he killed, and sell the other half.

"Oh," said Marie, who heard this, "poverty will induce Lipkowski to cheat the proprietor, and thus he will fall at last into our hands."

Antonia heaped upon him every misery. The blossoms were consumed by mildew; caterpillars ate up the vegetables of his little garden. Agnes was taken ill; and Antonia, invisible to everyone, by the power of her enchanted wand, determined upon examining into their condition, with her own eyes. She approached the cottage. Agnes was sitting before the door, upon a miserable bench, with her eldest daughter. Both were spinning: the younger children were standing by the side of their mother, who was teaching them to pray. Antonia beheld the wan cheek of the friend of her youth and she felt a generous feeling awaken in her soul. At that moment Lipkowski approached. "Here is our dear father," cried the children. Agnes hastened a few steps to meet him, and threw herself into his arms. He gave each of them a small present. "There," said he to Agnes, "I have reserved the finest snipe for you; the other game that I have sold has produced sufficient for our maintenance for a few days. The good proprietor always supposes that I reserve for him more than I keep for myself, and, therefore, always returns me something back. But I am very weary." They sat themselves down upon the bench. "Have you a draught of milk?" said he to Agnes. Agnes could not refrain from tears.

"Oh," cried she, with a sob, "our last cow died suddenly last night."

"Then I will drink water," said Lipkowski, "and, by the side of thee, my dear wife, it is more delicious than the most costly wine." Agnes threw her arms around him, and kissed the tears away from his cheek.—"God gave me," continued he, "strength to suffer, and to work for you; be therefore, of good cheer, dear soul; we are still happier than many of our fellow creatures. I would not exchange my lot with the proud Antonia, and her magnificent castle."

"How may she be going on?" asked Agnes. The tone of voice in which she said this announced the heartfelt interest she took in her well-being.

"I heard strange things reported in the town," replied Lipkowski. "In the inn, where I just sold my game, two gentlemen were speaking of her; one of them said she was mad; the other, that something lay heavy at her heart; for the evil conscience that devours her is visible in her countenance."

"Poor Antonia," cried Agnes, "I loved thee as my sister; oh! I can now do nothing for thee: but I and my children will pray for thee, and God will not suffer the cries of innocence to pass unheard."

Antonia had not expected a scene like this. She could hardly support herself; and, almost unconscious of what she did, she cried out, with inward emotion, and in an audible voice, the name of Agnes. "My God!" said the latter, "that is Antonia's voice!" They all looked round, but no one could perceive her.

"Perhaps," suggested Lipkowski, "she has this moment disappeared."

"God be merciful to the poor soul."

Antonia felt herself moved, nay, partly consoled by the conviction that she had not rendered those wholly unhappy whom she had done so much mischief to; and, this reflection, together with the sight of the wretched situation in which she found the friend of her early youth, suppressed that envy of their happiness, which had hitherto raged in her bosom. In a sorrowful state of mind she returned to her castle. Passing through the rooms, in which, in her youth, she had often sat by the side of Agnes, she came, unconscious of having any purpose in view, into the sleeping room of her deceased father, which had never been inhabited since his death, and which she had consequently never visited. She opened the door softly, and stood still, quaking with fear; for she instantly perceived opposite to her the portrait of the venerable Damasus, with a cross in his hand. A travelling painter had taken his likeness in this manner a few months before his death, and her deceived father had ordered the picture, out of respect to the deceased, to be placed in his own chamber. "Oh, that it were possible," thought Antonia, "that holy spirits could stand around us as guardian angels! Could this cross, which the pious Damasus offered me in a warning dream, bring me salvation!" She felt so glad, and at the same time so melancholy at heart; she stepped towards the window, which looked into the garden, opened it, and the sight of nature appeared to give her joy. She then heard a rustling noise, looked round about, and observed that the wind was turning over the leaves of a book, which was lying open. Upon drawing nearer, she perceived that it was the Holy Scriptures. She cast a look upon them, and noticed the place in the eighth chapter of the apostles, where Simon, the magician, was not thought unworthy of baptism; she read further, and found Paul's conversion. The darkness of her soul became illumined with a ray of hope. She struck her breast in a repentant manner, and cried out: "God be merciful to me a sinner!"

At this moment Marie entered the room. "In what manner didst thou get here?" said she in astonishment. "I was seeking for thee in all parts of the castle." Antonia disclosed to her everything that had passed; exhorted her also to repentance; and declared that she would go tomorrow to the bishop at Cracow, and open her state of mind to him. Marie made use of all her endeavours to dissuade her from this determination; and Antonia was at last induced to make the promise, at her entreaty, to defer her intention for three days; and, if she were in the same mind on the fourth day, then Marie promised to go with her to the bishop, for she confessed to her that the thirty years covenant with the evil spirit, were now passed, but that, could she induce another person to enter it, the benefit of this covenant would be extended to her for ten years. She had succeeded with Antonia; but, since that, nearly eight years had elapsed, and all endeavours to obtain another member of the covenant had been fruitless. Antonia now perceived for what reason she had been plunged into sin. She promised, however, to pardon the wicked Marie for all that she had done, if she would desist from crime, and return again to God. Marie appeared affected; she promised to try every effort for that purpose in the three days. Antonia confided in her, and spent her time for the most part, in the apartment, where, from her own conviction, God and the holy angels had been so merciful to her. Her heart being now more tranquil, the refreshing sleep, to which she had been so long a stranger, returned to her pillow. In the night of the third day, she felt disturbed in her sleep. She awoke, and beheld herself in a place perfectly strange to her. Marie, Zarowka, Ezekiel, with six other sorcerers were standing before her couch, in the attire so well known to her. "Thou designedst to betray us," said Marie, "for that reason, have we, thrice three sorcerers in council, taken away thy power, and banished thee to an uninhabited island in the Indian ocean. We have prepared for thee this abode; thy parrot will be thy only companion, and do all that is necessary for thee. Thou wilt not be missed in thy castle, for I assume thy form. Thou art not to reckon upon redemption, until I go down to the deity below, where, thou, however, wilt probably appear first, for I have already two maidens in the right road, to become sisters of the covenant." They all placed their hands upon Marie, who took upon herself the perfect form of Antonia. The latter trembled for fear when she beheld herself personified, and all the sorcerers now departed, setting up an hellish yell.

Antonia had a convenient abode. She wanted nothing necessary, although she adhered faithfully to her resolution of asking nothing of the parrot, who never moved from her side, and endeavoured to entertain her with various subjects. Solitude made not, upon Antonia, the disagreeable impression, which it otherwise would have done, since she was fully convinced that she had merited the contempt of all the world. The sorcerers transplanted much of her furniture and other materials to her new place of abode. They even provided her with books; but, upon casting her first look into them, she threw them from her in disgust, and afterwards committed them, together with various pictures which adorned her room, to the flames. Her thoughts were often employed upon the future; and she implored God, with tears in her eyes, to have compassion upon her soul. Upon various changes of the moon alone, could she, in some degree, calculate the period of her stay on the island. The trees had twice lost their leaves, and had been twice been covered again with fresh foliage. She accustomed herself to consider her fate as a deserved and mild chastisement, and she doubted not of the favour of the All-Merciful. The parrot, receiving no commissions from his mistress, but rarely presented himself. Short rambles were all the recreation she allowed herself. In a thick wood, she formed an arbour of the boughs of some trees near each other. Here she built a little altar of turf, placing thereon a picture of our Saviour on the cross, which she had carved with her knife. Before this she frequently prostrated herself; while the beating of her heart, the tears which rolled down her cheeks, the wringing of her hands in anguish, spoke more than words could express.

One day she approached the sea-side, where she discovered many remnants of wrecks of vessels, which had been thrown on the shore; and, upon turning an angle of the rock, she observed a human corpse. Notwithstanding the closed eyes and paleness of death which hung upon the countenance, she observed that the unfortunate stranger was a well formed young man. "Oh that there still be life in him, and that he may be sent to me, in this desert, for protection and consolation!" This idea arose in her mind. She knelt down by the side of him, rubbed his forehead and hands, placed her own hand upon his heart, and thought she felt a faint beating. She redoubled her endeavours. The cheeks of the youth appeared to redden, and her joy increased. He gradually opened his beautiful black eyes, and she raised her hands in gratitude to heaven. The parrot, at that moment, drew near. He softly enquired if she desired his assistance.

"Begone, thou curse!" cried Antonia, "I seek only assistance from God."

The youth still lay at her feet, and addressed her in the French language, calling her his deliveress, his benefactress, and kissing her hands and bedewing them with his tears. She ordered him to get up; but he was so faint that he staggered, and she was obliged to support him.

"Only come far from this place," said Antonia, "that the flood tide may not overtake you, and I will get you some cordial."

She with difficulty conducted him to her bower; but he sunk down in a swoon.

"Dost thou wish me to get medicine, or anything to strengthen him?" cried the parrot.

Antonia rushed into the bower quite distracted, seized the cross, held it up, and hastened to the swooner.

"Merciful God," cried she, "send me the means of saving him!"

A clap of thunder rolled through the clouds; the youth awoke, and changed himself into a negro of gigantic stature. The wings of a bat grew upon his shoulders; instead of feet he supported himself upon two frightful dragon's tails: and, in the place of each finger, a serpent sent forth his dreadful hisses.

"Dost thou not know the power whom thou servest, and with whom thou enteredst into covenant?" cried the horrid figure.

The earth burst under him; the monster sunk into the abyss, and, before this could close, flames of fire rushed upwards.

Antonia threw herself upon her knees and returned thanks to God. With the cross in her hand, she now hastened to her abode, and found that it had disappeared. In place of it stood a rock, in which she observed a cavern. She looked into it; and beheld, to her astonishment, her bed and furniture. She immediately became liberated from the illusion which had hitherto hung around her. She stepped softly into the cavern; but found not the smallest article of provision. "He who has hitherto assisted me, and preserved my soul from perishing," said she

196

in humble reliance upon God, "will take farther care of me." She fasted and prayed. On the following morning she began to feel the cravings of hunger, and made all haste in search of nourishment. The sun was burning fiercely; and she wandered among the shrubs; her strength failed her. "Eternal God," cried she, "am I to die of hunger!" The parrot drew near, and offered her some delicious grapes; but she made the sign of the cross, looked towards heaven, and the tempter disappeared. She came from among the shrubs to the borders of the sea; there all was rocky and desolate. The waves were rumbling at her feet. A voice appeared to whisper to her soul: "Throw thyself into them, and put an end to misery," but she gained strength, and thought of God. Casting her eyes accidentally upon the ground, she saw, with extreme joy, some oysters at her feet; she satisfied her hunger, thanked God, and picked up some of the oysters to keep in store. She now endeavoured to find her cavern again, although she suffered greatly from thirst. At that moment she heard the delightful singing of a bird: "The Creator who preserves this bird," said she, "will also not suffer me to perish," she then hastened to the spot where the notes of the bird proceeded, and immediately came to a well, surrounded with fine Cocoa-trees. Here she quenched her thirst, and sunk into a refreshing slumber in which she continued a considerable time. Upon her awaking, the morning sun was just rising. She found herself in her own home, with Ezekiel standing before her.

"I come to apprize thee," said he in an anxious manner, "in order that I may not be suspected, when thou goest into thy former chamber. Marie has come to her end in it, the foregoing night. She had succeeded in adding another sister to the covenant, and considered herself secure, when the prince of darkness appeared to her yesterday evening, just as I was with her. He exclaimed in a terrific voice:

"Hold thyself ready about midnight; for, since Antonia has escaped me, the other sister, added to the covenant, was only serviceable for the ten years that are past.' It is not in my power to describe the horror which seized Marie; and her rage was heightened by the reflection that thy spell is now over. Come, behold the room in which she came to her end, and thou wilt convince thyself of the necessity of no one observing what has happened."

Antonia followed him, and found the apartment filled with a sulphurous vapour: the walls and the ground were stained with Marie's blood, and some lacerated members were still lying scattered about. On which she returned thanks to God, that she had escaped such a fate. Ezekiel then offered to remove and inter the scattered remains: and, upon Antonia exhorting him to repentance and baptism, he promised to obey her, but instantly disappeared, and no farther account was ever heard of him.

Antonia now resumed the management of her own affair; and the domestics and vassals whom Marie, under the assumption of Antonia's form, had treated with tyrannical severity, were at a loss to account for the difference of treatment, they at present experienced. She preferred occupying the chamber of her deceased father; and sent messengers to invite Count Ignatius and Constance, to come and see her, with the least possible delay. The following morning, she ordered her carriage to be got ready and drove to see Agnes, who still lived in the same cottage. The children, as well as Agnes and her husband, came rushing out, when they saw the magnificent equipage approach. Antonia hastened to meet them, and encircled Agnes in her arms.

"Forgive me," said she, "my worthy, pious friend, for all that is past. I will endeavour to recompense you, as far as it is possible, and reward you too for your sufferings, in your children."

She then prevailed upon them all to get into the carriage with her, in order to take possession of a part of the castle. Lipkowski was appointed superintendent of the estates; and the tenants and dependants were forgiven all their debts. She lowered their rents, and lightened their services. Antonia now heard only grateful blessings, saw only tears of gladness, and returned thanks to heaven, from the inmost of her soul, that she had been brought back to the path of righteousness. She then hastened to Cracow, where the bishop of this place, a venerable old man, enjoyed the highest character for piety. The day following her return, Constance and Ignatius, who had paid attention to the pressing invitation given them, arrived; upon which she ordered the lawyers to be sent for, who drew up a deed of gift, whereby Constance was to receive one half and Agnes the other, of her whole estates, and they were both earnestly entreated to accept the donation.

"I," said Antonia, "want nothing further. It is my intention to undertake a pilgrimage, to the holiest place of Christendom, and, when I have accomplished it, I will pass the remainder of my days in solitude, or in a nunnery. I have only to make one request of you, that is, to open the room which I have barred up, three years hence, and then you will find everything disclosed to you."

She fixed an early period for entering upon her pilgrimage: nor could all the entreaties, and representations, which her friends made against such an intention, detain her among them.

"For the last time," said she, "we are assembled here, but perhaps it may be God's pleasure, that above we be united forever."

It was a beautiful spring evening, and they were sitting together in the garden; the blossoms sent forth their fragrance and the nightingale was heard in the neighbouring woods, when Antonia stepped before them.

"Oh, my beloved," said she, "answer me one question more! what do you now think, and what are your present feelings, concerning your past sorrows?"

"I have indeed," said Ignatius, "lost my eye sight; but my good angel, Constance, guides me through life: without her, I should have idly wandered through the world,—should not have known the real value of existence, and probably should only have had this life in view, nor have ever directed my thoughts to heaven."

"And you Constance?" asked Antonia, with emotion.

"Never," said she, "had it not been for the misfortune, which befell my husband, should I have performed my duties as I now do, or have rendered myself so worthy of his affection. I therefore thank Providence for having given me the means of obtaining a joyful existence here, together with the hope of a still more blissful one hereafter."

"But what are the sentiments you entertain?" said Antonia to Agnes.

"Had it not been for the oppression of poverty, and the wants we suffered;—had it not been for those innumerable proofs of sincerest affection, which my husband daily gave me, I never could have loved and revered him as I have done, from the bottom of my heart,—never have gained the strength to discharge the most laborious duties of a wife, and a mother. I therefore would not forego the recollection of our past sorrows for worlds."

"Nor I, certainly," said Lipkowski, as he pressed the hand of his spouse tenderly to his breast.

"Eternal God," cried Antonia, as the tears rolled down her checks: "Eternal God, thou who convertest even the wicked unto goodness, praised be thy mercy, and thy forgiveness. As yet," continued she, "you understand me not, but you shall in time learn everything."

The whole of the vassals and dependants of the estates were assembled at the desire of Antonia, who came amongst them in a pilgrim's attire; and took her leave of them, and her friends. Having distributed her money among the poor and sick, she proceeded to church, attended by all present; and prayed with fervour, whilst all joined in prayer for her. They afterwards accompanied her some distance; and she was followed by the benediction of everyone.

Aided by their husbands, Agnes and Constance did everything to make the vassals that were given over to them, as happy as possible, as they had promised their friend they would. Heaven blessed their endeavours; and the estates were brought to the highest pitch of prosperity.

Thus three years rolled away, when agreeably to the promise given to Antonia, they opened the room which had been closed up; where neither the vapour of sulphur was gone, nor had the traces of the dreadful death of Marie been entirely effaced. Upon the table lay a note in Antonia's handwriting, which ran thus: "The pious bishop of Cracow, will, if you address yourselves to him, three years after my departure, impart to you, my unhappy and dreadful history. Pardon me, for all the harm I have occasioned you, and pray for me and my soul." They went, therefore, to the venerable pastor at Cracow, whose court chaplain had written down Antonia's history, under the seal of confession, just as it has been here detailed, and now imparted it to them, with the episcopal sanction, according to the commission Antonia had given him. Filled with astonishment at so terrible a narrative, they all heartily forgave her, remembered her with affection, and frequently prayed for her. At first they hoped to get some account of her, but were wholly disappointed. Agnes and Constance, who lived together as bosom friends, could never forget the truly unfortunate Antonia. A monk, who came from Rome, finally brought the intelligence that he had seen buried in the Convent of the Penitents, a nun who, according to report, was born in Poland, and who often lamented that she was the greatest sinner upon earth, and passed her life in acts of contrition—that she enjoyed the love and esteem of all her sisters, and had departed in peace and tranquillity, in hopes of the favour of the All-Merciful. Agnes and Constance ordered a letter to be written to Rome, and received for answer, that the deceased nun was—Antonia.

THE HARP

by Theodor Körner

THE secretary Sellner had begun to taste the first spring of happiness with his youthful bride. Their union was not formed on the vague and evanescent passion which often lives and dies almost in the same moment—sympathy and esteem formed the basis of their attachment. Time and experience, without diminishing the ardour, had confirmed the permanence of their mutual sentiments. It was long since they had discovered that they were formed for each other, but want of fortune imposed the necessity of a tedious probation: till Sellner, by obtaining the patent for a place, found himself of an easy competence, and on the following Sunday brought home in triumph his long betrothed bride. A succession of ceremonious visits for some weeks engrossed many of those hours that the young couple would have devoted to each other. But no sooner was this generous duty fulfilled than they eagerly escaped from the intrusion of society to their delicious solitude; and the fine summer evenings were but too short for plans and anticipation of future felicity. Sellner's flute and Josephine's harp filled up the intervals of conversations, and with their harmonious unison seemed to sound the prelude to many succeeding years of bliss and concord. One evening, when Josephine had played longer than usual, she suddenly complained of a head-ache; she had, in reality risen with the symptoms of indisposition, but concealed it from her anxious husband: naturally susceptible of nervous complaints, the attention which she had lent to the music, and the emotions it had caused in her delicate frame, had increased a slight indisposition to fever, and she was now evidently ill. A physician was called in, who so little anticipated danger, that he promised a cure on the morrow. But after a night spent in delirium, her disorder was pronounced a nervous fever, which completely baffled the effects of medical skill, and on the ninth day was confessedly mortal. Josephine herself was perfectly sensible of her approaching dissolution, and with mild resignation submitted to her fate.

Addressing her husband for the last time, she exclaimed, "My dear Edward, heaven can witness it is with unutterable regret that I depart from this fair world, where I have found with thee a state of supreme felicity; but though I am no longer permitted to live in those arms, doubt not thy faithful Josephine shall still hover round thee, and as a guardian-angel encircle thee until we meet again." She had scarcely uttered these words when she sunk on her pillow, and soon fell into a slumber, from which she awoke no more; and when the clock was striking nine, it was observed that she had breathed her last. The agonies of Sellner may be more easily conceived than described; during some days it appeared doubtful whether he would survive; and when, after confinement of some weeks, he was at length permitted to leave his chamber, the powers of youth seemed paralyzed, his limbs were enfeebled, his frame emaciated, and he sunk into a state of stupor, from which he was only to be roused by the bitterness of grief. To this poignant anguish succeeded a fixed melancholy; a deep sorrow consecrated the memory of his beloved; her apartment remained precisely in the state in which it had been left previous to her death; on the work-table lay her unfinished task; the harp stood in its accustomed nook untouched and silent; every night Sellner went in a sort of pilgrimage to the sanctuary of his love, and taking his flute, breathed forth, in deep plaintive tones, his fervent aspirations for the cherished shade. He was thus standing in Josephine's apartment, lost in thought, when a broad gleam of moon-light fell on the open window, and from the neighbouring tower the watchman proclaimed the ninth hour; at this moment, as if some invisible spirit, the harp was heard to respond to his flute in perfect unison. Thunderstruck at this prodigy, Sellner suspended his flute, and the harp became silent; he then began, with deep emotion, Josephine's favourite air, when the harp resumed its melodious vibrations, thrilling with ecstasy. At this confirmation of his hopes he sunk on the ground, no longer doubting the presence of the beloved spirit; and whilst he opened his arms to clasp her to his breast, he seemed to drink in the breath of spring, and a pale glimmering light flitted before his eyes. "I know thee, blessed spirit!" exclaimed the bewildered Sellner, "thou didst promise to hover round my steps, to encircle me with thy immortal love. Thou hast redeemed thy word; it is thy breath that glows on my lips; I feel myself surrounded by thy presence." With rapturous emotion he snatched the flute, and the harp again responded, but gradually its tones became softer, till the melodious murmurs ceased, and all again was silent. Sellner's feeble frame was completely disordered by these tumultuous emotions; when he threw himself on his bed, it was only to rave deliriously of the harp. After a sleepless night he rose only to anticipate the renewal of his emotions; with unspeakable impatience he awaited the return of evening, when he again repaired to Josephine's apartment; where, as before, when the clock struck nine, the harp began to play, in concert with the flute, and prolonged its melodious accompaniment till the tones gradually subsided to a faint and tremulous vibration, and all again was silent. Exhausted by this second trial, it was with difficulty that Sellner tottered to his chamber, where the visible alteration in his appearance excited so much alarm, that the physician was again called in, who, with sorrow and dismay, detected aggravated symptoms of the fever which had proved so fatal to Josephine; and so rapid was its progress that in two days the patient's fate appeared inevitable. Sellner became more composed, and revealed to the physician the secret of his late mysterious communications, avowing his belief that he should not survive the approaching evening. No arguments could remove from his mind this fatal presage; as the day declined, it gained strength and he earnestly entreated, as his last request, to be conveyed to Josephine's apartment. The prayer was granted Sellner no sooner reached the well-known spot than he gazed with ineffable satisfaction on every object endeared by affectionate remembrance.

The evening hour advanced; he dismissed his attendants, the physician alone remaining in the apartment. When the clock struck nine Sellner's countenance was suddenly illumined; the glow of hope and pleasure flushed his wan cheeks, and he passionately exclaimed—"Josephine, greet me once more at parting, that I may overcome the pangs of death." At these words the harp breathed forth a strain of jubilee, a sudden gleam of light waved round the dying man, who, on beholding the sign, exclaimed—"I come! I come to thee!" and sunk senseless on the couch. It was in vain that the astonished physician hastened to his assistance, and he too late discovered that life had yielded in the conflict. It was long before he could himself to divulge the mysterious circumstances which had preceded Sellner's dissolution; but once, in a moment of confidence, he was insensibly led to make the detail known to a few intimate friends and finally produced the harp, which he had appropriated to himself as a legacy from the dead.

WAKE NOT THE DEAD

by Ernst Raupach

Wake not the Dead:—they bring but gloomy night
And cheerless desolation into day;
For in the grave who mouldering lay.
No more can feel the influence of light,
Or yield them to the sun's prolific might;
Let them repose within their house of clay—
Corruption, vainly wilt thou e'er essay
To quicken:—it sends forth a pest'lent blight;
And neither fiery sun, nor bathing dew,
Nor breath of spring the dead can e'er renew.
That which from life is pluck'd, becomes the foe
Of life, and whoso wakes it waketh woe.
Seek not the dead to waken from that sleep
In which from mortal eye they lie enshrouded deep.

"WILT thou forever sleep? Wilt thou never more awake, my beloved, but henceforth repose forever from thy short pilgrimage on earth? O yet once again return! and bring back with thee the vivifying dawn of hope to one whose existence hath, since thy departure, been obscured by the dunnest shades. What! dumb? forever dumb? Thy friend lamenteth, and thou heedest him not? He sheds bitter, scalding tears, and thou reposest unregarding his affliction? He is in despair, and thou no longer openest thy arms to him as an asylum from his grief? Say then, doth the paly shroud become thee better than the bridal veil? Is the chamber of the grave a warmer bed than the couch of love? Is the spectre death more welcome to thy arms than thy enamoured consort? Oh! return, my beloved, return once again to this anxious disconsolate bosom."

Such were the lamentations which Walter poured forth for his Brunhilda, the partner of his youthful passionate love; thus did he bewail over her grave at the midnight hour, what time the spirit that presides in the troublous atmosphere, sends his legions of monsters through mid-air, so that their shadows, as they flit beneath the moon and across the earth, dart as wild, agitating thoughts that chase each other o'er the sinner's bosom— thus did he lament under the tall linden trees by her grave, while his head reclined on the cold stone.

Walter was a powerful lord in Burgundy, who, in his earliest youth, had been smitten with the charms of the fair Brunhilda, a beauty far surpassing in loveliness all her rivals; for her tresses, dark as the raven face of night, streaming over her shoulders, set off to the utmost advantage the beaming lustre of her slender form, and the rich dye of a cheek whose tint was deep and brilliant as that of the western heaven; her eyes did not resemble those burning orbs whose pale glow gems the vault of night, and whose immeasurable distance fills the soul with deep thoughts of eternity, but rather as the sober beams which cheer this nether world, and which, while they enlighten, kindle the sons of earth to joy and love. Brunhilda became the wife of Walter, and both being equally enamoured and devoted, they abandoned themselves to the enjoyment of a passion that rendered them reckless of aught besides, while it lulled them in a fascinating dream. Their sole apprehension was lest aught should awaken them from a delirium which they prayed might continue forever. Yet how vain is the wish that would arrest the decrees of destiny! as well might it seek to divert the circling planets from their eternal course. Short was the duration of this frenzied passion; not that it gradually decayed and subsided into apathy, but death snatched away his blooming victim, and left Walter to a widowed couch. Impetuous, however, as was his first burst of grief, he was not inconsolable, for ere long another bride became the partner of the youthful nobleman.

Swanhilda also was beautiful; although nature had formed her charms on a very different model from those of Brunhilda. Her golden locks waved bright as the beams of morn: only when excited by some emotion of her soul did a rosy hue tinge the lily paleness of her cheek: her limbs were proportioned in the nicest symmetry, yet did they not possess that luxuriant fullness of animal life: her eye beamed eloquently, but it was with the milder radiance of a star, tranquillizing to tenderness rather than exciting to warmth. Thus formed, it was not possible that she should steep him in his former delirium, although she rendered happy his waking hours—tranquil and serious, yet cheerful, studying in all things her husband's pleasure, she restored order and comfort in his family, where her presence shed a general influence all around. Her mild benevolence tended to restrain the fiery, impetuous disposition of Walter: while at the same time her prudence recalled him in some degree from his vain, turbulent wishes, and his aspirings after unattainable enjoyments, to the duties and pleasures of actual life. Swanhilda bore her husband two children, a son and a daughter; the latter was mild and patient as her mother, well contented with her solitary sports, and even in these recreations displayed the serious turn of her character. The boy possessed his father's fiery, restless disposition, tempered, however, with the solidity of his mother. Attached by his offspring more tenderly towards their mother, Walter now lived for several years very happily: his thoughts would frequently, indeed, recur to Brunhilda, but without their former violence, merely as we dwell upon the memory of a friend of our earlier days, borne from us on the rapid current of time to a region where we know that he is happy.

But clouds dissolve into air, flowers fade, the sands of the hourglass run imperceptibly away, and even so, do human feelings dissolve, fade, and pass away, and with them too, human happiness. Walter's inconstant breast again sighed for the ecstatic dreams of those days which he had spent with his equally romantic, enamoured Brunhilda—again did she present herself to his ardent fancy in all the glow of her bridal charms, and he began to draw a parallel between the past and the present; nor did imagination, as it is wont, fail to array the former in her brightest hues, while it proportionably obscured the latter; so that he pictured to himself, the one much more rich in enjoyment, and the other, much less so than they really were. This change in her husband did not escape Swanhilda; whereupon, redoubling her attentions towards him, and her cares towards their children, she expected, by this means, to reunite the knot that was slackened; yet the more she endeavoured to regain his affections, the colder did he grow—the more intolerable did her caresses seem, and the more continually did the image of Brunhilda haunt his thoughts. The children, whose endearments were now become indispensable to him, alone stood between the parents as *genii* eager to affect a reconciliation; and, beloved by them both, formed a uniting link between them. Yet, as evil can be plucked from the heart of man, only ere its root has yet struck deep, its fangs being afterwards too firm to be eradicated; so was Walter's diseased fancy too far affected to have its disorder stopped, for, in a short time, it completely tyrannized over him. Frequently of a night, instead of retiring to his consort's chamber, he repaired to Brunhilda's grave, where he murmured forth his discontent, saying: "Wilt thou sleep forever?"

One night as he was reclining on the turf, indulging in his wonted sorrow, a sorcerer from the neighbouring mountains entered into this field of death for the purpose of gathering, for his mystic spells, such herbs as grow only from the earth wherein the dead repose, and which, as of the last production of mortality, are gifted with a powerful and supernatural influence. The sorcerer perceived the mourner, and approached the spot where he was lying.

"Wherefore, fond wretch, dost thou grieve thus, for what is now a hideous mass of mortality—mere bones, and nerves, and veins? Nations have fallen unlamented; even worlds themselves, long ere this globe of ours was created, have mouldered into nothing; nor hath any one wept over them; why then should'st thou indulge this vain affliction for a child of the dust—a being as frail as thyself, and like thee the creature but of a moment?"

Walter raised himself up:—"Let yon worlds that shine in the firmament," replied he, "lament for each other as they perish. It is true, that I who am myself clay, lament for my fellow-clay: yet is this clay impregnated with a fire—with an essence, that none of the elements of creation possess—with love: and this divine passion, I felt for her who now sleepeth beneath this sod."

"Will thy complaints awaken her: or could they do so, would she not soon upbraid thee for having disturbed that repose in which she is now hushed?"

"Avaunt, cold-hearted being: thou knowest not what is love. Oh! that my tears could wash away the earthy covering that conceals her from these eyes;—that my groan of anguish could rouse her from her slumber of death!—No, she would not again seek her earthy couch."

"Insensate that thou art, and couldst thou endure to gaze without shuddering on one disgorged from the jaws of the grave? Art thou too thyself the same from whom she parted, or hath time passed o'er thy brow and left no traces there? Would not thy love rather be converted into hate and disgust?"

"Say rather that the stars would leave yon firmament, that the sun will henceforth refuse to shed his beams through the heavens. Oh! that she stood once more before me;—that once again she reposed on this bosom!—how quickly should we then forget that death or time had ever stepped between us."

"Delusion! mere delusion of the brain, from heated blood, like to that which arises from the fumes of wine. It is not my wish to tempt thee;—to restore to thee thy dead; else wouldst thou soon feel that I have spoken truth."

"How! restore her to me," exclaimed Walter casting himself at the sorcerer's feet. "Oh! if thou art indeed able to effect that, grant it to my earnest supplication; if one throb of human feeling vibrates in thy bosom, let my tears prevail with thee; restore to me my beloved; so shalt thou hereafter bless the deed, and see that it was a good work."

"A good work! a blessed deed!"—returned the sorcerer with a smile of scorn; "for me there exists neither good nor evil; since my will is always the same. Ye alone know evil, who will that which ye would not. It is indeed in my power to restore her to thee: yet, bethink thee well, whether it will prove thy weal. Consider too, how deep the abyss between life and death; across this, my power can build a bridge, but it can never fill up the frightful chasm."

Walter would have spoken, and have sought to prevail on this powerful being by fresh entreaties, but the latter prevented him, saying: "Peace! bethink thee well! and return hither to me tomorrow at midnight. Yet once more do I warn thee, 'Wake not the dead.'"

Having uttered these words, the mysterious being disappeared. Intoxicated with fresh hope, Walter found no sleep on his couch; for fancy, prodigal of her richest stores, expanded before him the glittering web of futurity; and his eye, moistened with the dew of rapture, glanced from one vision of happiness to another. During the next day he wandered through the woods, lest wonted objects by recalling the memory of later and less happier times might disturb the blissful idea that he should again behold her—again fold her in his arms, gaze on her beaming brow by day, repose on her bosom at night: and, as this sole idea filled his imagination, how was it possible that the least doubt should arise; or that the warning of the mysterious old man should recur to his thoughts?

No sooner did the midnight hour approach, than he hastened before the grave-field where the sorcerer was already standing by that of Brunhilda. "Hast thou maturely considered?" inquired he.

"Oh! restore to me the object of my ardent passion," exclaimed Walter with impetuous eagerness. "Delay not thy generous action, lest I die even this night, consumed with disappointed desire; and behold her face no more."

"Well then," answered the old man, "return hither again tomorrow at the same hour. But once more do I give thee this friendly warning, 'Wake not the dead.'"

All in the despair of impatience, Walter would have prostrated himself at his feet, and supplicated him to fulfil at once a desire now increased to agony; but the sorcerer had already disappeared. Pouring forth his lamentations more wildly and impetuously than ever, he lay upon the grave of his adored one, until the grey dawn streaked the east. During the day, which seemed to him longer than any he had ever experienced, he wandered to and fro, restless and impatient, seemingly without any object, and deeply buried in his own reflections, inquest as the murderer who meditates his first deed of blood: and the stars of evening found him once more at the appointed spot. At midnight the sorcerer was there also.

"Hast thou yet maturely deliberated?" inquired he, "as on the preceding night?"

"Oh, what should I deliberate?" returned Walter impatiently. "I need not to deliberate; what I demand of thee, is that which thou hast promised me—that which will prove my bliss. Or dost thou but mock me? if so, hence from my sight, lest I be tempted to lay my hand on thee."

"Once more do I warn thee." answered the old man with undisturbed composure, "'Wake not the dead'—let her rest."

"Aye, but not in the cold grave: she shall rather rest on this bosom which burns with eagerness to clasp her."

"Reflect, thou mayst not quit her until death, even though aversion and horror should seize thy heart. There would then remain only one horrible means."

"Dotard!" cried Walter, interrupting him, "how may I hate that which I love with such intensity of passion? how should I abhor that for which my every drop of blood is boiling?"

"Then be it even as thou wishest," answered the sorcerer; "step back."

The old man now drew a circle round the grave, all the while muttering words of enchantment. Immediately the storm began to howl among the tops of the trees; owls flapped their wings, and uttered their low voice of omen; the stars hid their mild, beaming aspect, that they might not behold so unholy and impious a spectacle; the stone then rolled from the grave with a hollow sound, leaving a free passage for the inhabitant of that dreadful tenement. The sorcerer scattered into the yawning earth roots and herbs of most magic power, and of most penetrating odour, so that the worms crawling forth from the earth congregated together, and raised themselves in a fiery column over the grave, while rushing wind burst from the earth, scattering the mould before it, until at length the coffin lay uncovered. The moonbeams fell on it, and the lid burst open with a tremendous sound. Upon this the sorcerer poured upon it some blood from out of a human skull, exclaiming at the same time, "Drink, sleeper, of this warm stream, that thy heart may again beat within thy bosom." And, after a short pause, shedding on her some other mystic liquid, he cried aloud with the voice of one inspired: "Yes, thy heart beats once more with the flood of life: thine eye is again opened to sight. Arise, therefore, from the tomb."

As an island suddenly springs forth from the dark waves of the ocean, raised upwards from the deep by the force of subterraneous fires, so did Brunhilda start from her earthy couch, borne forward by some invisible power. Taking her by the hand, the sorcerer led her towards Walter, who stood at some little distance, rooted to the ground with amazement.

"Receive again," said he, "the object of thy passionate sighs: mayest thou never more require my aid; should that, however, happen, so wilt thou find me, during the full of the moon, upon the mountains in that spot and where the three roads meet."

Instantly did Walter recognize in the form that stood before him, her whom he so ardently loved; and a sudden glow shot through his frame at finding her thus restored to him: yet the night-frost had chilled his limbs and palsied his tongue. For a while he gazed upon her without either motion or speech, and during this pause, all was again become hushed and serene; and the stars shone brightly in the clear heavens.

"Walter!" exclaimed the figure; and at once the well-known sound, thrilling to his heart, broke the spell by which he was bound.

"Is it reality? Is it truth?" cried he, "or a cheating delusion?"

"No, it is no imposture; I am really living:—conduct me quickly to thy castle in the mountains."

Walter looked around: the old man had disappeared, but he perceived close by his side, a coal-black steed of fiery eye, ready equipped to conduct him thence; and on his back lay all proper attire for Brunhilda, who lost no time in arraying herself. This being done, she cried; "Haste, let us away ere the dawn breaks, for my eye is yet too weak to endure the light of day." Fully recovered from his stupor, Walter leaped into his saddle, and catching up, with a mingled feeling of delight and awe, the beloved being thus mysteriously restored from the power of the grave, he spurred on across the wild, towards the mountains, as furiously as if pursued by the shadows of the dead, hastening to recover from him their sister.

The castle to which Walter conducted his Brunhilda, was situated on a rock between other rocks rising up above it. Here they arrived, unseen by any save one aged domestic, on whom Walter imposed secrecy by the severest threats.

"Here will we tarry," said Brunhilda, "until I can endure the light, and until thou canst look upon me without trembling as if struck with a cold chill." They accordingly continued to make that place their abode: yet no one knew that Brunhilda existed, save only that aged attendant, who provided their meals. During seven entire days they had no light except that of tapers: during the next seven, the light was admitted through the lofty casements only while the rising or setting-sun faintly illumined the mountain-tops, the valley being still enveloped in shade.

Seldom did Walter quit Brunhilda's side: a nameless spell seemed to attach him to her; even the shudder which he felt in her presence, and which would not permit him to touch her, was not unmixed with pleasure, like that thrilling awful emotion felt when strains of sacred music float under the vault of some temple; he rather sought, therefore, than avoided this feeling. Often too as he had indulged in calling to mind the beauties of Brunhilda, she had never appeared so fair, so fascinating, so admirable when depicted by his imagination, as when now beheld in reality. Never till now had her voice sounded with such tones of sweetness; never before did her language possess such eloquence as it now did, when she conversed with him on the subject of the past. And this was the magic fairy-land towards which her words constantly conducted him. Ever did she dwell upon the days of their first love, those hours of delight which they had participated in together when the one derived all enjoyment from the other: and so rapturous, so enchanting, so full of life did she recall to his imagination that blissful season, that he even doubted whether he had ever experienced with her so much felicity, or had been so truly happy. And, while she thus vividly portrayed their hours of past delight, she delineated in still more glowing, more enchanting colours, those hours of approaching bliss which now awaited them, richer in enjoyment than any preceding ones. In this manner did she charm her attentive auditor with enrapturing hopes for the future, and lull him into dreams of more than mortal ecstasy; so that while he listened to her siren strain, he entirely forgot how little blissful was the latter period of their union, when he had often sighed at her imperiousness, and at her harshness both to himself and all his household. Yet even had he recalled this to mind would it have disturbed him in his present delirious trance? Had she not now left behind in the grave all the frailty of mortality? Was not her whole being refined and purified by that long sleep in which neither passion nor sin had approached her even in dreams? How different now was the subject of her discourse! Only when speaking of her affection for him, did she betray anything of earthly feeling: at other times, she uniformly dwelt upon themes relating to the invisible and future world; when in descanting and declaring the mysteries of eternity, a stream of prophetic eloquence would burst from her lips.

In this manner had twice seven days elapsed, and, for the first time, Walter beheld the being now dearer to him than ever, in the full light of day. Every trace of the grave had disappeared from her countenance; a roseate tinge like the ruddy streaks of dawn again beamed on her pallid cheek; the faint, mouldering taint of the grave was changed into a delightful violet scent; the only sign of earth that never disappeared. He no longer felt either apprehension or awe, as he gazed upon her in the sunny light of day: it was not until now, that he seemed to have recovered her completely; and, glowing with all his former passion towards her, he would have pressed her to his bosom, but she gently repulsed him, saying:—"Not yet—spare your caresses until the moon has again filled her horn."

In spite of his impatience, Walter was obliged to await the lapse of another period of seven days: but, on the night when the moon was arrived at the full, he hastened to Brunhilda, whom he found more lovely than she had ever appeared before. Fearing no obstacles to his transports, he embraced with all the fervour of a deeply enamoured and successful lover. Brunhilda, however, still refused to yield to his passion. "What!" exclaimed she, "is it fitting that I who have been purified by death from the frailty of mortality, should become thy concubine, while a mere daughter of the earth bears the title of thy wife: never shall it be. No, it must be within the walls of thy palace, within that chamber where I once reigned as queen, that thou obtainest the end of thy wishes—and of mine also," added she, imprinting a glowing kiss on the lips, and immediately disappeared.

Heated with passion, and determined to sacrifice everything to the accomplishment of his desires, Walter hastily quitted the apartment, and shortly after the castle itself. He travelled over mountain and across heath, with the rapidity of a storm, so that the turf was flung up by his horse's hooves, nor once stopped until he arrived home.

Here, however, neither the affectionate caresses of Swanhilda, or those of his children could touch his heart, or induce him to restrain his furious desires. Alas! is the impetuous torrent to be checked in its devastating course by the beauteous flowers over which it rushes, when they exclaim:—"Destroyer, commiserate our helpless innocence and beauty, nor lay us waste?"—the stream sweeps over them unregarding, and a single moment annihilates the pride of a whole summer.

Shortly afterwards did Walter begin to hint to Swanhilda that they were ill-suited to each other; that he was anxious to taste that wild, tumultuous life, so well according with the spirit of his sex, while she, on the contrary, was satisfied with the monotonous circle of household enjoyments:—that he was eager for whatever promised novelty, while she felt most attached to what was familiarized to her by habit: and lastly, that her cold disposition, bordering upon indifference, but ill accorded with his ardent temperament: it was therefore more prudent that they should seek apart from each other that happiness which they could not find together. A sigh, and a brief acquiescence to his wishes was all the reply that Swanhilda made: and, on the following morning, upon his presenting her with a paper of separation, informing her that she was at liberty to return home to her father, she received it most submissively: yet, ere she departed, she gave him the following warning: "Too well do I conjecture to whom I am indebted for this our separation. Often have I seen thee at Brunhilda's grave, and beheld thee there even on that night when the face of the heavens was suddenly enveloped in a veil of clouds. Hast thou rashly dared to tear aside the awful veil that separates the mortality that dreams from that which dreameth not? Oh! then woe to thee, thou wretched man, for thou hast attached to thyself that which will prove thy destruction."

She ceased: nor did Walter attempt any reply, for the similar admonition uttered by the sorcerer flashed upon his mind, all obscured as it was by passion, just as the lightning glares momentarily through the gloom of night without dispersing the obscurity.

Swanhilda then departed, in order to pronounce to her children a bitter farewell, for they, according to national custom, belonged to the father; and, having bathed them in her tears, and consecrated them with the holy water of maternal love, she quitted her husband's residence, and departed to the home of her father.

Thus was the kind and benevolent Swanhilda driven an exile from those halls where she had presided with grace;—from halls which were now newly decorated to receive another mistress. The day at length arrived on which Walter, for the second time, conducted Brunhilda home as a newly made bride. And he caused it to be reported among his domestics that his new consort had gained his affections by her extraordinary likeness to Brunhilda, their former mistress. How ineffably happy did he deem himself as he conducted his beloved once more into the chamber which had often witnessed their former joys, and which was now newly gilded and adorned in a most costly style: among the other decorations were figures of angels scattering roses, which served to support the purple draperies whose ample folds o'ershadowed the nuptial couch. With what impatience did he await the hour that was to put him in possession of those beauties for which he had already paid so high a price, but, whose enjoyment was to cost him most dearly yet! Unfortunate Walter! revelling in bliss, thou beholdest not the abyss that yawns beneath thy feet, intoxicated with the luscious perfume of the flower thou hast plucked, thou little deemest how deadly is the venom with which it is fraught, although, for a short season, its potent fragrance bestows new energy on all thy feelings.

Happy, however, as Walter was now, his household were far from being equally so. The strange resemblance between their new lady and the deceased Brunhilda filled them with a secret dismay,—an undefinable horror; for there was not a single difference of feature, of tone of voice, or of gesture. To add to these mysterious circumstances, her female attendants discovered a particular mark on her back, exactly like one which Brunhilda had. A report was now soon circulated, that their lady was no other than Brunhilda herself, who had been recalled to life by the power of necromancy. How truly horrible was the idea of living under the same roof with one who had been an inhabitant of the tomb, and of being obliged to attend upon her, and acknowledge her as mistress! There was also in Brunhilda much to increase this aversion, and favour their superstition: no ornaments of gold ever decked her person; all that others were wont to wear of this metal, she had formed of silver: no richly coloured and sparkling jewels glittered upon her; pearls alone lent their pale lustre to adorn her bosom. Most carefully did she always avoid the cheerful light of the sun, and was wont to spend the brightest days in the most retired and gloomy apartments: only during the twilight of the commencing or declining day did she ever walk abroad, but her favourite hour was when the phantom light of the moon bestowed on all objects a shadowy appearance and a sombre hue; always too at the crowing of the cock an involuntary shudder was observed to seize her limbs. Imperious as before her death, she quickly imposed her iron yoke on everyone around her, while she seemed even far more terrible than ever, since a dread of some supernatural power attached to her appalled all who approached her. A malignant withering glance seemed to shoot from her eye on the unhappy object of her wrath, as if it would annihilate its victim. In short, those halls which, in the time of Swanhilda were the residence of cheerfulness and mirth, now resembled an extensive desert tomb. With fear imprinted on their pale countenances, the domestics glided through the apartments of the castle; and in this abode of terror, the crowing of the cock caused the living to tremble, as if they were the spirits of the departed; for the sound always reminded them of their mysterious mistress. There was no one but who shuddered at meeting her in a lonely place, in the dusk of evening, or by the light of the moon, a circumstance that was deemed to be ominous of some evil: so great was the apprehension of her female attendants, they pined in continual disquietude, and, by degrees, all quitted her. In the course of time even others of the domestics fled, for an insupportal horror had seized them.

The art of the sorcerer had indeed bestowed upon Brunhilda an artificial life, and due nourishment had continued to sup-port the restored body: yet this body was not able of itself to keep up the genial glow of vitality, and to nourish the flame whence springs all the affections and passions, whether of love or hate; for death had forever destroyed and withered it: all that Brunhilda now possessed was a chilled existence, colder than that of the snake. It was nevertheless necessary that she should love, and return with equal ardour the warm caresses of her spell-enthralled husband, to whose passion alone she was indebted for her renewed existence. It was necessary that a magic draught should animate the dull current in her veins and awaken her to the glow of life and the flame of love—a potion of abomination—one not even to be named without a curse—human blood, imbibed whilst yet warm, from the veins of youth. This was the hellish drink for which she thirsted: possessing no sympathy with the purer feelings of humanity; deriving no enjoyment from aught that interests in life and occupies its varied hours; her existence was a mere blank, unless when in the arms of her paramour husband, and therefore was it that she craved incessantly after the horrible draught. It was even with the utmost effort that she could forbear sucking even the blood of Walter himself, reclined beside her. Whenever she beheld some innocent child whose lovely face denoted the exuberance of infantine health and vigour, she would entice it by soothing words and fond caresses into her most secret apartment, where, lulling it to sleep in her arms, she would suck from its bosom the raw, purple tide of life. Nor were youths of either sex safe from her horrid attack: having first breathed upon her unhappy victim, who never failed immediately to sink into a lengthened sleep, she would then in a similar manner drain his veins of the vital juice. Thus children, youths, and maidens quickly faded away, as flowers gnawn by the cankering worm: the fullness of their limbs disappeared; a sallow line succeeded to the rosy freshness of their cheeks, the liquid lustre of the eye was deadened, even as the sparkling stream when arrested by the touch of frost; and their locks became thin and grey, as if already ravaged by the storm of life. Parents beheld with horror this desolating pestilence devouring their offspring; nor could spell or charm, potion or amulet avail aught against it. The grave swallowed up one after the other; or did the miserable victim survive, he became cadaverous and wrinkled even in the very morn of existence. Parents observed with horror this devastating pestilence snatch away their offspring—a pestilence which, neither herb however potent, nor charm, nor holy taper, nor exorcism could avert. They either beheld their children sink one after the other into the grave, or their youthful forms, withered by the unholy vampire embrace of Brunhilda, assume the decrepitude of sudden age.

At length strange surmises and reports began to prevail; it was whispered that Brunhilda herself was the cause of all these horrors; although no one could pretend to tell in what manner she destroyed her victims, since no marks of violence were discernible. Yet when young children confessed that she had frequently lulled them asleep in her arms, and elder ones said that a sudden slumber had come upon them whenever she began to converse with them, suspicion became converted into certainty, and those whose offspring had hitherto escaped unharmed, quitted their hearths and home—all their little possessions—the dwellings of their fathers and the inheritance of their children, in order to rescue from so horrible a fate those who were dearer to their simple affections than aught else the world could give.

Thus daily did the castle assume a more desolate appearance; daily did its environs become more deserted; none but a few aged decrepit old women and grey-headed menials were to be seen remaining of the once numerous retinue. Such will in the latter days of the earth be the last generation of mortals, when childbearing shall have ceased, when youth shall no more be seen, nor any arise to replace those who shall await their fate in silence.

Walter alone noticed not, or heeded not, the desolation around him; he apprehended not death, lapped as he was in a glowing elysium of love. Far more happy than formerly did he now seem in the possession of Brunhilda. All those caprices and frowns which had been wont to overcloud their former union had now entirely disappeared. She even seemed to dote on him with a warmth of passion that she had never exhibited even during the happy season of bridal love; for the flame of that youthful blood, of which she drained the veins of others, rioted in her own. At night, as soon as he closed his eyes, she would breathe on him till he sank into delicious dreams, from which he awoke only to experience more rapturous enjoyments. By day she would continually discourse with him on the bliss experienced by happy spirits beyond the grave, assuring him that, as his affection had recalled her from the tomb, they were now irrevocably united. Thus fascinated by a continual spell, it was not possible that he should perceive what was taking place around him. Brunhilda, however, foresaw with savage grief that the source of her youthful ardour was daily decreasing, for, in a short time, there remained nothing gifted with youth, save Walter and his children, and these latter she resolved should be her next victims.

On her first return to the castle, she had felt an aversion towards the offspring of another, and therefore abandoned them entirely to the attendants appointed by Swanhilda. Now, however, she began to pay considerable attention to them, and caused them to be frequently admitted into her presence. The aged nurses were filled with dread at perceiving these marks of regard from her towards their young charges, yet dared they not to oppose the will of their terrible and imperious mistress. Soon did Brunhilda gain the affection of the children, who were too unsuspecting of guile to apprehend any danger from her; on the contrary, her caresses won them completely to her. Instead of ever checking their mirthful gambols, she would rather instruct them in new sports: often too did she recite to them tales of such strange and wild interest as to exceed all the stories of their nurses. Were they wearied either with play or with listening to her narratives, she would take them on her knees and lull them to slumber. Then did visions of the most surpassing magnificence attend their dreams: they would fancy themselves in some garden where flowers of every hue rose in rows one above the other, from the humble violet to the tall sunflower, forming a parti-coloured broidery of every hue, sloping upwards towards the golden clouds where little angels whose wings sparkled with azure and gold descended to bring them delicious cakes or splendid jewels; or sung to them soothing melodious hymns. So delightful did these dreams in short time become to the children that they longed for nothing so eagerly as to slumber on Brunhilda's lap, for never did they else enjoy such visions of heavenly forms. They were most anxious for that which was to prove their destruction:—yet do we not all aspire after that which conducts us to the grave—after the enjoyment of life? These innocents stretched out their arms to approaching death because it assumed the mask of pleasure; for, while they were lapped in these ecstatic slumbers, Brunhilda sucked the life-stream from their bosoms. On waking, indeed, they felt themselves faint and exhausted, yet did no pain nor any mark betray the cause. Shortly, however, did their strength entirely fail, even as the summer brook is gradually dried up: their sports became less and less noisy; their loud, frolicsome laughter was converted into a faint smile; the full tones of their voices died away into a mere whisper. Their attendants were filled with horror and despair; too well did they conjecture the horrible truth, yet dared not to impart their suspicions to Walter, who was so devotedly attached to his horrible partner. Death had already smote his prey: the children were but the mere shadows of their former selves, and even this shadow quickly disappeared.

The anguished father deeply bemoaned their loss, for, notwithstanding his apparent neglect, he was strongly attached to them, nor until he had experienced their loss was he aware that his love was so great. His affliction could not fail to excite the displeasure of Brunhilda: "Why dost thou lament so fondly," said she, "for these little ones? What satisfaction could such unformed beings yield to thee unless thou wert still attached to their mother? Thy heart then is still hers? Or dost thou now regret her and them because thou art satiated with my fondness and weary of my endearments? Had these young ones grown up, would they not have attached thee, thy spirit and thy affections more closely to this earth of clay—to this dust and have alienated thee from that sphere to which I, who have already passed the grave, endeavour to raise thee? Say is thy spirit so heavy, or thy love so weak, or thy faith so hollow, that the hope of being mine forever is unable to touch thee?" Thus did Brunhilda express her indignation at her consort's grief, and forbade him her presence. The fear of offending her beyond forgiveness and his anxiety to appease her soon dried up his tears, and he again abandoned himself to his fatal passion, until approaching destruction at length awakened him from his delusion.

Neither maiden, nor youth, was any longer to be seen, either within the dreary walls of the castle, or the adjoining territory:—all had disappeared; for those whom the grave had not swallowed up had fled from the region of death. Who, therefore, now remained to quench the horrible thirst of the female vampire save Walter himself? and his death she dared to contemplate unmoved; for that divine sentiment that unites two beings in one joy and one sorrow was unknown to her bosom. Was he in his tomb, so was she free to search out other victims and glut herself with destruction, until she herself should, at the last day, be consumed with the earth itself, such is the fatal law to which the dead are subject when awoke by the arts of necromancy from the sleep of the grave.

She now began to fix her blood-thirsty lips on Walter's breast, when cast into a profound sleep by the odour of her violet breath he reclined beside her quite unconscious of his impending fate: yet soon did his vital powers begin to decay; and many a grey hair peeped through his raven locks. With his strength, his passion also declined; and he now frequently left her in order to pass the whole day in the sports of the chase, hoping thereby to regain his wonted vigour. As he was reposing one day in a wood beneath the shade of an oak, he perceived, on the summit of a tree, a bird of strange appearance, and quite unknown to him; but, before he could take aim at it with his bow, it flew away into the clouds, at the same time letting fall a rose-coloured root which dropped at Walter's feet, who immediately took it up and, although he was well acquainted with almost every plant, he could not remember to have seen any at all resembling this. Its delightfully odoriferous scent induced him to try its flavour, but ten times more bitter than wormwood it was even as gall in his mouth; upon which, impatient of the disappointment, he flung it away with violence. Had he, however, been aware of its miraculous quality and that it acted as a counter charm against the opiate perfume of Brunhilda's breath, he would have blessed it in spite of its bitterness: thus do mortals often blindly cast away in displeasure the unsavoury remedy that would otherwise work their weal.

When Walter returned home in the evening and laid him down to repose as usual by Brunhilda's side, the magic power of her breath produced no effect upon him; and for the first time during many months did he close his eyes in a natural slumber. Yet hardly had he fallen asleep, ere a pungent smarting pain disturbed him from his dreams; and, opening his eyes, he discerned, by the gloomy rays of a lamp that glimmered in the apartment what for some moments transfixed him quite aghast, for it was Brunhilda, drawing with her lips, the warm blood from his bosom. The wild cry of horror which at length escaped him, terrified Brunhilda, whose mouth was besmeared with the warm blood. "Monster!" exclaimed he, springing from the couch, "is it thus that you love me?"

"Aye, even as the dead love," replied she, with a malignant coldness.

"Creature of blood!" continued Walter, "the delusion which has so long blinded me is at an end: thou are the fiend who hast destroyed my children—who hast murdered the offspring of my vassels."

Raising herself upwards and, at the same time, casting on him a glance that froze him to the spot with dread, she replied. "It is not I who have murdered them—I was obliged to pamper myself with warm youthful blood, in order that I might satisfy thy furious desires—thou art the murderer!"—These dreadful words summoned, before Walter's terrified conscience, the threatening shades of all those who had thus perished, while despair choked his voice.

"Why," continued she, in a tone that increased his horror, "why dost thou make mouths at me like a puppet? Thou who hadst the courage to love the dead—to take into thy bed one who had been sleeping in the grave, the bed-fellow of the worm—who hast clasped in thy lustful arms, the corruption of the tomb—dost thou, unhallowed as thou art, now raise this hideous cry for the sacrifice of a few lives?—They are but leaves swept from their branches by a storm.—Come, chase these idiot fancies, and taste the bliss thou hast so dearly purchased." So saying, she extended her arms towards him; but this motion served only to increase his terror, and exclaiming: "Accursed Being,"—he rushed out of the apartment.

All the horrors of a guilty, upbraiding conscience became his companions, now that he was awakened from the delirium of his unholy pleasures. Frequently did he curse his own obstinate blindness, for having given no heed to the hints and admonitions of his children's nurses, but treating them as vile calumnies. But his sorrow was now too late, for, although repentance may gain pardon for the sinner, it cannot alter the immutable decrees of fate—it cannot recall the murdered from the tomb. No sooner did the first break of dawn appear, than he set out for his lonely castle in the mountains, determined no longer to abide under the same roof with so terrific a being; yet vain was his flight, for, on waking the following morning, he perceived himself in Brunhilda's arms, and quite entangled in her long raven tresses, which seemed to involve him, and bind him in the fetters of his fate; the powerful fascination of her breath held him still more captivated, so that, forgetting all that had passed, he returned her caresses, until awakening as if from a dream he recoiled in unmixed horror from her embrace. During the day he wandered through the solitary wilds of the mountains, as a culprit seeking an asylum from his pursuers; and, at night, retired to the shelter of a cave; fearing less to couch himself within such a dreary place, than to expose himself to the horror of again meeting Brunhilda; but alas! it was in vain that he endeavoured to flee her. Again, when he awoke, he found her the partner of his miserable bed. Nay, had he sought the centre of the earth as his hiding place, had he even imbedded himself beneath rocks, or formed his chamber in the recesses of the ocean, still had he found her his constant companion; for, by calling her again into existence, he had rendered himself inseparably hers, so fatal were the links that united them.

Struggling with the madness that was beginning to seize him, and brooding incessantly on the ghastly visions that presented themselves to his horror-stricken mind, he lay motionless in the gloomiest recesses of the woods, even from the rise of sun till the shades of eve. But, no sooner was the light of day extinguished in the west, and the woods buried in impenetrable darkness, than the apprehension of resigning himself to sleep drove him forth among the mountains. The storm played wildly with the fantastic clouds, and with the rattling leaves, as they were caught up into the air, as if some dread spirit was sporting with these images of transitoriness and decay: it roared among the summits of the oaks as if uttering a voice of fury, while its hollow sound rebounding among the distant hills, seemed as the moans of a departing sinner, or as the faint cry of some wretch expiring under the murderer's hand: the owl too, uttered its ghastly cry as if foreboding the wreck of nature. Walter's hair flew disorderly in the wind, like black snakes wreathing around his temples and shoulders; while each sense was awake to catch fresh horror. In the clouds he seemed to behold the forms of the murdered; in the howling wind to hear their laments and groans; in the chilling blast itself he felt the dire kiss of Brunhilda; in the cry of the screeching bird he heard her voice; in the mouldering leaves he scented the charnel-bed out of which he had awakened her. "Murderer of thy own offspring," exclaimed he in a voice making night, and the conflict of the element still more hideous, "paramour of a blood-thirsty vampire, reveller with the corruption of the tomb!" while in his despair he rent the wild locks from his head. Just then the full moon darted from beneath the bursting clouds; and the sight recalled to his remembrance the advice of the sorcerer, when he trembled at the first apparition of Brunhilda rising from her sleep of death;—namely, to seek him at the season of the full moon in the mountains, where three roads met. Scarcely had this gleam of hope broke in on his bewildered mind than he flew to the appointed spot.

On his arrival, Walter found the old man seated there upon a stone as calmly as though it had been a bright sunny day and completely regardless of the uproar around. "Art thou come then?" exclaimed he to the breathless wretch, who, flinging himself at his feet, cried in a tone of anguish:—"Oh save me—succour me—rescue me from the monster that scattereth death and desolation around her.

"Wherefore a mysterious warning? why didst thou not rather disclose to me at once all the horrors that awaited my sacrilegious profanation of the grave?"

"And wherefore a mysterious warning? why didst thou not perceivest how wholesome was the advice—'Wake not the dead.'

"Wert thou able to listen to another voice than that of thy impetuous passions? Did not thy eager impatience shut my mouth at the very moment I would have cautioned thee?"

"True, true:—thy reproof is just: but what does it avail now;—I need the promptest aid."

"Well," replied the old man, "there remains even yet a means of rescuing thyself, but it is fraught with horror and demands all thy resolution."

"Utter it then, utter it; for what can be more appalling, more hideous than the misery I now endure?"

"Know then," continued the sorcerer, "that only on the night of the new moon does she sleep the sleep of mortals; and then all the supernatural power which she inherits from the grave totally fails her. 'Tis then that thou must murder her."

"How! murder her!" echoed Walter.

"Aye," returned the old man calmly, "pierce her bosom with a sharpened dagger, which I will furnish thee with; at the same time renounce her memory forever, swearing never to think of her intentionally, and that, if thou dost involuntarily, thou wilt repeat the curse."

"Most horrible! yet what can be more horrible than she herself is?—I'll do it."

"Keep then this resolution until the next new moon."

"What, must I wait until then?" cried Walter, "alas ere then, either her savage thirst for blood will have forced me into the night of the tomb, or horror will have driven me into the night of madness."

"Nay," replied the sorcerer, "that I can prevent;" and, so saying, he conducted him to a cavern further among the mountains. "Abide here twice seven days," said he; "so long can I protect thee against her deadly caresses. Here wilt thou find all due provision for thy wants; but take heed that nothing tempt thee to quit this place. Farewell, when the moon renews itself, then do I repair hither again." So saying, the sorcerer drew a magic circle around the cave, and then immediately disappeared.

Twice seven days did Walter continue in this solitude, where his companions were his own terrifying thoughts, and his bitter repentance. The present was all desolation and dread; the future presented the image of a horrible deed which he must perforce commit; while the past was empoisoned by the memory of his guilt. Did he think on his former happy union with Brunhilda, her horrible image presented itself to his imagination with her lips defiled with dripping blood: or, did he call to mind the peaceful days he had passed with Swanhilda, he beheld her sorrowful spirit with the shadows of her murdered children. Such were the horrors that attended him by day: those of night were still more dreadful, for then he beheld Brunhilda herself, who, wandering round the magic circle which she could not pass, called upon his name till the cavern re-echoed the horrible sound. "Walter, my beloved," cried she, "wherefore dost thou avoid me? art thou not mine? forever mine—mine here, and mine hereafter? And dost thou seek to murder me?—ah! commit not a deed which hurls us both to perdition—thyself as well as me." In this manner did the horrible visitant torment him each night, and, even when she departed, robbed him of all repose.

The night of the new moon at length arrived, dark as the deed it was doomed to bring forth. The sorcerer entered the cavern; "Come," said he to Walter, "let us depart hence, the hour is now arrived." And he forthwith conducted him in silence from the cave to a coal-black steed, the sight of which recalled to Walter's remembrance the fatal night. He then related to the old man Brunhilda's nocturnal visits and anxiously inquired whether her apprehensions of eternal perdition would be fulfilled or not. "Mortal eyes," exclaimed the sorcerer, "may not pierce the dark secrets of another world, or penetrate the deep abyss that separates earth from heaven." Walter hesitated to mount the steed. "Be resolute," exclaimed his companion, "but this once is it granted to thee to make the trial, and, should thou fail now, nought can rescue thee from her power."

"What can be more horrible than she herself?—I am determined." And he leaped on the horse, the sorcerer mounting also behind him.

Carried with a rapidity equal to that of the storm that sweeps across the plain they in a brief space arrived at Walter's castle. All the doors flew open at the bidding of his companion, and they speedily reached Brunhilda's chamber, and stood beside her couch. Reclining in a tranquil slumber, she reposed in all her native loveliness, every trace of horror had disappeared from her countenance; she looked so pure, meek and innocent that all the sweet hours of their endearments rushed to Walter's memory, like interceding angels pleading in her behalf. His unnerved hand could not take the dagger which the sorcerer presented to him. "The blow must be struck even now," said the latter. "Shouldst thou delay but an hour, she will lie at daybreak on thy bosom, sucking the warm life drops from thy heart."

"Horrible! most horrible!" faltered the trembling Walter, and turning away his face, he thrust the dagger into her bosom, exclaiming—"I curse thee forever!"—and the cold blood gushed upon his hand. Opening her eyes once more, she cast a look of ghastly horror on her husband, and, in a hollow dying accent said—"Thou too art doomed to perdition."

"Lay now thy hand upon her corpse," said the sorcerer, "and swear the oath."

Walter did as commanded, saying, "Never will I think of her with love, never recall her to mind intentionally, and, should her image recur to my mind involuntarily, so will I exclaim to it: be thou accursed."

"Thou hast now done everything," returned the sorcerer;—"restore her therefore to the earth, from which thou didst so foolishly recall her; and be sure to recollect thy oath: for, shouldst thou forget it but once, she would return, and thou wouldst be inevitably lost. Adieu—we will see each other no more." Having uttered these words he quitted the apartment, and Walter also fled from this abode of horror, having first given direction that the corpse should be speedily interred.

Again did the terrific Brunhilda repose within her grave; but her image continually haunted Walter's imagination, so that his existence was one continued martyrdom, in which he continually struggled to dismiss from his recollection the hideous phantoms of the past; yet, the stronger his effort to banish them, so much the more frequently and the more vividly did they return; as the night-wanderer, who is enticed by a fire-wisp into quagmire or bog, sinks the deeper into his damp grave the more he struggles to escape. His imagination seemed incapable of admitting any other image than that of Brunhilda: now he fancied he beheld her expiring, the blood streaming from her beautiful bosom: at others he saw the lovely bride of his youth, who reproached him with having disturbed the slumbers of the tomb; and to both he was compelled to utter the dreadful words, "I curse thee forever." The terrible imprecation was constantly passing his lips; yet was he in incessant terror lest he should forget it, or dream of her without being able to repeat it, and then, on awaking, find himself in her arms. Else would he recall her expiring words, and, appalled at their terrific import, imagine that the doom of his perdition was irrecoverably passed. Whence should he fly from himself? or how erase from his brain these images and forms of horror? In the din of combat, in the tumult of war and its incessant pour of victory to defeat; from the cry of anguish to the exultation of victory—in these he hoped to find at least the relief of distraction: but here too he was disappointed. The giant fang of apprehension now seized him who had never before known fear; each drop of blood that sprayed upon him seemed the cold blood that had gushed from Brunhilda's wound; each dying wretch that fell beside him looked like her, when expiring, she exclaimed,—"Thou too art doomed to perdition"; so that the aspect of death seemed more full of dread to him than aught beside, and this unconquerable terror compelled him to abandon the battle-field. At length, after many a weary and fruitless wandering, he returned to his castle. Here all was deserted and silent, as if the sword, or a still more deadly pestilence had laid everything to waste: for the few inhabitants that still remained, and even those servants who had once shewn themselves the most attached, now fled from him, as though he had been branded with the mark of Cain. With horror he perceived that, by uniting himself as he had done with the dead, he had cut himself off from the living, who refused to hold any intercourse with him. Often, when he stood on the battlements of his castle, and looked down upon desolate fields, he compared their present solitude with the lively activity they were wont to exhibit, under the strict but benevolent discipline of Swanhilda. He now felt that she alone could reconcile him to life, but durst he hope that one, whom he so deeply aggrieved, could pardon him, and receive him again? Impatience at length got the better of fear; he sought Swanhilda, and, with the deepest contrition, acknowledged his complicated guilt; embracing her knees as he beseeched her to pardon him, and to return to his desolate castle, in order that it might again become the abode of contentment and peace. The pale form which she beheld at her feet, the shadow of the lately blooming youth, touched Swanhilda. "The folly," said she gently, "though it has caused me much sorrow, has never excited my resentment or my anger. But say, where are my children?" To this dreadful interrogation the agonized father could for a while frame no reply: at length he was obliged to confess the dreadful truth. "Then we are sundered forever," returned Swanhilda; nor could all his tears or supplications prevail upon her to revoke the sentence she had given.

Stripped of his last earthly hope, bereft of his last consolation, and thereby rendered as poor as mortal can possibly be on this side of the grave, Walter returned homewards; when, as he was riding through the forest in the neighbourhood of his castle, absorbed in his gloomy meditations, the sudden sound of a horn roused him from his reverie. Shortly after he saw appear a female figure clad in black, and mounted on a steed of the same colour: her attire was like that of a huntress, but, instead of a falcon, she bore a raven in her hand, and she was attended by a gay troop of cavaliers and dames. The first salutations being passed, he found that she was proceeding the same road as himself; and, when she found that Walter's castle was close at hand, she requested that he would lodge her for that night, the evening being far advanced. Most willingly did he comply with this request, since the appearance of the beautiful stranger had struck him greatly, so wonderfully did she resemble Swanhilda, except that her locks were brown, and her eye dark and full of fire. With a sumptous banquet did he entertain his guests, whose mirth and songs enlivened the lately silent halls. Three days did this revelry continue, and so exhilarating did it prove to Walter that he seemed to have forgotten his sorrows and his fears; nor could he prevail upon himself to dismiss his visitors, dreading lest, on their departure, the castle would seem a hundred times more desolate than beforehand, his grief being proportionally increased. At his earnest request, the stranger consented to stay seven, and again another seven days. Without being requested, she took upon herself the superintendence of the household, which she regulated as discreetly and cheerfully as Swanhilda had been wont to do, so that the castle, which had so lately been the abode of melancholy and horror, became the residence of pleasure and festivity, and Walter's grief disappeared altogether in the midst of so much gaiety. Daily did his attachment to the fair unknown increase; he even made her his confidant; and, one evening as they were walking together apart from any of her train, he related to her his melancholy and frightful history. "My dear friend," returned she, as soon as he had finished his tale, "it ill beseems a man of thy discretion to afflict thyself on account of all this. Thou hast awakened the dead from the sleep of the grave and afterwards found what might have been anticipated, that the dead possess no sympathy with life. What then? thou wilt not commit this error a second time."

"Thou hast however murdered the being whom thou hadst thus recalled again to existence—but it was only in appearance, for thou couldst not deprive that of life which properly had none. Thou hast, too, lost a wife and two children: but at thy years such a loss is most easily repaired. There are beauties who will gladly share thy couch, and make thee again a father. But thou dreadst the reckoning of hereafter:—go, open the graves and ask the sleepers there whether that hereafter disturbs them." In such manner would she frequently exhort and cheer him, so that, in a short time, his melancholy entirely disappeared. He now ventured to declare to the unknown the passion with which she had inspired him, nor did she refuse him her hand. Within seven days afterwards the nuptials were celebrated, and the very foundations of the castle seemed to rock from the wild tumultuous uproar of unrestrained riot. The wine streamed in abundance; the goblets circled incessantly; intemperance reached its utmost bounds, while shouts of laughter almost resembling madness burst from the numerous train belonging to the unknown. At length Walter, heated with wine and love, conducted his bride into the nuptial chamber: but, oh! horror! scarcely had he clasped her in his arms ere she transformed herself into a monstrous serpent, which, entwining him in its horrid folds, crushed him to death. Flames crackled on every side of the apartment; in a few minutes after, the whole castle was enveloped in a blaze that consumed it entirely: while, as the walls fell in with a tremendous crash, a voice exclaimed aloud—"Wake not the dead!"

ACKNOWLEDGEMENTS

LUDWIG FRANZ ADOLF JOSEF VON BACZKO (1756-1823) was a Prussian historian and legal scholar. Whilst a student at the University of Königsberg he lost his eyesight to smallpox, a tragedy which did not prevent him from authoring numerous literary works including histories, social critiques, dramas, novels, and theological treatises as well as editing a newspaper and running a charitable society for the blind. "Die Zauberer" (tr. as "The Sorcerers") originally appeared in his *Legenden, volkssagen, gespenster und zaubergeschichten*, a three volume collection of novellas inspired by northern German and Polish folk legends.

LOUISE BRACHMANN (1777-1822) was a poet who first began to publish her verse on the urging of her youthful friend Georg Friedrich von Hardenberg, the famous mystic and Romantic poet who wrote under the name of Novalis. In addition to poetry she authored several knightly romances and plays, which were admired by De La Motte Fouqué and Friedrich Schiller, the latter of whom published her in his literary periodical *Musen-Almanach* (1789). Despite this, she never achieved the recognition she and her supporters felt she deserved. After a failed love affair and a series of family tragedies she took her own life by drowning.

HEINRICH CLAUREN was the pen name of Johann Gottlieb Samuel Carl Heun (1771-1854), a Prussian author, Mason and civic official. A prolific writer, Clauren was one of the most popular sentimental playwrights and novelists of the early nineteenth century, his collected works numbering over a hundred volumes, though his reputation suffered as a result of an ongoing literary feud with the Romantic poet and author Wilhelm Hauff. "Die graue Stube" (tr. as "The Grey Chamber") first appeared in the April issues of *Der Freimüthige* (1810), a Berlin newspaper, and soon became one of the most popular and frequently pastiched of German ghost stories, quickly being translated into French two years later as part of Jean-Baptiste Benoît Eyriès' famous anthology *Fantasmagoriana* (1812).

BARONESS CAROLINE PHILIPPINE DE LA MOTTE FOUQUÉ (1773-1831) was a novelist, editor and socialite. After a failed marriage to an officer she married the Romantic writer Baron Friedrich de la Motte Fouqué, and began her career as an author, writing novels, fairy-tales and short stories in a style commonly thought more restrained than her husband's. Many of her works were written with a female audience in mind and she also authored multiple treatises dealing with the controversial issue of the appropriate education for young women. "Valerie" first appeared in *Weihnachtsgabe Drei Erzahlungen* (1826).

BARON FRIEDRICH DE LA MOTTE FOUQUÉ (1777-1843) was a Prussian nobleman, military officer and one of the most important prose writers of German Romanticism. He was part of the literary group organised by August Wilhelm Schlegel, under whose patronage he began to publish a series of chivalric novels set in a legendary medieval period heavily influenced by German folklore and the Norse sagas, which were to be major precursors to modern fantasy fiction, as well as an inspiration for the operas of Richard Wagner. His major works include the popular fairy-tale *Undine* (1811) and the epic novel *Der Zauberring* (1812), an influence on J.R.R. Tolkien's *Lord of the Rings* trilogy. "Das Galgenmännlein" (tr. as "The Bottle Imp") first appeared in the second issue of the journal, *Pantheon*, in 1811.

FRIEDRICH GOTTSCHALCK (1772-1854) was a Saxon scholar and librarian, who played a part in the popularisation of Germanic folklore. Following his appointment as Councillor to the ducal court, he collected and published multiple collections of regional legends retold in a Romantic style, including his *Die Sagen und Volksmärchen der Deutschen*, an important precursor to the works of the Brothers Grimm. "Der Burggeist auf Scharzfeld" (tr. as "The Castle Spectre of Scharzfeld") first appeared within that volume.

CARL THEODOR KÖRNER (1791-1813) was a poet and cavalry officer who fought in the Wars of Liberation against Napoleon. As a child he was introduced to poetry by Friedrich Schiller, a family friend, and on admission to university soon proved a natural polymath, composing verse and drama along with short romantic stories and folk legends. He took part in the popular uprisings against occupying French forces, in which he fought with great bravery, even composing rousing sonnets impromptu as he lay wounded. His patriotic verse and his death on the battlefield at the age of twenty-two led to his being remembered as a national hero for much of the nineteenth century. "Die Harfe: Ein Beitrag zum Geisterglauben" (tr. as "The Harp") was first published in 1811 and has been translated into English several times.

LUISE MÜHLBACH was the pen name of Clara Maria Regina Müller (1814–1873), an extremely prolific writer of historical novels, plays and short stories. Luise and her husband, the writer Theodor Munt, were active in the Young Germany movement, and she herself wrote often on the unjust position of women in society and of female authors. Her fiction often deals with the affairs of the eighteenth century and emphasises psychology over explicitness. By the time of her death she was described as the German George Sand.

JOHANN KARL AUGUST MUSÄUS (1735-1786) was a Weimar intellectual and man of letters. After a failed ecclesiastical career Musäus resolved to live by his pen alone, writing numerous parodies and critiques of then-contemporary novels, as well as publishing his *Volksmärchen der Deutschen*, a compilation of German folktales retold in a satirical vein. "Die Entführung" (tr. as "The Elopement") appeared in the fifth volume in 1786 and was an important inspiration for Matthew Gregory Lewis's famous Gothic novel, *The Monk* (1796).

ERNST BENJAMIN SALOMO RAUPACH (1778-1854) was a student of theology turned dramatist who, after having taught at the University of Saint Petersburg for some years, eventually settled in Berlin, where his plays were produced to great acclaim. Although fêted as the next Schiller and enjoying royal patronage, his dramas were neglected after his death. His "Lass die Todten Ruhen" (tr. as "Wake Not The Dead") was one of the earliest modern vampire stories and the first to feature a female vampire. Originally published in 1822 in the annual *Minerva: Taschenbuch für das Jahr 1823*, upon translation into English the following year it was misattributed to the Romantic theorist and poet Johann Ludwig Tieck, a confusion that continues to this day.

GOTTFRIED PETER FRIEDRICH RAUSCHNICK (1778-1835) was originally a doctor who turned to travel writing to supplement his income, eventually producing several respected studies of German history as well as several novels. His

Gespenstersagen (1818 and 1820) was a two-volume collection of ghost stories, patterned after the style of the popular "ghost-books" of the previous century, compilations of allegedly true hauntings often with rationalising explanations. It was from the first of these volumes that *Blackwoods Magazine* translator Robert Pearse Gillies selected the piece here titled "The Warning" for his landmark anthology *German Stories* (1826).

ALOIS WILHELM SCHREIBER (1761-1841) lectured on Aesthetics and held the position of Dean of the Philosophy Faculty at the University of Heidelberg. In addition to his academic duties he produced many volumes of plays and travel writings, the latter a colourful mixture of local history traditions and folk legends; these proved very popular and were quickly taken up as guidebooks by tourists to the Rhine Valley and environs.

JOHANN HEINRICH DANIEL ZSCHOKKE (1771-1848) was Prussian-Swiss novelist and theologian. Following a tumultuous youth during which he fled higher education to live incognito as a part of a wandering theatre troop for a while he wrote one of the earliest Gothic novels, *Aballino, der grosse Bandit* (1793), which was translated into English as *The Bravo of Venice* (1804) by M.G. Lewis. Later in life he published a number of histories and short novellas, many with a philosophical bent. Intellectually he was influenced by the mysticism of Emanuel Swedenborg and believed himself to have minor clairvoyant faculties.

A PARTIAL LIST OF SNUGGLY BOOKS

MAY ARMAND BLANC *The Last Rendezvous*
G. ALBERT AURIER *Elsewhere and Other Stories*
CHARLES BARBARA *My Lunatic Asylum*
S. HENRY BERTHOUD *Misanthropic Tales*
LÉON BLOY *The Desperate Man*
LÉON BLOY *The Tarantulas' Parlor and Other Unkind Tales*
ÉLÉMIR BOURGES *The Twilight of the Gods*
CYRIEL BUYSSE *The Aunts*
JAMES CHAMPAGNE *Harlem Smoke*
FÉLICIEN CHAMPSAUR *The Latin Orgy*
BRENDAN CONNELL *Unofficial History of Pi Wei*
BRENDAN CONNELL *Metrophilias*
RAFAELA CONTRERAS *The Turquoise Ring and Other Stories*
ADOLFO COUVE *When I Think of My Missing Head*
QUENTIN S. CRISP *Aiaigasa*
LUCIE DELARUE-MARDRUS *The Last Siren and Other Stories*
LADY DILKE *The Outcast Spirit and Other Stories*
CATHERINE DOUSTEYSSIER-KHOZE
    The Beauty of the Death Cap
ÉDOUARD DUJARDIN *Hauntings*
BERIT ELLINGSEN *Now We Can See the Moon*
ERCKMANN-CHATRIAN *A Malediction*
ALPHONSE ESQUIROS *The Enchanted Castle*
ENRIQUE GÓMEZ CARRILLO *Sentimental Stories*
DELPHI FABRICE *Flowers of Ether*
DELPHI FABRICE *The Red Spider*
BENJAMIN GASTINEAU *The Reign of Satan*
EDMOND AND JULES DE GONCOURT *Manette Salomon*
REMY DE GOURMONT *From a Faraway Land*
REMY DE GOURMONT *Morose Vignettes*
GUIDO GOZZANO *Alcina and Other Stories*
GUSTAVE GUICHES *The Modesty of Sodom*
EDWARD HERON-ALLEN *The Complete Shorter Fiction*
EDWARD HERON-ALLEN *Three Ghost-Written Novels*
RHYS HUGHES *Cloud Farming in Wales*
J.-K. HUYSMANS *The Crowds of Lourdes*
J.-K. HUYSMANS *Knapsacks*
COLIN INSOLE *Valerie and Other Stories*
JUSTIN ISIS *Pleasant Tales II*

www.ingramcontent.com/pod-product-compliance
Lightning Source LLC
Chambersburg PA
CBHW050307110726
47899CB00007B/2147